# Dear Reader:

Thanks for picking up a copy of the cutting-edge novel *Serial Typical* by Michelle Janine Robinson. Michelle is one of my "discovered talents" via my numerous anthologies comprised of erotica from some of the strongest voices in fiction. I often made her stories the flagship of collections. "The Quiet Room" was the lead-in story for *Succulent: Chocolate Flava 2*, which spent six weeks on the *New York Times* Bestseller List.

After admiring Michelle's talent, I had often wondered when she would write a full-length novel. After meeting her at one of my book signings in Harlem, I asked her about it, and ironically, she had several manuscripts ready to roll out for publication. It was a no-brainer for me, since I am one of her biggest fans. I then published *Color Me Grey* followed by her paranormal erotica title, *More Than Meets the Eye*.

I'm pleased to introduce Michelle's third title, *Serial Typical*, wherein she showcases her versatility, leaping from erotica to mystery. Detectives Brandon Simms and Kimberly Watson team up to capture an elusive killer. They develop an attraction for each other, however, Kimberly avoids being intimate. She consistently hides aspects of her life that become as much of a mystery as the case they're trying to solve. Michelle cleverly crafts a novel that will keep readers guessing to the last page. And what is revealed will be a shocking surprise.

Michelle Janine Robinson is a wonderful writer and I am sure that you will enjoy this novel, as well as her next one: *Strange Fruit*.

Thanks for the support of the Strebor authors. To find me on the web, please go to www.eroticanoir.com or join my online social network, www.planetzane.org

Blessings,

*Zane*

Publisher
Strebor Books International
www.simonandschuster.com/streborbooks

ALSO BY MICHELLE JANINE ROBINSON
*More Than Meets the Eye*
*Color Me Grey*

ZANE PRESENTS

# SERIAL TYPICAL

## MICHELLE JANINE ROBINSON

SBI

STREBOR BOOKS

NEW YORK  LONDON  TORONTO  SYDNEY

Strebor Books
P.O. Box 6505
Largo, MD 20792
http://www.streborbooks.com

This book is a work of fiction. Names, characters, places and incidents are
products of the author's imagination or are used fictitiously. Any resemblance
to actual events or locales or persons, living or dead, is entirely coincidental.

ISBN 978-1-59309-305-1
ISBN 978-1-4391-8400-4 (ebook)
LCCN 2011938447

First Strebor Books trade paperback edition June 2012

Cover design: www.mariondesigns.com
Cover photograph: © Keith Saunders/Marion Designs

10  9  8  7  6  5  4  3  2  1

Manufactured in the United States of America

For information regarding special discounts for bulk purchases,
please contact Simon & Schuster Special Sales at 1-866-506-1949
or business@simonandschuster.com

The Simon & Schuster Speakers Bureau can bring authors to your live event.
For more information or to book an event, contact the Simon & Schuster Speakers
Bureau at 1-866-248-3049 or visit our website at www.simonspeakers.com.

FOR MY SONS, JUSTIN AND STEFAN,
for allowing me a wonderful "sneak-peek"
into the lives of the admirable men
you will one day become and already are

IN MEMORY
Tessa Charles-Lewis
*You were always an angel*
*Now you have your wings*

# GRAVEYARD

My dad is the graveyard exit
There to help you but so far away
My mom is the gravestone
Beautiful and creative in the beginning
 but slowly fades after time
My brother is the grave keeper
Keeping everything together
 but getting scared at night
My older brother is the dirt
Keeping everyone linked in a way
 but separate
I am the corpse in the grave
Isolated from the outside world
Left for eternity to think

—Justin Taylor Moniquette

# ACKNOWLEDGMENTS

Real life, unlike the stories you find between the pages of a book, can be unbelievably unpredictable and so the saying goes, *If you want to make God laugh, just tell Him your plans*. For so long this was little more than a humorous quote for me, one I attributed to filmmaker Woody Allen. However, 2011, with its tumultuous ride, was an all-too-real representation of the meaning of this haunting truism.

As I look back, I find it so hard to believe that so much could have happened. In little more than 365 days, I saw my second book published and available around the world. I met notable actors, writers and producers whom I've respected for years. I watched as the boys I gave birth to evolved into young men before my very eyes, as they now prepare for college. I also helped to record the memoirs of an industrialist, progressive public policy advocate and philanthropist, while I gained an understanding of what it means to live in the moment. In that same 365 days I lost what I thought would be one of the great loves of my life, only to regain what I hope will be a lifelong friendship. Within that same time period, I lost a job as well, only to learn that maybe, just maybe, there is an even better job waiting patiently for me to arrive. That same job I *lost*, at which I worked for close to four years, subjected me to the lowest and most debilitating form of discrimination and harassment I've ever experienced in my entire life as a woman of color. That experience proved to me what I've often told my sons is indeed true: no one ever said life was fair. It also helped me to embrace what is *really* important.

It would seem that the editing of each of my books always occurs close on the heels of my birthday, initiating a desire for a greater understanding of my inner-self and not only how my experiences have shaped me, but how I have shaped my experiences. This year I learned how expansively the lack of a father, or even a father figure, in my formative years, impacted my choice of men throughout my entire life. I also learned that within me I possess a great power to change the course of my life, but only if the desire is strong enough.

Close to two years ago, when my first book, *Color Me Grey*, was published, an interviewer asked me why I made all of my characters in the book so extremely damaged. I was interviewed by a radio station a few months later and to my surprise, was asked the very same question again. At the time, it was my belief that my stories represented what I considered the fabric of much of society's lives. I now believe otherwise.

Often it's so easy to believe that your own reality is the same for others. As a writer, I often pen stories and ideas that are hard to believe and sometimes difficult to embrace. But there is one thing I am sure of, for every story that is told that leaves another shaking their head in disbelief, there could be yet another who is living that very same tale in real life.

Recently, I was talking to a friend about how much I'd like to throw a huge party to celebrate my fiftieth birthday. While discussing it, I was surprised to learn that a small emotional detail of my life, while silently tucked away in my subconscious, still managed to make an appearance in one of my books. I mentioned to her how much I wanted the cake of all cakes at that party, because in forty-eight years on this planet, I had only had three birthday cakes. The first wasn't until I was an adult, but was baked by a family member who loves me very much; the second was bought by an enemy disguised as a friend; and the third was from a man I dated many years ago, who went out for the proverbial *pack of cigarettes* one day, and never returned. I watched as her face became shrouded, first in disbelief, and then in pity. At first I was hurt to think that she might not believe me, then it was the look of pity that hurt most of all. However, once I got past that initial pain, I remembered that first cake and the person who baked it, my wonderful aunt.

This year I got quite the scare when that same aunt was in the hospital. I've always thought of her as one of the strongest people I know, so it was quite a shock to see her in the hospital. She's always been there for me through thick and thin. However, as the years have ticked by and life's challenges have piled themselves one atop another, I haven't spent nearly as much time with my *Aunt Dot* as I know I should. Yearly trips to the Bahamas, Vegas and Jamaica have become little more than an occasional turkey dinner together every other year. The experience forced me to take a good, hard look at the value of the time I spend with others. As I sat in the hospital with my family, I was suddenly struck by the love that existed between us all. All it took was a couple of phone calls and there we all were, worried, but not only supporting the patient, but one another as well.

Through health scares, vocational and financial worries, as well as a multitude of concerns that I can't even begin to count, I have muddled through this year, often afraid of what might be waiting around the next corner. However, when it seemed things had reached bottom, it was the love and support of my mother, Sylvia Payne, that got me through—further proving to me that a mother's love is like no other love that exists on this planet. Thank you, Mom. I was drowning and you breathed life back into me.

And to my cousins, Linda Tillery, Nicole Tillery and Cynthia Tillery, thanks for ALWAYS shooting straight from the hip. You always tell it like it is and not *how I would like it to be*. Thanks, also, for reminding me to ALWAYS keep my head up and *maintain*—NO MATTER WHAT. Nicole, thank you for not only aiding me in my physical upkeep, but my spiritual upkeep as well. For so long I've resisted faith, but somehow now I feel it's restored.

This past year many notable people lost their lives. We mourned the lost lives of Joe Frazier, Nick Ashford, Elizabeth Taylor, Bubba Smith, Amy Winehouse and Heavy D. Steve Jobs also lost his life in 2011. I am constantly reminded of one of Mr. Jobs' quotes: "Your time is limited, so don't waste it living someone else's life. Don't be trapped by dogma—which is living with the results of other people's thinking. Don't let the noise of other's opinions drown out your own inner voice. And most important, have the courage to follow your heart and intuition. They some-how already know what you truly want to become. Everything else is secondary."

In life there are certain things that I know I must do, but when all obligations are complete, that free time is of great value and not to be wasted on the unworthy. Unfortunately, one of the things I also learned in 2011 is that there are those who do fall under the heading unworthy. I've never wanted to admit that, mostly because more than anything, I've wanted to believe in the intrinsic good in all people. This past year has allowed me to embrace the reality that often, even enemies come disguised as trusted friends. To waste valued time, which could otherwise be spent with those we love and who love and embrace us in return, is tantamount to a crime.

In that regard, I would like to thank my family and friends who have stood by me through it all, but most of all my beautiful sons, Justin and Stefan. I would also like to thank all of the folks at Strebor who have been so much like family and who have helped to make a lifelong dream come true, especially Zane, Charmaine Roberts Parker, Yona Deshommes and Nane Quartay. In addition, I thank all of the book clubs, bookstores and readers who have welcomed me with open arms.

As I eagerly have entered 2012 and kissed 2011 goodbye, I endeavor to embrace the many plans I have for my own life, not the least of which is love, security, truth and happiness. I hope that those I encounter in this new year will love me unconditionally and without unhealthy strings attached....and I wish these same things for all those whose paths I cross. I know better than anyone that these are the things of which a good life is built upon.

Please enjoy *Serial Typical* and as you read, always remember... though this is a work of fiction, the message is clear: our actions have consequences and what is *truly* in our hearts and minds will eventually be revealed.

"**W**hat are you doing here?" he whispered to his wife, through clenched teeth. "Haven't I told you to *never*, *ever* bring that thing to my place of business?"

"But Samuel, it won't stop crying. I don't know what to do. I've tried everything."

Her husband forbade her to call the child by name. Therefore, Marie did not. She did *exactly* as she was told, always. The only order she didn't follow was to kill the child.

"I don't care what you do. Just get it out of here! That is your cross to bear, not mine. In fact, if it were up to me, I would sacrifice that evil to the heavens and gain favor with the Lord. Surely, we would be granted entry through the gates of heaven, if we did.

"This abomination has been visited upon us because of the evil we have committed. You must atone for your sins, Marie. You must repent for luring me with your wicked and wanton ways. Maybe God will forgive you and free us from this hell. The sins of the flesh, Marie; the sins of the flesh."

Marie often wondered what the people of Lobeco would think of her and Samuel, if they could see them now. All the girls back at the South Carolina church she once attended had vied for the attention of the handsome and articulate Samuel Richardson. His crisp, cocoa-brown complexion and granite pecs, coupled with his extensive knowledge of the Bible, and his quick wit and intelligence, made him quite the catch. He was the complete package: handsome, articulate, intelligent, financially stable and God-fearing, to boot. But Marie had been the one who'd caught his eye. Most people would have described Marie as a plain Jane. She wasn't an ugly girl, but she was stick thin, without so much as a bump or a curve. Even her breasts were little more than molehills, with her 32A-bra size. Her wheat-colored complexion, while flawless and free of even the hint of a blemish, was sallow at best. Her clothes consisted mostly of items recovered from Goodwill. She had large feet, at least by female standards, and wore a size-twelve shoe, which made it close to impossible to find anything even bordering on attractive. Marie and her family were quite poor. She had three brothers and one sister, and their single mother barely survived, caring for them all on public assistance. Their father had abandoned them long ago, and her mother had made it clear to her eldest daughter, Marie, that her only escape from poverty would be to marry well.

Samuel's father, on the other hand, was Lobeco's town pastor, and everyone assumed Samuel would eventually follow in his father's footsteps. Samuel's mother had affluent parents, and when she died of cancer, she left both Samuel and his father well-fixed in the way of money.

Therefore, most of the people in their hometown, especially the young women, were quite surprised when Samuel chose to spend most of his time with the poor, plain and painfully shy Marie.

Samuel's father could not forgive him when he discovered that Marie had gotten pregnant. He had always had high hopes for his only son, and he'd assumed that Marie was a temporary dalliance that he would eventually tire of. The pair had married quickly and had left South Carolina, at the Pastor's insistence. It was his fear that their dirty little family secret would be revealed and his reputation would be ruined.

Marie was crestfallen. For the longest time, she believed that Sam's father accepted her. At first, she thought his father's reaction was purely because they were having a child out of wedlock. After accidentally overhearing a conversation between Sam and his father, she knew it was more. That conversation was one of the most difficult things she had ever come to terms with, and the most difficult conversation to ever forget.

"How could you choose her, of all people? You could have had your pick of girls. Why her? A girl like her belongs with her own kind."

"Dad, what are you saying? You're a preacher. You've built this entire family and your parishioners' lives on loving our fellow man. Now I see what you really meant. 'Fellow man' to you only includes the more affluent among us. I love Marie. She's got a heart of gold and she's got courage. She supports her family and gives me unconditional love, and she does all of this without having any money at all. Our child is going to be lucky to have her as a mother."

"You have brought shame to this family. I spent my life building our place in this community, and I will not have you and that urchin ruin the reputation I spent so much time creating."

"What are you saying?"

"I'm saying, if you must be with this woman, it needs to be someplace other than here."

"So, you would drive us out of our own community, in order to preserve an image?"

"What we have is more than an image; we have a responsibility. I have a responsibility to set a good example. and what kind of example would I be, if my own son was irresponsible enough to bring a bastard child into the world?"

"Thanks, Dad. Thanks a lot. You've made this so much easier for me. This has been the only home I've ever known, but now I think I *can* leave. I want to leave. I know now better than ever why I chose her. She's more real than any of you in this *community* will ever be. You think I could have done better just because she doesn't have any money, and because her home and clothing doesn't fit some sort of misguided image you have. There's one thing I know for sure, though. None of those girls you handpicked for me would have wanted a thing to do with me without my family name or without my money. None of them would have had the sheer will to survive what Marie has survived. She's got something none of them will ever have. Hell, she's got something you and I will probably never even have. She's got strength. Her life has been so damn tough, but she's still here, still standing. She hasn't given up."

Marie remembered standing there as her pain melted away into overwhelming love for Samuel. She was afraid of leaving the only home she had ever known, but she knew with Samuel by her side, she would be fine.

Samuel never knew Marie had heard the entire conversation, and he was not eager to share it with Marie, so he convinced her that moving away would be best for all of them. He explained that he would never be able to fulfill his father's dream of becoming a preacher. He'd decided that more than anything, he wanted to create another life, someplace faraway. Samuel had always been very creative, and he decided he would try his hand at being an artist of some sort. He was talented and loved sculpting and painting, and convinced Marie that New York was the place for them.

In order to ease the fear and tension of Marie leaving her entire family behind, he assured her that once the baby was born, they would return to South Carolina so everyone could get to know their new addition. He had no real desire to return but had every intention of keeping his promise for Marie's sake. He hoped that once they settled in New York, she would love it so much that their return to South Carolina would be nothing more than a brief visit. All of that changed once the baby was born.

Marie's pregnancy had been a difficult one. She had suffered through morning sickness from the beginning until the end. And from five months until the time she gave birth, she was constantly being rushed to the hospital with false contractions which she had to be medicated for, since it was too early in her pregnancy to have a safe birth. For months, Samuel reasoned that it was little more than the stress of being in a large new city and being away from her family. He told himself that as long as she and the baby got through the pregnancy safely, everything would be fine, that is until after Marie gave birth and it was readily apparent that their baby was not exactly *normal*.

It didn't take long for Marie to witness the change in Samuel. Within minutes after she'd given birth, he'd left her in the delivery room and didn't return until the next day. When he'd returned, Marie was surprised to find him holding something she never expected to see. In his hand was a Bible. Although Samuel had never voiced with anyone else how torn he was about his father's expectations for him, he and Marie had often discussed how disinterested he was in becoming a preacher, and how conflicted he was about religion, in general.

Eventually, the baby was released from the hospital. However, the doctors made it clear that there were certain hard decisions that would have to be made by both her and Samuel, as the parents. With each passing day, Marie watched as Samuel sunk deeper and deeper into despair. Whenever she mentioned all that had been discussed with her regarding their baby's care, he became angry and then sullen. He would lock himself in the basement of their home, and she would hear all sorts of banging. She assumed he was working on some sort of artwork and was happy that he had found an outlet for his pain. She decided she wouldn't bother him and would take on all the responsibility of caring for their baby alone, for as long as she had to. It went on that way for several months. By the time Samuel resurfaced, he was a mere shell of the handsome, vibrant suitor she had once known. In addition, where he had once been doubtful as to whether or not he wanted to follow in his father's footsteps, he had now become obsessed with religion; so much so that Marie became more than a bit concerned. Not a word was spoken nor a deed carried out that didn't revolve around the words of the Bible. Although Marie had been raised in the church, she could clearly see the difference between a healthy reverence of God and an unhealthy obsession.

While she loved her baby, she was devoted to Samuel. Any thoughts she had, any desires she held, took a back seat to his. When he first voiced his wish that they abandon their baby, Marie was shocked, but knew that she would never give in to what he wanted. She hoped that eventually, he would snap out of it and see things for what they were. They were a family with a child that wasn't born like most children, but it was nothing that couldn't be dealt with. As time moved on, Samuel was even more vocal about his wishes. However, he had gone from putting the baby up for adoption, to abandoning it at a church somewhere, to eventually insinuating that there were ways they could ensure it was like the child never even existed. That's when Marie started to get frightened and decided she could never leave Samuel alone with their baby. That was also when she decided she would do anything and everything else he wanted. She believed if she cared for him well enough, and made him happy enough, everything would be okay. She never contradicted any of his other wishes. As time passed, she considered it a miracle that the child was even still alive, given Samuel's thoughts on the matter. From the moment she left the hospital, and Samuel demanded they leave the hospital without the baby, the only times she ever shirked his authority was when it involved the baby. Marie had wanted a baby more than anything, and it didn't matter what their child looked like. All she cared about was that it was created by her and Samuel. He, on the other hand, considered their child a spawn of the devil, and frequently referred to their baby as an "abomination."

According to Samuel, their *situation* was simply punishment, because they had *lain together in sin*. After multiple conversations and constant coaxing from Marie, Samuel had made it quite clear that he would never acknowledge the child as his own. One day, in particular, the baby had been crying more than usual. Marie was all alone in a big city with no friends or family to help her, and the perfect marriage she always thought she would have with Samuel, was little more than a shambles. However, he was all that she had, so she decided to visit him at work, hoping that he would, once and for all, help her or at the least, feel empathy for their small baby's discomfort. From the moment she arrived at his office and saw the look on his face, she knew she had made a terrible mistake.

"Woman, why are you standing there looking like a damn fool? I have work to do. Why on earth are you here?"

"I'm sorry, Samuel. I didn't know what to do. The baby's been crying since you left. I've tried everything."

"You know what you need to do. I've told you time and time again what needs to be done. Just go home, now, and do it! And, tonight, we will pray together for redemption."

As she left, Samuel knew that she had no intention of following through with the instructions he had so often given her; to put a stop to the baby's endless wails. Therefore, he would have no other alternative but to handle its discipline himself.

Eventually, the baby wasn't a baby anymore, and Samuel began working longer hours. Marie welcomed the ten to fourteen hours a day he spent at work. Trying to run interference between him and a toddler was exhausting for her, especially when she began to realize that when she wasn't quick enough, it was their child who paid the price.

The bruises were the first thing she noticed. At first, she tried to convince herself they were normal bumps and bruises that every child got. Eventually, she realized it was so much more. Samuel was angry one day and locked the child in the basement. When Marie first heard the cries and the pounding on the door, she did everything she could do to make it right. It was the first time Marie was truly afraid. She was afraid for both of them and not sure what Samuel would do, so she didn't open the door. She did everything she could to make the basement a comfortable place for the child, and it eventually became a permanent bedroom. For a while, she thought that would ease the tension, until she realized Samuel made it a point to visit the basement often and antagonize the child as frequently as possible. It wasn't until Marie was in a minor car accident, and had to go to the hospital, that she realized the fragility of the situation. She had only been at the hospital for a few hours, but by the time she returned home, she found blood on the walls. And what she found in the basement was the most frightening thing she had ever seen. Samuel had never lied about anything he'd done. However, this time, he swore to God that he had nothing to do with what happened, and Marie couldn't help but believe him. She did her best to make everything right again. This time, she had to be more than a mother and protector. She had to use what little skill she possessed to nurse her child back to health.

# EIGHTEEN YEARS LATER

It had been a long hard ride, but Marie had done everything in her power to make this day possible. Despite the pain endured, it was hard to believe that eighteen years had passed and her *baby* was now going off to college.

"Thank you, Mom."

There were three small words, spoken in a whisper in passing, that Marie never expected to hear. She considered herself no better than Samuel. She was sure the guilt she felt would never leave her, but knowing that her child appreciated what little she had done, was enough to ease her guilt a small bit.

Freedom had finally arrived. There would be no more weekends that stretched into endless darkness, never knowing the difference between night and day; no more dull aches of hunger, the withdrawal of food imposed at the simplest infraction. There would be no more beatings or any of the other atrocities perpetuated from the confines of that dank basement that had become a prison. Freedom had arrived in the form of education. College awaited; college and the greatest gift anyone could ever imagine—sweet freedom.

Marie sat in the living room, listening as her only child packed, knowing it would probably be the last time they ever saw each other. She had tried to be a good mother but was aware she had failed. Her last redeeming act had been to ensure that her child went to college. She had been very secretive in her efforts, hiding books anywhere and everywhere, so that Samuel would never find them. As soon as Samuel went off to work, she would spring into action, first researching how best to homeschool her child, and eventually ensuring that her education efforts met the standards that allowed this day to come to pass. Her self-esteem had always been so low, but somehow, her teaching efforts allowed her to feel some level of self-pride. If not for her efforts, this day would never have happened. She had done it. In her mind, it was the very least that she could do. That is, until today. Her work wasn't finished. There was one last self-sacrificing act that only she could carry out. It would be the only way to ensure some semblance of a life for her child. She hoped that the departure would be uneventful, and there would be no need to carry out her plans. Somehow, though, she knew it would not and she would be forced to take a stand, once and for all. She knew Samuel would never allow their child to leave quietly.

Throughout the years, his descent into madness had been progressive, but great. He was now little more than a vicious wielder of punishment, doling out his form of justice, first to their baby and eventually to Marie as well. Sex with him had become some twisted form of worship, release and punishment, that Marie was sure she would never understand. After all, how could a sane person understand the actions of the insane? While she often considered leaving, her love of Samuel, albeit illogical, had not abated. She still adored him as much as she ever had. In fact, her adoration had been replaced with a certain protectiveness, since she fully knew that he was stark-raving mad, and subject to confinement at any time—that is, if anyone ever discovered what went on behind closed doors.

Downstairs, in the basement, Samuel stood in the doorway, smiling, silently taunting the only child he had ever known, the same child he never acknowledged as his own. His words spewed forth like venom.

"The world knows what you are," Samuel said. "You are, and will always be, an abomination, and college and moving away will never change that. Even the doctors can't fix what you are. God knows, I tried. I know exactly what you are and soon the world will know. You will never know peace. There is no peace for those created in the demon's image."

"You might be right. But, if the world knows what I am, then it knows what you are as well. After all, didn't you help to create me? I don't just mean your rancid seed. I'm referring to the hell you have subjected me to all these years. Everything that I am, I owe to you—you and my poor, disillusioned mother. You are a sick and evil man, who shrouds his evil in the name of The Lord. You can keep your *Lord*. I don't need Him or you. You have made life for me here hell on earth, so how much worse can it get for me? Yes, you can keep your *Lord*. I don't need him, and I definitely don't need you! My only regret is that my mother will die here, never having known what life could have been like if she hadn't been married to a sick fucking bastard like you!"

Samuel's face contorted into a shape and had taken on a hue reminiscent of complete and utter evil. Suddenly, he realized he no longer had any power. For years, he had waited for the constant reminder of his inadequacies to meet with some obvious and ill-fated destiny, yet it had never come to pass. Here it stood, taunting him, ridiculing him, and taking the name of the Lord in vain, all while standing triumphantly in his own home. He would not stand for it!

Upstairs in the living room, Marie sat biting at her last remaining fingernail; the others now painfully gnawed to the quick. The silence was more deafening to her ears than all eighteen years of screams and wails she had been forced to helplessly listen to. The threat of impending doom reverberated throughout her entire being. It occurred to Marie that she had never been a champion to her only child, but today, God willing, she would be. The slamming of the basement door was the last sound she heard, after what seemed like endlessly agonizing moments of silence. Marie raced downstairs, taking steps two at a time.

Throughout the years, Marie had proven to be artful at turning a deaf ear to all she heard. But, somehow, she had always avoided *seeing* anything altogether. The moment she entered the basement, she was mortified. The full realization of how her child had probably been tortured by her husband, time and time again, became a far too tangible reality. Memories swirled around her, dizzying her, crippling her, until she saw what he held in his hand. It was a crude object, of twisted metal, carefully handcrafted by an evil man with evil intentions, for the sole purpose of inflicting pain; the same object that had probably harmed her child so many years ago. Marie felt as though she had risen from some invisible tomb, stronger than she had ever been, maybe even invincible.

"You bastard!" she yelled. "There never was an accident! How could you? How could you mutilate your own child? I always knew! I always knew it was you!"

From the moment Marie rose from her bed early that morning, her actions had been set on autopilot. She went about her usual day, preparing breakfast, making the beds. Everything had been all so commonplace, that is, until she took her place in the living room while her child prepared to leave. Marie settled in and waited. As she sat, she maintained a firm grasp on the Glock she had purchased from a neighborhood thug a few days earlier.

"Marie? What are you doing? Where did you get that? Now, now calm down. I was just... Now hold on a damn minute! You mean to tell me, you're holding a gun on me in my own home! This is me, Marie. What are you doing? It's me, me! There is no reason..."

While Samuel pleaded with his typically dutiful wife to lower the gun she was holding, Marie considered the implications and watched and listened as Samuel alternated between being apologetic, angry and confused. As he approached her, fully prepared to pounce, Marie Richardson aimed the gun and fired.

# CHAPTER ONE

"It's women like her...women like her that make the bad things happen. Yes, it is. Women like her have to go away or they make the world an ugly place. Yes, ugly women, ugly world. They wear disguises, really good disguises, these women, and masks, yes, masks and costumes to fool everyone. But, they don't fool me, for *I* am one of his disciples. No, I'm not fooled at all and I must save the world from the corruption of these demons. Yes, that's what they are, demons, and I can see beyond their disguises. So, I must save the world by destroying the monsters. They are everywhere, here, where I live, where I work, at the supermarket, movie theaters, restaurants, walking down the street as if they belong. They're even with the innocent children. They are everywhere. They pretend to be normal, just like *her*, but they're not. Oh no. Just like *her*, they have been sent here from hell, sent to alter the decency of our world, sent to alter this world to hell on earth. But, I *will* stop them! I will stop them *all*! And, I know just where to start."

Scattered throughout the tiny, damp, downtown apartment, were countless fashion magazines and newspapers, piled one on top of another, practically from floor to ceiling. Food was discarded throughout and flies, roaches and mice competed for residency. If anyone had ever gotten an opportunity to see inside, the place probably would have been declared an uninhabitable fire hazard. Along with the magazines, there were hundreds of cutouts of beautiful women, indiscriminately lining every available corner of wall space. Violent splotches of red clung to the walls. The pungent odor of cigarette smoke clung to the tattered black curtains, occupying the space like dense fog. Each and every window had been thickly coated with black paint, undoubtedly to completely block out any and all hope of sunshine entering, or anyone peeping inside. There was no furniture, not even a bed occupying the tiny studio. Instead, there was a dirty old mattress in one corner of the room, piled high with blankets, and at the center of the room, was a large metal container, filled with water.

"I exorcise thee in the name of God the Father almighty, and in the name of Jesus Christ His Son, our Lord, and in the power of the Holy Ghost, that you may be able to put to flight all the power of the enemy, and be able to root out and supplant that enemy and his apostate angels, through the power of our Lord Jesus Christ, who will come to judge the living and the dead and the world by fire.

"God, Who for the salvation of the human race, has built Your greatest mysteries upon this substance, in Your kindness hear our prayers and pour down the power of Your blessing into this element, prepared by many purifications. May this, Your creation, be a vessel of divine grace to dispel demons and sicknesses, so that everything that it is sprinkled on in the homes and buildings of the faithful will be rid of all unclean and harmful things. Let no pestilent spirit, no corrupting atmosphere, remain in those places. May all the schemes of the hidden enemy be dispelled. Let whatever might trouble the safety and peace of those who live here, be put to flight by this water, so that health, gotten by calling Your holy name, may be made secure against all attacks. Through the Lord, Amen.

"I am Your humble servant, Lord, one of Your angels, dispatched to earth to rid this world of the pestilent, festering boils of society. I will do Your work, Lord. I will destroy them, those that seek to corrupt and leave us all unclean.

"My work has only just begun. And it all will end as You intended, Lord. It all shall end with fire.

"I don't deny that this battle has become an exhausting one. Each day there are more. Who knew there were so many? As quickly as I destroy them, their numbers increase. Don't worry. I sit at the threshold of their arrival. The sooner I eradicate them, the better. It's only a matter of time before they will all be gone and my work here will be done. I *will* stay the course.

"I am so very tired. There is no rest for the chosen. Yet, it is my destiny to purify this earth, one way or another.

"More than anything, I long for the day when I no longer have to hide from those who simply don't understand. We have the same purpose. Yet, they continue to challenge me every step of the way. If only they were to join me in the fight, retribution would be even more swift and dealt with a far more crushing blow. I *will* make them see. I have faith. They will join me. My cause will become their own. Finally, the world will be pure."

Cloaked in layers of clothing and hunched over a vat of many months' worth of collected holy water, a nameless, faceless threat clipped even more pages from magazines. This time, instead of pictures of beautiful women, they were men—handsome, movie star-looking men. After a sufficient number of pictures were clipped, they were glued side by side with the pictures of women that lined every corner of the wall.

As much as the project appeared random, there was nothing random about it. The trained eye could have detected how carefully the male and female pictures were matched to look alike.

For every female photo, there was a matching male photo that could have easily been a sibling. The closer the photos matched, the more feverishly the work continued.

"No matter how much you look alike, you will never be one. It's not how it was meant to be. It was foretold long, long ago. This is my one true purpose, to maintain the balance of things. This unity was never meant to be. The others shall not divert me from my plan."

Searching for more pictures in the countless magazines that lined the floor, suddenly a clever advertising tool between the pages of a *Cosmopolitan* magazine revealed a mirror. It was likely nothing more than an attempt to grab its readers' attention, get them to stop and eventually buy the product being pitched. But, for the occupant crouched on the floor, crazily clipping pages, it was a trigger. In a fit of rage, a set of sharp scissors previously used only to clip pictures, was raised, impaling not only the magazine and its paper mirror, but the leg upon which the magazine rested.

As blood seeped slowly from the wound, the injured party appeared to feel nothing.

**C**andace listened to the sound of the buzzer, announcing her next client. She was tired. Recently, she had begun considering whether or not she needed to take a sabbatical. Between her practice, her support group, the work she did at the prison, and her own personal life, she was beyond overwhelmed. Helping others was what gave her life meaning, but she realized she was ignoring the same advice that she gave many of her clients. She wasn't taking care of herself. It was like the instructions given to passengers on a flight about securing your own oxygen before assisting others. She couldn't be there for everyone else, if she allowed herself to sink. She had three more clients to see today and she was free. Somehow it seemed as though her days were getting longer and longer. She had doubled her client load over the past year, in the hopes that the extra money would help her to have her long-awaited surgery much more quickly. Candace had chosen the field of psychiatry so that she could help others. She also had chosen psychiatry, and her unique specialty, to tackle her own demons.

Soon, she would be embarking on one of the greatest challenges in her life. She was sure she was ready, but hoped that it would still allow her to practice as a psychiatrist. She loved her career and found great fulfillment in helping others. She especially enjoyed the support group she had been conducting for the past several months. She often invited her patients to participate in the group, if she thought it might serve them well. In the beginning, she had been tight-lipped about her more personal reasons for feeling passionate about the work the group was doing. She felt it lacked professionalism to allow her patients a peek inside of her personal life.

Candace had spent so many years of her own life living in the shadows, she hadn't realized how damaging it had become, not only for herself, but for most of her patients, to spend most of their lives hiding from the world. One of her patients was so career-obsessed and adamant about Candace not documenting any sessions that Candace began to become concerned that her patient was slipping into a world where the lines of reality were becoming dangerously blurred and paranoia reigned supreme. Candace did understand better than anyone, since there was always that chance that her practice might suffer after her own transformation was complete. She had known since she was a child what had to be done. Yet, it was only now that her dreams were becoming real. As she encouraged her patients to discover, there were certain decisions in life that no one could or should make for you. All those many years ago, her parents had decided what they thought was best. They had been premature and had probably lacked a clear understanding of what they were dealing with. As far as Candace was concerned, it was high time she rectified their decision, and lived the life she was *truly* meant to live. If that meant abandoning her career, she was prepared to make that sacrifice.

Her next client concerned her a great deal. Candace had become expert at recognizing the subtle clues that indicated a patient was in real trouble. To start, she was sure that Shelly was not her real name. However, that was the least of it. With each visit, Candace became increasingly concerned about Shelly. Since her initial visit, she had presented signs of irritability, difficulty sleeping, and an obvious lack of emotion. Many of her thoughts and ideas were rambling, and often seemed to have no basis in reality. In addition, she demonstrated dangerous promiscuity on more than one occasion, while expressing a lack of desire to connect with anyone. She would pick up random partners frequently, and on many occasions, would become angered by their desire to see her again.

"Hi, Shelly. How are you today?"

"Everything is everything."

"I'm not sure what that means, Shelly."

"It means, nothing has changed. I still can't sleep. I'm still pissed off, and don't know why. Everybody annoys me. I can't even walk down the street without thinking about how much I'd like to trip some random stranger up. I've stopped riding the subway to every place but here, because it's way too stimulating. Every time I get on the subway, I find myself thinking the most evil thoughts. Is that normal? Tell me. This is New York. Maybe my behavior is normal. What do you think, Doc?"

"That's what we're going to figure out, here, together."

"Yeah, I know that, but *when* am I gonna figure it out? I've been coming to you for months now and things are exactly the same. In fact, I think they may have actually gotten worse. Now, I'm starting to think I have a drinking problem. I woke up in a hotel last night alone and I couldn't even remember how I got there."

"Tell me the last thing you remember."

Shelly sat quietly for a moment, then she spoke.

"Okay. So, I remember leaving the hospital and walking to the bus stop. Then, it all gets fuzzy. I might have gone to a bar, but I'm not sure."

"We've established that things were a little fuzzy for you after you left work. What about before?"

"Nothing out of the ordinary...oh, except there's this one patient that I think the staff has been slacking on, since he's so incapacitated and incapable of voicing his concerns. I found these scars on his body. I'm not sure what to make of it, but something doesn't seem right. I only work part-time, but I make it a point to check in on him whenever I'm at the hospital. I believe he was the last person I saw before I left."

"Let's go back further than that?"

"All I remember is a smell. That morning when I woke up, there was this awful smell in my apartment. It smelled like someone had left some food out somewhere, but I couldn't find it or remember leaving any food laying around. It smelled like old bananas or corroded apples or something, but it was so strong, like an entire stock of fruit had spoiled over time in a supermarket and had never been thrown away. That's the only thing I remember."

"Could that have been the reason you were at the hotel?"

Shelly seemed miles away. Her eyes were suddenly vacant and empty. Candace thought she might be drifting off to sleep.

"Shelly? Shelly?"

Nothing seemed to be registering, then suddenly, like a light bulb had been turned on, her eyes blinked and she resumed where the conversation had left off.

"Yeah, Doc. You might be right. Maybe that's why I was at The Mercer."

"Shelly, you've never mentioned your parents. Are they still alive?"

"Uh...No. Actually, I'm not sure. I was adopted."

Candace sensed that she was lying, but resisted the urge to

persist. She assumed that if Shelly was lying, she might retreat and maybe even leave. That's what she had done once, earlier in her treatment, when Candace had tried to persuade her to discuss her sexual trysts. She still would have liked to have known a bit about Shelly's parents.

"What do my parents have to do with anything?"

"Often, our childhood is the root of where many of our troubles begin. Even many sleep difficulties begin in childhood. They can manifest in different ways. For instance, as a child, one might sleep-walk, but when they grow up, the sleepwalking may be replaced with insomnia."

"Well, I don't remember anything about mine, so I guess we'll have to take another discovery route."

Shelly's show of agitation was nothing new, but what happened next most certainly was.

Candace watched as she shifted position. It was a small motion that, for most, would have been inconsequential, but for Shelly it was not. Her small adjustment brought about an obvious change. Her eyes appeared smaller and a bit squinted. Her posture was much more upright, so much so, she actually seemed taller, and her smile was broad and uncustomary.

"This is the first time I've ever noticed how beautiful your eyes are."

Shelly's tone was purposely seductive and meant to express her intent. The octave of her voice was of an obvious lower pitch.

She chuckled.

"Awww, you're so cute. Did my little compliment make you uncomfortable? I didn't mean it, really. I tried so hard to keep it tame. There are a lot better things we could be doing than sitting here and exploring the inner psyche."

"Like what?" Candace asked.

"Hmmm. Like fucking. I can smell your pussy over here and your nipples are so hard, pushing against that conservative silk top you're wearing. I can tell you feel it, too. We'd make incredible fuck buddies."

"We should explore why you imagine yourself suddenly attracted to me, sexually."

"I'm all for exploring. How about I start? I'd like to explore what your nipples taste like inside my mouth, or how much harder they'll get if I run my teeth against them."

Shelly stood up; her gait was seductive, yet lacked much of the sway her hips typically executed. There was a swagger to her step, similar to a man on the hunt. She crossed the room to where Candace was sitting.

"Shelly, I would like for you to go back and sit down where you were."

"Shelly? Shelly who? Shelly isn't here, Doc."

"You're not Shelly?"

"You can call me Kay."

She sat down next to Candace.

Shelly touched her own groin area, rubbing her hand back and forth.

"Oh, Dr. Phipps, you make me so fucking hot," she moaned.

Candace considered asking her to leave, but she would have to witness this transformation firsthand in order to make an informed assessment of what was happening with Shelly. She did, however, make a threat.

"If you don't move, I'm going to have to ask you to leave, *Kay*."

"Okay, don't get your panties in a bunch. I thought you needed tightening up."

"We're here to talk about you."

"You know this isn't going to work, don't you, Dr. Phipps?"

"What isn't going to work?"

"Trying to *fix* something that isn't broken."

"What is it you think I'm trying to fix?"

"Shelly."

It didn't go unnoticed by Candace that Shelly was speaking of herself in the third person.

"Aren't you Shelly?"

She laughed.

"Ever the shrink, huh?"

"What makes you say that?"

"Aren't you Shelly?" she said, mimicking Candace in a high-pitched, squeaky voice.

"I'm so much more than just *Shelly*. I thought you would have figured that out by now."

"Yes, I get it."

"Yeah, sure you do."

Just as easily as Shelly had slipped into her new persona, Kay, the *old* Shelly suddenly returned and the subject was immediately changed.

"Doc, I really wish your office was in another location. This is the only place that I now take the subway to; a bus to your office is a pain in the ass. I see by the clock on the wall our session is over."

"Don't worry about that. In fact, Shelly, I was thinking maybe you might want to add an additional day a week to your sessions."

"Wow! That's big. Am I really that fucked up?"

"No. You're not *fucked up*. I think it would be a lot easier to get to the root of things, if we had more time."

"I'll see you next week, Doc; *same bat time, same bat channel*. I'll think about that additional session."

As Shelly left Candace's office, Candace realized it was moments like these that made it more difficult to consider cutting back on her client load.

# CHAPTER THREE

"Dad, I don't have time. I've got to be in court with Mr. Fishman early this morning."

Caitlin silently wished she hadn't answered the phone. She seldom got calls from anyone other than her office or her parents this early in the morning. From the moment the phone rang at six-thirty, she knew it could be no one but her mom or dad.

"I have to be in court at ten o'clock this morning."

Caitlin contemplated simply hanging up the phone. After all, what difference would it make? No matter what she did or what accomplishments she made, nothing would ever be good enough for her parents, especially her father. They had both carried around some sort of silent shame from the moment she was born. She had done everything to please them, but she knew in her heart, none of it would ever be enough.

"Okay, Dad, I'll meet you at Sebastian's at eight o'clock. But it's got to be quick, because I absolutely *have* to be in court by ten."

Caitlin's father was early, as usual, when she arrived.

She arrived at five minutes after eight, waving at her father from the doorway as she entered. Even the simple act of her waving seemed to annoy him, or was it simply her presence, she wondered. Her kiss on his cheek was met with his usual steely veneer.

"Hi, Dad. Have you been waiting long?"

"You said eight o'clock on the dot, and I was here at eight *on the dot*."

"Sorry. I wanted to make sure I had everything for court this morning before I left the apartment."

"Haven't I always cautioned you to prepare the night before? You'll never make partner with such fly-by-the-seat-of-your-pants thinking."

"I did prepare the night before. I still like to double-check things the same day."

"Isn't that what you have an assistant for? You do have an assistant, don't you?"

"Of course, I have an assistant. Dad, I don't have much time. What was it you wanted to discuss?"

"Your mother tells me you've joined some sort of support group."

"Yes, I have."

She wasn't sure why she had told her mother about the support group. She guessed it was her desire to move forward or maybe to gain some understanding of who she was. It was her hope that her parents might embrace what she was trying to do or possibly even help her on her journey. Somehow, though, she knew it was little more than a pipe dream.

"Do you know what would happen if anyone found out about this? You could kiss any hopes of ever becoming partner good-bye."

"I doubt anyone is going to find out about some obscure little support group I've joined somewhere on the other side of town."

"You'd be surprised at what can be unveiled."

"Besides which, why should I be ashamed? I've done nothing wrong."

"Caitlin, don't be so naive. This *situation* is much bigger than right or wrong. You're oversimplifying again, and it's going to cost you. It's going to cost all of us."

"I've spent my entire life living for you and Mom. When do I get a chance to live for me? When do I get to take care of me for a change? I need this. I need a chance to heal."

"My dear, I thought once you passed the bar, and I helped secure you a position at one of the most respected law firms in the country, you would have gotten over your love of all things theatrical."

Caitlin didn't have a violent bone in her body, but it was times like these, when her father was condescending to her, yet again, that she wanted to wring his neck.

"I'll take it under advisement," she responded sarcastically.

"Make sure you do that, young lady. There's but so much I can do to help you."

"Have I ever asked you for anything?"

"No, as a matter of fact, you haven't. But, what am I supposed to do? I can't exactly shirk my responsibilities."

"No, I guess you can't."

"I was considering leaving the group anyway," she lied.

"I think that would be for the best."

"Of course."

"Any word on the partnership?"

"Not yet. I'm going to hear something soon, though."

"All the more reason to leave that support group as soon as possible."

"Okay, Dad, I get the point. I have to go. Mr. Fishman will be waiting for me."

Leaving the restaurant, Caitlin glanced quickly behind her, just in time to see the look of disgust on her father's face. It was unmistakable. She often wondered why he even bothered. He could have easily disowned her years ago. He probably would have, if it wasn't for his need to keep up appearances. The one and only time he didn't care what people thought was when he decided not to bring his daughter into the firm in which he was a partner. He was more concerned about what people might find out than the questions that were sure to arise about why his only daughter wasn't an attorney at his prestigious firm.

Despite her obvious distractions, Caitlin couldn't help but wonder again whether she was being followed. For weeks, she'd felt the presence of someone near. There was the telltale sound of footprints and the unmistakable chemical smell that soon followed. It was eerily frightening. There was a presence she knew was there, but could not see. She didn't consider for a moment that her mind might be playing tricks on her. If nothing else, Caitlin's history had ensured her a life firmly entrenched in reality. She knew there was someone there, watching and waiting. What they were waiting for, she wasn't sure. After speaking with her father, the most she was worried about was that someone had discovered her secret. She stayed vigilant, ever-mindful of what she had to lose. It occurred to her that maybe her father was right. Maybe she needed to quit the group. She wished she didn't have to make that decision. It was the only place she had ever felt like something other than a freak.

Several feet behind her, the person following Caitlin saw her as nothing other than a freak—a freak that needed to be eradicated, in all due time.

Caitlin glanced at her watch, realizing how late she was.

"Enough worries about the boogeyman," she uttered quietly to herself. "You've got work to do."

Five minutes after arriving at her office, the phone rang. Right about the time she began to feel like she was being followed, she also began receiving odd phone calls. The calls were little more than sounds, but she was sure it was connected. Wendy answered before she could grab the phone.

It never ceased to amaze Wendy. It seemed as though whenever the phone rang, her boss, Caitlin Schwartz, began speaking, as if it never occurred to her that carrying on two conversations simultaneously was ill-advised and rude to all parties concerned. Nevertheless, she was once again shouting at her from her office, mere seconds after the phone rang.

"Wendy, is that Mr. Fishman?"

"No," Wendy responded quickly.

"Mr. Fishman and I will be in court all day today. Also, please start revising the brief I left on your desk. Scan my mark-up when you're done and email me both the mark-up and the revised version."

It had been one of those weird phone calls again, with no one on the other end, so Wendy simply hung up.

"Okay, Ms. Schwartz."

Wendy had worked with Caitlin Schwartz for five years now, but she still couldn't bring herself to call her by her first name, despite her initial request that Wendy do so. Ms. Schwartz didn't seem to mind all that much, either. She was every bit the *J.A.P.* (Jewish American Princess). Caitlin only wore gray, black or blue Brooks Brothers suits. She wore sensible shoes, horn-rimmed glasses and never, ever wore her hair in anything other than a bun securely, bound in the back of her head. The only jewelry she ever wore was a very small single strand of cultured pearls with a matching pair of equally understated earrings. On the rare occasions when she removed her glasses, the beauty of her blue eyes was unmistakable. Not only that, her hair actually appeared to be naturally blonde. Despite these assets, she appeared to be doing everything in her power to camouflage her beauty. Wendy, along with many of the other secretaries in the office, had two theories: either Ms. Schwartz felt the only way to climb the ladder of success and achieve the coveted prize of partner was to downplay her femininity, or she was really a closet freak and wanted to keep her secret safe. Wendy was betting on the latter. On more than one occasion, Wendy had walked in on conversations that Ms. Schwartz clearly didn't want Wendy to hear. Wendy's best guess was that Ms. Schwartz and the firm's partner, Samuel Fishman, were doing the horizontal mambo on a regular basis. Wendy would eventually find out her boss' secret life was much more convoluted than that. Ms. Schwartz had a father who was a partner at another top ten law firm and a mother who was an internist at New York Presbyterian Hospital. From Wendy's point of view, Ms. Schwartz had it all. However, you wouldn't know it to look at her. Her face was permanently etched in a terminal scowl. Wendy often wondered what on earth this woman for whom *she* worked had to look so damn miserable about. Wendy had grown up in a Detroit slum in a one-bedroom apartment with her single mom, brother and sister. Wendy couldn't work up too much sympathy for her boss' type—girls like Ms. Schwartz, who were obviously born with a silver spoon in their mouths.

Ms. Schwartz's words broke into Wendy's thoughts.

"Wendy, did you order me a car?"

"Yes, Ms. Schwartz. The car's ETA is ten minutes. You have Car Number Four Six Seven, Kenton Car Service."

"Thanks, Wendy. Please call Mr. Fishman and let him know what time the car will be here. Tell him I'll meet him downstairs in the lobby.

"Oh, one more thing, Wendy; did you order my regular five forty-five car for Wednesday night?"

"Yes, Ms. Schwartz, you have a standing order for *every* Wednesday night at five forty-five."

"Thanks, Wendy. I just wanted to check. It's going to be a busy week and I want to make sure that the car is in place, in case I get so wrapped up in work, I forget to ask you to reserve one."

"Don't worry. I set up a standing order with Kenton for every Wednesday at five forty-five, so, that's the reservation until you decide you don't need it anymore."

"Thanks again. I'll email you, if I need anything else. Oh, by the way, who was that on the phone?"

"The phone? I think maybe someone thinks your number is a fax number. It rings and rings, and then when I pick up, there's this piercing tone and the line disconnects."

"That's weird, isn't it?"

"Yeah, it is a little weird. Usually, if someone thinks it's a fax number, they eventually figure it out after a couple of days of trying to send. This has been happening for weeks now."

"Does a number pop up on the phone display? Maybe you could call it back and find out who it is?"

"No, nothing comes up. It appears to be blocked."

"Don't worry about it. I guess it will stop eventually."

Wendy was sure not to mention that the tone was unlike anything she had ever heard before. Initially, it sounded like something electronic, but with each subsequent call, it was starting to sound more and more like the sound of someone or something wailing. She didn't dare mention this to Ms. Schwartz for fear of being thought a complete nut. She assumed, like Ms. Schwartz, that eventually it would stop.

As Caitlin Schwartz got on the elevator to head to court, the phone rang again and Wendy answered. Once again, it was that familiar wail, only this time it was more pronounced and followed up with three small words spoken in monotone: *God has spoken.*

# CHAPTER FOUR

D isgusted, yet watching with glee as they all filed into the dark, musty room, there was one among them that was not there to heal. Each week, there were far more than anticipated. Overwhelmed, yet brimming with a sense of purpose, their executioner waited, anxious to decide who would be next.

Chairs were arranged in a circle for optimum sharing. Some had been here often, while others were new to the group. The dates of their arrival meant little. Watching and waiting, the killer knew they would all be eradicated in time.

Before Candace arrived, two of the members seemed to already be embroiled in a heated exchange.

"I not only feel like you're not being honest with us; I feel like you're not even being honest with yourself," a member named Christina said. "How could anyone feel *lucky* to be born this way?"

"I'm not going to try to convince you of what *I* feel, but I will continue to reiterate what I said in our last session. And I'll even elaborate a bit, if only to help anyone else here that might feel tortured by their circumstances," Sydney responded. "I *do* feel lucky. I feel like we're all lucky. We have had a unique opportunity, that few others have, from early in our lives, to not only be confronted with the reality of our own sexuality, but also to be in a position to make a decision about who and what we want to be. This is not the first group I've been involved with. I joined several groups before I found the one that I felt fit for me. Through-out that process, I have met the most incredible, spectacular people. In one group, I met a man who struggled for years with his sexuality. On the surface, he believed himself to be a straight man and eventually, he married and had children. Unfortunately, he wasn't prepared for what followed when he was confronted with the fact that at his core, he was a man who wanted to be with other men. His wife felt betrayed, his children were ashamed, and he was hard-pressed to explain to either his wife or children how he could deceive them so, especially when he didn't feel as though he had deceived anyone. He didn't know who he was. We are lucky in that sense. We have had to deal with figuring out where our sexuality lies. We've had no other choice."

"And you think having no choice makes us *lucky?*"

"Yes, I do."

"You've got a hell of an idea of what the meaning of luck is. I've never felt like anything other than a freak. The world made sure I knew that was exactly what I was from the time I was a little kid. How could anyone feel lucky about that?"

"It's all subject to interpretation. I've walked in the same shoes you've walked in. I've been called the same names. But, I've adapted, and excuse the cliché, but I've tried to turn lemons into lemonade and I'm happy to say it's worked for me. I truly do feel lucky to have had this opportunity. I'm not going to say it hasn't been hard, or that if I had been given an opportunity early on not to be born this way, I wouldn't have grabbed it, but, I am who I am and I can't change that. I see the disadvantages, but I also see the advantages it has granted me. I fully believe that my life will be, and has been, no different than anyone else's who hasn't lived these circumstances. I've fallen in love, I'm going to get married one day and even have children, because that's what I want and there's nothing to keep me from having that."

"What are you, fucking Pollyanna? What you just said is nothing but bullshit!"

"You can call it whatever you want to call it, but, I'm fine. You are the one full of anger, and what has it gotten you?"

"My feet are firmly planted on the ground, and I'm dealing with reality. That's what it's gotten me! What has your Pollyanna approach gotten you?"

"It's gotten me peace."

Sydney suddenly noticed Candace was there and was happy to have someone there to mediate.

"I see you all got started without me," Candace said. "I'm sorry I'm late. I had a session with a client I couldn't end."

"I don't know how the hell you do it."

"Do what, Christina?"

"Deal with nut cases all day."

"I don't consider the people I counsel *nut cases*. They are simply people that need a little bit of help figuring things out."

"You mean like us."

"Yes."

"Speaking of nuts, did you all hear about Caitlin?"

"Caitlin?" one of the participants asked.

"Yeah, Caitlin Schwartz. Don't you read the papers? She was part of our group. Although, she really never shared much, but, she had been coming for at least a month or two. You know the one, the lawyer. She was tall, pretty, a little stuck-up."

"Oh, yeah. I didn't even realize that was her," another member of the group chimed in. "It was in all the papers. Wasn't she burned to death?"

"Yeah. Whoever did it burned her so fucking bad they weren't even sure at first whether she was a man or a woman."

"It's horrific. This city has become a fucking toilet. It's full of miscreants and the dregs of society," Christina chimed in.

One member of the group was content to listen, especially fascinated by Christina's comment about the city being full of miscreants and dregs of society. It was baffling how she could consider others dregs, and not consider herself one.

"How much you wanna bet it was a hate crime?" offered another member.

"I don't think so. They also said she was raped. Besides, it's not like anyone knew."

"Don't you know?" Christina responded. "*Someone* always knows. That's the thing about secrets; they don't stay buried for long. That's why I make sure my life is an open book."

"Oh, really? So, you're saying you wouldn't care if someone found out why you come here?" Brandy, one of only two black members of the group, asked.

"I couldn't care less. Weren't you listening during my shares? I spent close to five years of my life selling pictures of myself, in all my glory. People are willing to pay good money to see freaks, so I gave them a freak to gawk at."

"Why would you do something like that?" another member asked.

"Because I'm sick and tired of all the damn secrecy. Think about it. If it weren't for all the secrets, the people who victimized us wouldn't have had all the power they had. I remember Caitlin and she was just one of many trapped by her secrets. It's a shame, too, because it almost seemed like she might be breaking free of her parents and the influence they had on her, especially that father."

"Christina, I agree with you on one level, but on another level, some of us have jobs that depend on that very same secrecy. I'm not ashamed of who I am, but if my job were to find out, it might cause problems for me at work. People can be very close-minded. I'm a teacher. I can just imagine what some of the parents might say if they knew. I love my job. As much as I would like to be a role model for some of the kids I teach, kids that are hiding behind their own walls of shame, I know that I can't be there for any of my kids if I can't teach."

"I understand where both of you are coming from, and in the end, it has to be a personal decision. Some decide to keep it private while others are quite vocal about it. I do think far more people keep it a secret, though," Candace added.

"Let me ask you something, Teri? That's your name, right?"

"Yes."

"Are you so frightened that you really believe with all the civil rights laws and the EEOC and the union, that you could still be fired because of this?" Christina asked.

"Absolutely."

"Her concerns are definitely warranted," said Brandy. "I used to work at this law firm before I started working as a writer. My office manager at the firm would make all these racially inappropriate comments about everything from dating practices to the way African-Americans wore their hair. She even declined to promote me, explaining that she didn't want to promote a black woman, and preferred instead to hire someone of the same ethnic background as herself. When I was truly fed up with it all, I informed her superiors, who surprisingly told me they were well aware of *all* of the comments. They told me they didn't condone her behavior and that it would be addressed. However, within months of me telling them, I was fired after working there for years. Every other week, there was some new complaint, but in the end, it was all about maintaining the racially inappropriate conduct that the firm was obviously okay with. I hired an attorney to sue. They went back and forth with letters and phone calls, but when all was said and done, the attorney dumped me as a client, telling me it would involve too much work and drag on far too long for them to continue on a contingency basis. Not only that, after trusting the firm that was representing me for several months, I was informed by the EEOC that the time to file a complaint had expired. That's your legal process. If you've got money, and lots of it, the legal process works just fine, but if you don't, you are decidedly screwed. The truth is, it's *the green* that calls all the shots."

"Well, I've got money and the legal process doesn't always work all that well for me, either."

Just when Candace believed there was a break in the conversation, a member who seldom, if ever, spoke.

"*Colossians 3:5: Put to death, therefore, whatever belongs to your earthly nature: sexual immorality, impurity, lust, evil desires and greed, which is idolatry.*"

The words were spoken so quietly, many of the members barely heard. Candace heard the words but wasn't quite sure what the meaning was—especially in the context of what they were all discussing.

"Could you repeat that? I don't think everyone heard you," said Candace.

"*Colossians 3:5-Put to death, therefore, whatever belongs to your earthly nature: sexual immorality, impurity, lust, evil desires and greed, which is idolatry.*"

This time, the words were spoken much louder and clearer. Candace was glad to see the member finally actively participating in the discussion. However, before Candace could encourage further discussion, Christina jumped in.

"What the fuck did you say?" she asked.

The look of rage and shock on the face of the quiet member was undeniable.

"Well, did you hear me? What are you trying to say? Are you

calling me and the other members here immoral, impure and evil? I'll give you greed, because I ain't gonna lie: I'm greedy and I don't have a problem with claiming that. But what makes you think *any* of us should be judged immoral, impure or evil?"

"It's in the Bible, Galatians 5:19: The acts of the sinful nature are obvious: sexual immorality, impurity and debauchery; idolatry and witchcraft; hatred, discord, jealousy, fits of rage, selfish ambition, dissensions, factions and envy; drunkenness, orgies, and the like. I warn you, as I did before, that those who live like this will not inherit the kingdom of God."

"Oh, I get it. You're one of those. Do you even belong in this group, or are you just here to pass judgment and quote passages from the Bible? This is some bullshit!" Christina said. "I don't come here to be judged by some Bible thumper."

"Christina, I don't think you're being judged. Through time, many have looked to the Bible to make sense of the world."

"Yeah, right; it sure sounds like a judgment to me."

When it appeared that things had quieted down, Candace decided it would be a perfect time to jump in and discuss her principal topic for the evening.

"I'm happy to see that you all have gotten started without me and are already *sharing*. Is there anyone else that has something they would like to discuss?"

No one responded, so Candace continued.

"I do have something I would like to discuss with all the members of the group."

"What is it, Candace?" Sydney asked.

"I've been trying to figure out whether or not I should contact the police regarding Caitlin."

"Do you know anything about her murder?" asked Teri.

"I don't believe so, but it occurs to me that I may have information about Caitlin that may be helpful to the investigation."

"I thought when you started this group, you said everything would be strictly confidential?"

"Teri, I said that, but this is a special situation. A woman is dead."

"It's not like one of us threatened to kill her. I don't know if you heard what we were talking about, but I came to this group expecting privacy. I could lose my job if anyone found out about me. Sienna and I are trying to have a baby. In fact, I'm sure she's probably pregnant already. I need my job now more than ever."

Candace knew Teri's concerns were real. She didn't know what she should do.

"Besides, as a psychiatrist, I thought you only had to contact the police if someone told you they were going to kill someone else. That's not what happened here."

"You're right, Teri, but I'm not talking about my legal obligation here. I brought this up as it relates to *all* of our moral obligations. Don't you feel some sort of obligation to Caitlin as one of our former members?"

"I hate to sound like a hard ass, because I'm not, but no, I don't feel any obligation to contact the police," Brandy said.

"Okay, so that brings me to what I thought would be the best alternative. I'd like all of you to search your own personal circumstances and vote on whether or not I should contact the police."

Before Candace could continue any further, two members of the group left. She was not surprised and assumed she would most likely lose members from the moment she brought it up.

She was more than a bit disappointed. She'd had such high hopes when she started the group. Now, it seemed it would probably end long before it really got started.

# CHAPTER FIVE

"Aw hell, what the fuck are you doin', man? Who let this rookie in here? He touched the fucking bracelet with his fingers, no gloves, no nothing! Why do I have fucking amateurs trudging through my crime scene?"

"Brandon Simms, do you know any other word besides 'fuck'?" Detective Kimberly Watson said as she approached.

"Let me bum one of those," Watson asked a nearby officer.

"Since when did you start smoking?"

"Probably right about the time you acquired that mouth you've got."

"The Commissioner's fu...," Simms began. "I mean... We need some leads on this. The Commissioner's breathing down our necks big-time and we got diddly. And, what do I see, this rookie rooting through the crime scene without gloves, and leaving his cigarette butts at the crime scene. What the hell is that?"

"I doubt his ineptness will make much of a difference," Watson said. "It's the same, isn't it? I'm guessing that once again, the body is charred beyond recognition. The first one was so bad, we still don't know whether it's even a man or a woman. Thank goodness the second victim didn't have a tire to aid burning, or enough time to burn, or we'd still be trying to figure out who she was."

"Yeah. That one sad little bone was enough for us to connect her to a missing person's report and compare the DNA to the couple that reported their daughter missing. Right now, she's all we've got. I wish they were more cooperative. That father is a piece of work. His daughter is burnt to a crisp and he's still criticizing her," said Simms.

"You know what they say; you can't pick your family."

"Speaking of family, Watson, you got any?"

For years, Watson had been as much of a mystery as many of the cases they'd tried to solve. She was tight-lipped about her family, her social life, even what she did before she entered the academy. He learned long ago to lighten up with the questions, but every now and then, when he saw an opening, he would give it a shot.

"I would think you'd have better things to jaw about than me. The guy we're looking for is a fucking mole, and if we don't find him, he *will* hit again. We may know who the second victim is, but we still don't have anything on the killer or the first victim. If we don't have anything on him, we can't trap him. We have no clear-cut picture of what the prototype is for his victims. One victim is still unidentified, the second was a hot-shot lawyer at a prestigious law firm, and now we've got a third. All we know so far is that they were all murdered on Wednesday night."

"You know, Watson, that could just be a coincidence."

"It's no coincidence. You better believe there's some significance to all three murders being committed the same night of the week. We need to figure out what the connection is, and we'll be that much closer to nailing this dirt bag. Not only that, all of these guys have a type, and you better believe, he has one, too."

Simms watched his partner in awe. He had been with the New York City Police Department long enough to see the demographics of the department change considerably. Detective Watson was a clear example. She was incredibly beautiful and her femininity was not to be denied, yet she made it quite clear, female or not, she was not to be fucked with. Many a criminal had underestimated her and mistaken her sexiness for weakness. Watson was part of the new breed of female detectives. Long gone were the days of female officers who looked more like men than women.

*Look at her*, Simms thought to himself: voluptuous lips, perky breasts, a flat six-pack, gorgeous firm, round ass, and runner's legs that made his heart stop every time he was lucky enough to see her in a skirt. Those legs had to be Watson's most outstanding feature. He often daydreamed about those legs wrapped tightly around him as he showed her exactly how much he thought of her and how often. Simms quickly changed his focus. He was conscious that sometimes there were things a man simply couldn't control. When it came to matters of sex, a man's Johnson was one of those things. The more he thought of Kimberly's beautiful brown, smooth, athletic legs, the more he could feel his nature begin to rise. He tried to focus, think of something, anything else. As if her beauty wasn't enough, she was a damn good detective. Often, he watched her alternate between being tough-as-nails to using her femininity to her advantage, and the mere thought made his dick hard. He wasn't sure whether to be in awe of her or fear her. One thing was for sure; he was glad she was his partner. Watson had worked her magic on more than one occasion to *both* their advantages, not only out in the field, but with their own colleagues.

"Was this victim also burned in the truck of a stolen car, with a tire under the body?" Watson asked. "That's the only reason we were able to identify the second victim; there was no tire. I guess the car he stole that time didn't have a spare. I'll bet this time, there was complete bone destruction again."

"You're probably right," Simms agreed.

"The medical examiner explained it to me. The body lies on the tire, and while the rubber burns, the body is suspended on the metal rim, giving it greater access to the intense heat. Undoubtedly, the trunk takes on the same properties of a mini-crematorium. What I don't understand is, according to the medical examiner, the body would have to burn for at least five hours in order to cause that kind of destruction to the bone and tissue. How could a fire burn for that long without anyone noticing?"

"That's easily explained," said Simms. "The time of death for the last victim was estimated at approximately midnight. The vic is killed around midnight in the middle of the week. The body burns and no one notices until everyone gets up to start their day the next morning. Even if someone does notice late at night, people don't want to get involved, especially where there's no obvious victim, and the car is usually parked in an alleyway somewhere. So, even the threat of fire isn't enough of a motivator. People are scared. They don't want to get involved, especially if they don't feel it affects them in any direct way.

"One thing we do know for sure is that the bastard is trying to leave some sort of a message," Simms continued. "The same sterling silver bracelets were left at the scene of both crimes. We know the second victim was incapacitated with diethyl ether, and he used that same ether to start the fire. With all these bells and whistles, no one noticed a thing. It's like the guy is fucking invisible. I haven't seen anyone as elusive as this guy in a long time. He makes no mistakes and what's with the burning of the bodies? Is it simply to hide evidence or could it be part of his message?"

"I guess we've got our work cut out for us."

"You ain't kidding," Simms agreed. "What are you smiling about?"

Watson was amused by the attention her partner got from the

young female officers. One at the scene was watching every move Simms made.

"You've got a fan."

He turned to find a uniformed female officer smiling at him. She was attractive enough, but Simms' attention was elsewhere. He seldom dated other officers, but if he were going to, it wouldn't be someone random. He had his eyes on someone a little closer to home.

"Go for it!" Watson encouraged.

"Not my type."

"She's female and she has a pulse. I thought that *was* your type. Who knows? She could be wife number three."

"Yeah, that's all I need."

"At least if you get married again, you'll wake up in the same place on a regular."

It was clear to Simms that Watson would never take him seriously as anything other than her partner. That comment spoke volumes. He knew his trysts with women were legendary, but he had always hoped that Watson could see beyond the hype.

"Despite what you may think, I am *very* selective," he responded, annoyed.

Watson knew she had gone too far and hurt his feelings. She knew he had a little crush on her, but she also knew there could never be anything between them. It wasn't as if she didn't recognize his obvious charm and good lucks, or his beautiful blue eyes. He was quite a man, masculine and teeming with testosterone. Once, when they were just starting out together, Watson almost gave in to an impulse to sleep with Simms, but she was glad she hadn't. It was important that they maintain their professionalism, and partners against crime was all they could ever hope for. However, she couldn't help but remember the burn of his lips on her own. It was a memory that had not easily faded.

Lost in thought, Watson didn't hear Simms calling to her.

"Watson! Watson!"

He tapped her on the shoulder.

"Where were you?"

"You know me. The wheels are always turning, always thinking. We've got a murder to solve, don't we?"

Simms turned to find the media heading toward them.

"Your turn," he said, referring to whose turn it was to address the news stations.

Just as quickly as he spoke those words, Watson was gone, again.

Realizing that Watson had disappeared, he decided to call her on her cell.

"What is it with you and the media anyway?" he asked when Watson answered the phone.

"That's more your schtick than mine. I'll let you shine."

"Well, aren't you just the shrinking violet," Simms replied sarcastically.

"So, Madame Violet, have you gotten any info yet on those bracelets?"

"I'm working on it. As a matter of fact, I'm on my way to a spot called Come Again now. You want to meet me there? It's on Fifty-third Street."

"I thought you did that already?"

"No. I'm doing it now. I've had a full plate, okay?"

"Whoa, partner. Lighten up. No judgments here. I was checking in on my own memory. I thought I remembered you stopping by there already."

"Oh," was all she said.

"While you're having fun at the sex boutique, I'll stick around here. I can't wait to see what forensics has got to say about the latest victim. Besides, I don't think you're going to uncover much there. That would be too easy."

"You might be right, but the first victim had a business card from Come Again inside her appointment book. Also, while I'm there, I can see whether or not the store knows anything about these bracelets and their significance. I looked them up on Google images, and they call them slave bracelets. I tried to figure out why they're called that, but I couldn't find anything on the Internet. It may only be because of the way it links a bracelet to a ring by way of chains, but there's always that possibility there may be some underground meaning, and what better place to start than a sex shop."

"You go ahead. After I leave here, I'm going to head over to the second victim's office and check out her client list again; maybe ask a few questions about her colleagues. There might have been something we missed. You'd be surprised what information is shared standing around the water cooler."

"Simms, your age is showing. Don't you know there are no more water coolers? Everybody drinks bottled water these days," Watson joked.

"Well then, I'll just have to sniff around for information around the refrigerator. Don't forget we've got reports to do tonight."

"Yeah, don't remind me."

"A bunch of us are going over to Flanagan's. How about it, Watson; you wanna come along after we're done with our reports?"

"No, I already made plans."

"You always got plans. What you got; a hot date or something?"

Suddenly the phone went dead.

"Watson! Watson! Shit! She did it to me again!"

"Let me guess. That was your elusive partner on the other end of that line. What's up with her, anyway? She's so damn secretive. Every night, she's off to places unknown. What's the deal?"

Detective Johnson was a pig. Simms knew it. Watson knew it. Hell, the whole damn New York City detective squad probably knew it. His sole purpose in life seemed to be to nail the next woman in his path. He was surprisingly effective at his goal, except, of course, when it came to Watson. Johnson made it very clear that didn't sit well with his ego.

"What are you worried about it for? What do you think; if she spends some time with you at Flanagan's, maybe she'll get drunk enough to spread her legs for you?"

"Sounds like projection, if you ask me, or are you going to stand there and tell me the thought of fucking that sexy bit of chocolate hasn't crossed your mind?" Detective Johnson quipped.

Everyone at the Nineteenth Precinct knew Detective Simms was slightly bedeviled by his sexy partner. At that moment, he wanted to knock Johnson on his ass. Instead, he controlled himself.

"I'm not the one worried about what she does with her free time," said Simms.

"Yeah right. The only reason you try to act like you're not interested is because you don't want to piss her off. Everybody knows you're scared of her, or maybe it's just that you're afraid she might decide not to work with you if she knew how smitten you are. You wouldn't be able to stand not being with her every day, not smelling her, not watching those lips of hers speak."

"Fuck you," Simms said, then walked away.

Even as he tried in earnest to ignore Detective Johnson, Simms wondered himself where she went every night and how he would feel if he couldn't be with her all the time.

About six o'clock, Simms joined Watson at the station to work on their reports.

"So Watson, did your sex shop, fact-finding mission turn up anything?"

"No, nothing."

"Too bad."

Simms was surprised to find that she didn't elaborate, but he didn't press her for information. He figured if there was anything to tell, she would have.

"I'm gonna head out. I'm finished here," Watson announced after a half-hour.

"You sure you don't want to stop by Flanagan's?"

"Yeah, I'm sure. I'm beat. I'll see you tomorrow."

While Simms continued his paperwork, he once again wondered how Watson spent her time. She never spoke of boyfriends, parents, even girlfriends. She hardly ever spent time with any of her colleagues, including him, unless she was badgered into it. It was hard to believe that such a beautiful, intelligent woman could spend her life so isolated. Work seemed to be all she did.

Seconds after Watson left, Simms was on his way out of the door when he heard a cell phone ringing. He searched in his jacket pocket and it wasn't his. Then, he realized the sound was coming from Watson's desk. He heard footsteps on the stairs and hoped that maybe Watson had been stopped on the way out and was still in the building. He called to her, hoping that she could still hear him, but got no response. A smile spread across Simms' lips. He and his partner engaged in an ongoing joke about how often she left her cell phone behind and how often he neglected to charge his. He raced down the stairs to catch up with her. He saw Watson and called to her, but she didn't hear him. Simms watched as she got into her car and drove away. He decided he would catch up with her and return her phone.

Driving behind Watson, Simms, at first, assumed she was on her way home, until he realized she was going in the opposite direction. For a moment, he considered turning back. He started to feel like he might be invading her privacy. Instead, he convinced himself that she would probably need her phone and continued. If he had been honest with himself, he would have admitted that he was intrigued with discovering where she was going.

Within a half-hour, Watson pulled up in front of a church. Simms knew the place well. He had attended an Alcoholics Anonymous meeting there with his first wife before they'd split up. It suddenly all made sense to Simms. Obviously, Watson must have been a recovering alcoholic. It wasn't surprising. Many cops were in recovery. She probably was, too. Instead of taking the risk that she would see him, and be embarrassed or maybe even angry, he decided to turn back.

# CHAPTER SIX

U pon arriving home, Detective Kimberly Watson opened her mailbox, only to find more of the same envelopes piling up. She had hoped they would eventually stop coming, but she'd had no such luck. The letters unnerved her and angered her all at the same time. She discussed the letters at the meetings, but no one seemed to understand, and that only made her feel even more isolated. The stories she heard were all variations on the same theme. She had hoped that she might feel less alone, if she was part of something. Instead, the meetings she attended made her feel even more out of sorts. More than anything, she wanted to feel more grounded. However, with each passing day, she felt more and more like she was losing her grip. If she didn't have a hold on anything else, she always believed she was in control of her work. She was a good detective, or at least she always thought she was, until recently. Lately, she wasn't following up on her cases the way that she should, and she had even begun lying to her partner. Even though she'd told him she had gone to Come Again to question the owner about the bracelets being left at the scene of the burn murders, she still hadn't.

She didn't want to have a drink, but at that moment, she felt she *needed* to have one. Kimberly poured herself a glass of rum. She wasn't sure why she'd chosen rum again. She had a fully stocked bar, even though she rarely drank anymore, but on the rare occasions when she did choose to drink, it was the same signature rum *he* drank. Two glasses was all she needed before she was out like a light.

"Are you there?" she called out.

The pitiful sound of children crying seemed close enough, but no matter how hard she tried, she couldn't reach them. She called.

"Where are you? Don't worry. I've come to save you."

Sharp metal objects dropped from the ceiling, barely missing her, as she continued in her search for the children she had come to save. Suddenly, the walls appeared to bleed. It was a little at first. Then, torrents of bright red blood cascaded from the ceiling to the floor. She attempted to walk, but sharp objects began poking through the floor on which she walked. With each step, safe areas to walk became smaller and smaller, until she was being cut from above and below. However, that did not deter her from her objective. She was still hell-bent on saving the children she heard crying. For a moment, she was hopeful when the objects in the floor seemed to disappear. That's when the blood began to quickly fill the floor, mimicking the feel of cement. The harder she tried to walk, the more difficult it became. Just as she thought the blood was going to stop, the walls began to close in. The space got smaller and smaller. She thought she would be crushed to death. That's when she heard the gunshot. The sound of the children crying was replaced with their laughter.

Kimberly screamed and woke up.

"Shit!" she said.

She turned on the television, hoping it would help put her back to sleep. All she found was a flashing Time Warner Cable symbol, indicating her service had been turned off. She had put such an effort into avoiding the mail lately, she realized she had also neglected to pay her bills. She was happy it wasn't something more important, like her electric bill. She gathered the voluminous stack of mail that had built up and began opening it. After going online and paying everything that needed to be paid, she glanced at the remaining mail. Most of it was tossed back into the pile, except for several that she systematically ripped into tiny pieces and threw into a large metal trash can, then set it all on fire.

Kimberly gazed intently into the flames, before suddenly becoming aware of her reckless action. She quickly doused the trash can with water, went into the kitchen and made herself a turkey sandwich and pulled an Express catalog from the pile. While flipping through it, she discovered one of the envelopes hidden between the pages. If discovered earlier, it probably would have been burned with all the others. Instead, for some reason, she did something she hadn't done in years. She opened the envelope and began reading it.

By the time she finished reading the letter, she bore no resemblance to the calm, self-assured woman who had entered her apartment earlier.

She rose from her chair and threw it across the room. That was only the beginning. She began upsetting all of the furniture and throwing anything she could get her hands on. Glasses, plates, appliances were all hurled against the walls.

She simply screamed at first. Then the idle screaming turned into words.

"Leave me alone!" she screamed. "Why can't you just *leave me alone!*"

She yelled the same words over and over again while she violently ripped the pages that seemed to send her into the rage she was now in.

Sweaty and disheveled, she was mid-scream when there was a knock at her door.

Just as quickly and easily as she had become enraged, her mental state seemed to suddenly adjust. She pulled a paper towel off of the roll in the kitchen, dabbed at her face and arms, and smoothed down her hair, before calmly calling out.

"Just a minute."

She looked through the peephole to find one of her neighbors. He had been trying to fuck her since she'd moved in. He'd tried everything from common interests to chivalry to encourage her interest. However, she was not in the least bit interested and believed he was probably to be avoided.

"Who is it?" she asked.

"It's 4G. Everything okay in there?"

She didn't want to let him in but decided the conversation was less likely to be heard by all of her neighbors if she did.

"Are you alone?" he asked as he entered the apartment and looked around.

Kimberly looked around the room like she was seeing it for the very first time.

"Oh, this," she said. "I got some news I didn't want or need to hear, and I guess I lost it."

"You're not kidding."

4G's first thought was that he had dodged the bullet with this one. However, he still couldn't help but wonder, if this might be an optimum time to "hit it and quit it."

"I could help you clean up, if you'd like."

"No. Don't worry about this. It's not as bad as it looks."

He glanced at the shattered LCD TV, the toppled couch and chair, and the toaster on the floor, and wondered what she was looking at.

The uncomfortable silence was more than she could stand, so she asked him if he'd like something to drink. Kimberly was thinking a glass of water or a soda to go. Instead, he glanced at what remained on the ample bar.

"Some Courvoisier would be nice."

"Courvoisier, it is."

"Aren't you going to join me?"

Kimberly glanced at the shattered bottle of rum and her first thought was at least some good had come of her meltdown.

She decided she would try something new.

"Have a seat," she said.

He turned over the couch.

"You're stronger than you look."

"Yeah, I guess I am."

"You know, I don't think I even know your name."

"It's Troy. I told you before, but I guess maybe I wasn't that memorable, huh?"

"No, not at all. I'm sorry. I mean no, I remember you. You are memorable," she stuttered.

"Yeah, sure I am. I want you to know I am deeply wounded."

Kimberly gulped at her drink, anxious to ease a bit of the tension before filling her glass again.

The two sat drinking in silence.

"So, what happened here tonight? Don't tell me this was about a man."

"What makes you say that?"

"Because it usually is."

"I guess you're right, but not in the way that you think. It was about a man, but indirectly."

"That sounds like quite a story."

"It is."

"I've got time, if you do."

"Maybe some other time," she said, finishing her fourth drink. "I'd rather not talk about that tonight."

"What would you like to talk about?" he asked seductively.

"I'd rather not talk at all."

"I can help you with that."

He moved in slowly. She met his gaze full on, prepared for the kiss that was sure to come. At first she welcomed it, until his tongue began to sloppily roam about her mouth. He was a terrible kisser. She remembered the one and only time she had kissed her partner, Brandon. That kiss had been so different. She remembered wondering how a simple act, one that caused her thoughts to swirl about like she was dizzy, could bring her so much peace.

She knew what the rest of the precinct thought of her; that she was some sort of a freak. All she wanted was to be normal. She thought this would make her normal. So, she kissed Troy back, hoping it would get better. The kissing didn't get any better, but what he was doing to her breasts with his hands made up for it. When he moved on from kissing her lips and toying with her breasts with his hands, to nibbling at her nipples through her shirt, she forgot his lack of skill in the kissing department. Involuntary moans emitted from her lips, and she could feel him growing rock-hard against her thigh.

"Is there someplace more comfortable we can move this to?" he asked.

"Yes."

The alcohol eased Kimberly's usual tension and she led Troy to the bedroom without hesitation.

Within minutes, Troy bolted from the bedroom.

"I'm sorry, but...but, I can't."

Kimberly stood in the doorway, pain etched all over her face.

"You should have said something," he muttered before leaving.

Kimberly followed behind Troy and locked her door, never saying a word. Once the door was locked, she returned to her living room, sat down and continued to drink, while mumbling to herself.

"It doesn't matter. He's not important. I have much more important things to think about. I've got to go to Come Again tomorrow and find out something about those bracelets. I can't let all of these unimportant issues keep me from doing my job. The city needs me. Simms needs me."

She remembered now why she had stopped drinking. When she drank, she forgot, and when she forgot, she didn't prepare. Tonight was one of those nights when she hadn't *prepared*. She slowly rose from the couch, smoothing out her clothing and her hair, before returning to her bedroom.

# CHAPTER SEVEN

While Simms and Watson continued to work their case, Watson got the distinct impression that her partner was preoccupied with something more than work.

"You okay, Simms?"

"Yeah, I'm good. How about you?"

"I'm fine. You seem a little preoccupied, though."

"I'm a little worried about a friend, that's all," Simms said.

"A friend, huh? Who is she?"

"A very close friend with a problem. I don't understand why she doesn't feel she can come to me."

"Maybe she's not sure who she can trust," Watson responded.

Simms wasn't sure whether or not Watson was aware that he was referring to her.

"I'm starving. You wanna get some lunch?"

"Sure," said Watson. "What did you have in mind?"

"I was thinking some barbecue. How about we go to Hill Country and have some chicken and ribs?"

"After that, neither of us is gonna want to go back to work. We're gonna have a chronic case of 'itis.'"

"What the heck is 'itis'?"

"I'll explain it to you over lunch."

It was Simms' intention to take Watson to lunch and inform her he had followed her the previous night and knew her secret.

Instead, they enjoyed lunch together, and he decided not to dampen the day with such a heavy topic. All day, he considered bringing it up, but lost his nerve. By the end of the day, she seemed to be in such a good mood, he didn't have the heart to have anything to do with erasing the uncustomary smile on her face.

"Simms, I'm heading out. See you tomorrow."

"We could always do a double-header and have dinner also."

"Maybe another time," she said. "My apartment is a wreck and I need to clean up big-time. Can I get a rain check?"

Simms was shocked. It was more than she had ever offered.

"Absolutely. I'm going to hold you to that."

Simms could feel Detective Johnson watching the exchange between him and Watson.

"Johnson, don't you have anything better to do than mind my fucking business?"

"Whoa. Chill out, buddy. What are you feeling; like a bad ass now because you think you might get some play?"

"Sounds like projection to me. Looks like you're the one that's got the problem. I'm just doing me. Your problem is, you know she'll *never* do you. And, I'm not your fucking buddy!"

"Lucky me. If you ask me, that bitch is crazy anyway."

"Nobody's asking you."

Johnson laughed and walked away.

While Simms tried not to punch Johnson in the face, Kimberly was on her way home, enjoying a rare moment of feeling at ease. She drove home, hoping the feeling would last. She put the key to her apartment in the lock, only to find the door already open. She was sure she had locked it when she'd left. She never left her door open. She decided it was better to be safe than sorry, so she withdrew her firearm and entered the apartment.

Her apartment was small and most of it could be seen, at any angle, through her now cracked, living room mirror. She approached slowly, hoping to catch a glimpse of whoever might still be there in the mirror.

A male voice startled her so, she was surprised she didn't fire the gun she was holding.

"Hey, Sis!"

"Do you know I could have killed you? You can't keep doing this. You can't just stop by here whenever you like and break into my apartment."

He was sitting there waiting.

"What? I don't even get a hug?"

"Kadeem, I don't have any money."

"Sis, I gotta tell you, I'm hurt. You think the only thing I ever want from you is money?"

"Why else would you be here?"

"Actually, there is one other reason you usually return. You don't have a place to stay, do you?"

"Well, no, but that's not the real reason I'm here. I'm really here for Mom. She needs us...she needs you."

"What are you talking about?"

"You know Mom is up for parole soon, and a letter from a family member, who is also a police detective, would go a *long* way. I would do the letter myself, but I don't think my words are going to hold much weight."

"You're right. It probably won't. I'm still not doing the letter, though. You know how I feel about that whole situation. I made up my mind a long time ago what my level of involvement would be and I have no intention of changing that now."

"Why are you so angry? She wasn't that bad."

"She had gotten a bit more backbone by the time you were born. I was the one who suffered the most because she didn't know how to be anything but a victim. She reminds me of some of these women who call needing police help. I think it's why I became a cop. It makes me sick, thinking about how weak some women can be, letting men beat them and worse. I've spent my entire life making sure that would *never* happen to me. I would be a hypocrite if I were the one to jump in and attempt to save the day. She needs to learn how to do that herself."

"So, what you're telling me is that people shouldn't ask for help. Doesn't that make your entire life a contradiction? You are a cop, aren't you?"

"There's a big difference between help and a crutch. Besides, what I do is protect lives. What you're asking me to do has nothing to do with saving a life."

"That's where you're wrong. Helping our mother will save a life. It will save *her* life. Under the circumstances, don't you think she's spent enough time in that hellhole?"

"She hasn't served her sentence yet."

"Wow, Kay, you're a colder piece of work than I thought."

"I'm not cold and please don't call me Kay. You know I don't like that. I hated it when we were kids, and I still hate it."

"There is something *really* wrong when a person is more passionate about their name than they are about the woman who gave birth to them."

"Whatever. I didn't ask to be born."

"So, can I stay with you or what?"

"You know I don't like anyone in my place when I'm not here."

"So what else is new?" Kadeem whispered.

"What did you say?" she asked.

"Nothing. I'm not just anyone. I'm your other half."

Kimberly opened the refrigerator and removed some bacon and eggs. "You hungry?" she asked.

"Yeah, I could eat something."

They ate in silence, never once mentioning their mother.

"What are you working on these days?" Kadeem asked.

"Nothing you'd be interested in."

"Every time I think we're in the same place, you go and prove me wrong. I'm not trying to pry. I'm trying to connect with you on any level I can."

Kimberly lowered her head for a moment, considering what to say, and in that split second, between the time she lowered and then raised her head, Kadeem was gone. Oddly, she didn't hear the front door open and he was nowhere in the apartment.

She wasn't sure what time she'd drifted off to sleep, but when she woke up, it was obvious her brother had returned. There was jewelry on top of the coffee table and various items of clothing scattered throughout the apartment. Undoubtedly, the meal he had eaten with her had not been enough because her kitchen appeared to have been ransacked. Cold cuts were left out on the countertop, empty soda cans were also on the coffee table, and a pint of unfinished ice cream was left melting on top of the fridge.

She remembered why she limited her contact with her brother. Whenever he reappeared, he was always so damned annoying. He had little respect for her space and often left with not as much as a thank you, or even a goodbye. She hoped this time he wouldn't stay long.

In an effort to clean things up, Kimberly began moving about the apartment, cleaning up everything Kadeem had left. She started on the kitchen, then continued to the clothes and jewelry he'd left everywhere. Among the gold jewelry items was one piece of silver. Kimberly froze when she saw it. It was exactly the same as the silver bracelets being left at the crime scenes.

She knew Kadeem was irresponsible as hell, but she was sure

he wasn't a killer. What could she do? She couldn't conceal evidence, especially not evidence conveniently left in her own home. He couldn't be the killer. It didn't make sense. If he were, why would he leave evidence that could convict him in plain sight of his police detective sister?

"I'm sorry I left such a mess, Kay...I mean, Kimberly," Kadeem said, suddenly appearing.

"Dammit, Kadeem. Stop sneaking up on me. One of these days you're gonna get a hole blown through your gut like that."

"I didn't sneak up on you. I've been here all along."

"Oh yeah. Sure."

"This apartment barely has enough space to turn around in. I would know it if you were here with me. Where did you go, anyway?"

Kadeem smiled and touched Kimberly's face.

"Like I said, I've been here with you all along. I'm gonna turn in. I'm a little tired."

"Me, too. Kadeem?"

"Yeah, Sis?"

"Do you remember him?"

"Of course, I do. How could any of us forget? He made us what we are."

"You know she made us this way, too."

"That's where you're wrong, Kimberly. Our mother was like us. She was a victim of circumstance. Our father, he was the harbinger of evil. So, if you're going to hate anyone, you should hate him. Once you let go of your hatred of Mom and attach it to whom it belongs, we will all know peace. Wouldn't that be great, true peace? We need that. Otherwise, our entire world is going to implode."

"Will you be okay on the couch?" she asked.

"Absolutely."

Sleep had always been Kimberly's enemy. On the *good* nights, she tossed and turned endlessly, sleeping intermittently. On the bad nights, she never went to sleep at all. Tonight was a good night. The thought of Kadeem in the house helped her to sleep. For so long, he had been her only link to her former world, and despite her frequent complaints about him, she didn't feel complete without his presence. She tucked the covers around her shoulders and hoped morning wouldn't come too soon.

The pelting of the rain against the window is what awakened her. She stumbled half awake to the kitchen to make coffee and realized it had already been made. She smiled, enjoying another benefit of having her brother there. The sound of a female voice was the first indication something was different.

"Where's Kadeem?"

"Huh?"

"Where is my irresponsible brother?"

"I have no idea."

"You okay?"

"I'm fine. Why do you ask?"

"You seem a little off, that's all."

"I made some coffee. Do you want some? I'll make you a cup."

"Uh, yeah. Thank you. Two sugars..."

"Black, yeah, I know."

Kimberly retrieved the silver bracelet Kadeem had left at her place and showed it to the strange girl standing in her kitchen preparing coffee.

"Does this belong to you?"

"No. It's not mine. Maybe your brother's girlfriend left it here."

"This isn't my brother's place; this is my place."

"I know."

"You know a lot. Do you happen to know where the fuck my no-account brother is?"

The girl suddenly recognized how agitated Kimberly really was and decided it was best that she make a hasty exit.

"I'm gonna head out. It was really nice meeting you. I left my number on the fridge."

"So, is this what passes for normal encounters these days? You come to someone else's house, fuck my brother, and walk out the door like everything is normal."

"I'm not sure what's happening, honey, but give me a call when you straighten things out. I would love to hear from you."

"Don't you dare talk to me like you're managing me!" Kimberly yelled.

Kimberly stood dumbfounded and more than a little angry. It was moments like these that made her want to get rid of Kadeem, once and for all.

By the time she was leaving for work, Kadeem returned.

She passed him as she was leaving, but didn't want to make a scene, since she could see Simms sitting outside in his car, waiting for her.

"What are you doing?" she asked.

"There you go again with those rhetorical questions."

"I don't want to play these games, Kadeem."

"Neither do I."

She joined Simms and prepared to be briefed about what the plan was for the day. He seemed much more concerned about her.

"Kimberly, are you okay?"

"Of course, I'm okay. Why do you ask?"

"I can't tell a lie. I do my fair share of talking to myself. But, usually when you're having that heated an exchange with yourself, for all the world to see, it means you're either crazy, or you've got a lot on your mind. I'm assuming you're not crazy, so, what gives? You okay?"

Kimberly laughed.

"I should be asking you if you're okay. Do we need to get your eyes tested? Didn't you see my brother, Kadeem, coming in as I was leaving? It was him I was pissed off at. He left some chick in my apartment last night and went out, without so much as a heads-up."

"No. I didn't see him. But, I could see how that might piss you off. Was she fine?"

"Really, Simms? Are you *still* thinking with your small head, instead of the big one?"

Simms smiled.

"I got news for you; they're both big heads."

"Oh, real nice, partner."

"By the way, since when do you have a brother? I thought you were an only child."

"No. He's been here my whole life. He just went away for a while. He seems to only come back when I really need him."

"You need him now? Why? Is it anything I can help you with?"

"No. It's family stuff. Only Kadeem can help me. He always knows what to do."

Simms couldn't help but wonder what was going on with Watson and her family. It was his guess that there was probably more than a little drinking going on. Often, alcoholism could be genetic. He wondered if Kadeem, or other members of Watson's family, had the same problem she had.

# CHAPTER EIGHT

or the first five years, Marie Richardson had been numb. In one fell swoop, she was ripped from the only two people she ever loved. The guilt was overwhelming. The absence of one person from her life was the reason she found herself locked away in prison, and the absence of the other was a byproduct of her weakness. If only she had done something all those many years ago, maybe she could have saved both of them, and herself.

Now, she believed she was in a position to make it all right. All she had to do was get paroled.

It took prison for Marie to realize she had actually spent her entire life as a prisoner. First, there was her childhood and the limits her mother placed on her; and then, there was her marriage. The realization truly hit home when she was incarcerated. The restrictions of prison life were nothing new to her. In fact, she discovered a certain freedom she had to hide when she was married. Samuel had been obsessed with keeping no other books in the house but the Bible. He rationalized that all the other books were evil and meant to undermine the fabric of decency. But, Marie knew the truth. He would have done anything to keep their child from progressing. So, Marie hid books everywhere, so that she could not only read herself, but also so that she could prepare her child for a future. When he went to work, she would use the time to embrace the world outside through reading. She used every opportunity to read anything and everything she could get her hands on. When she wasn't reading, she was teaching her child. Often she was sure Samuel knew, and she would frequently change the hiding places for her books. While in prison, books were her salvation and the prison library was her God.

"Hey. Hey. Yoo-hoo!"

Marie pretended she didn't see her bunk mate, Patty, waving feverishly and loudly *whispering* from the other side of the room. It wasn't that she had anything against Patty, but she didn't have time for friendships and banter. She had to stay the course. She had a goal and the last thing she needed was to get sidetracked. Patty could also be a bit annoying at times. She was like a fly that keeps buzzing around you, no matter how many times you swat at it. Marie lowered her head and focused on the books and papers in front of her, hopeful that Patty would either get the message or simply assume she hadn't seen her. Marie noted the look on the face of one of the guards in the room, and it dawned on her that Patty and her loudness might cause problems for her. The last thing she needed was to lose her library privileges because of Patty, so she turned quickly and looked directly at Patty, cautioning her with her facial expression to stop. When that didn't work, she knew she had to speak up.

"Patty, would you please just shut up!"

Patty made a face and turned away.

Sitting in the library and reading over her parole paperwork, she allowed herself to believe she would be freed. After all, she was not an evil person. Once she told her story, they were bound to show mercy. Faced with what she thought was no other alternative, she had done the only thing she thought she could do.

Only days before that fateful night, she had watched a movie, *Enough*, with actress Jennifer Lopez. In the movie, Lopez' best friend assured her that *she had a God-given right to protect both herself and her offspring.* Hadn't she in fact had that same right? She knew that could not be her defense in getting herself freed from prison, but it at least allowed her to ease her guilty conscience, even if only for a moment.

As she examined the information regarding her parole hearing, it occurred to her that she had at least one advantage. There would be no one there from the outside to oppose her release. All she had to do was convince the Parole Commission that she was unlikely to commit any future crimes. They also needed to know that she was remorseful and that she understood why she was here. Although both her and her child were clearly victims of abuse, there were alternatives that she could have chosen that didn't involve violence. She was aware of that now. The task now at hand was to convince the Commission.

Sitting in the library, poring over reading materials, Marie couldn't help but notice all of the other women in the room. Although she kept to herself, she often heard their stories. Marie had been isolated from people for so long, it had never occurred to her that she was just a small part of a bigger picture. It had become so easy to believe that she was the only one trapped by horrible circumstances, that was, until she ended up in prison. It was then that she realized the countless stories of women who had been victimized by men, in one way or another, were not new. Her story, and so many others, were simply variations of the same theme. Some ended up in prison, some endured their dysfunction and others died, often with little more than a few tears shed by loved ones. Sadly, some never even got that.

The only thing that kept her going was that, in all this, her child had been saved. If she never saw the light of day again, that would offer her some solace. Yet, she knew her child had to blame her for not being more of a mother. More than anything, she needed an opportunity to explain. The only way she would have that chance was if she were freed.

Lost in thought, she didn't hear her bunk mate pull out a chair and join her.

"You working on your PF's (parole forms)?"

"Yeah."

Marie's guilt suddenly got the better of her.

"I'm sorry I yelled at you," said Marie.

"It's okay, girl. This place can bring out the worst in anyone. I don't take that shit personally. Is it true you're up for parole?"

"Yeah. I've got my parole hearing next month."

"What you gonna do, if you get outta here? You know you gonna miss us. You been with us a long time, Marie."

"I don't want to get my hopes up, so I'll cross that bridge when I come to it. But, it sure would be nice to see my baby again. It's been nearly fifteen years."

"I didn't know you had any kids."

"Yeah, just one."

"So, why you don't get no visitors, Marie? Don't your kid wanna visit?"

"I made some mistakes a long time ago, and I don't resent my kid for wanting to put that whole life behind. I just want a chance to try to make up for it."

"It's hard to imagine you doing anything bad to anyone, let alone your own kid."

"I let my husband hurt our child and that's just as bad."

"I'm gonna say one thing before I leave you alone to read: Don't get caught up in guilt and regret, Marie. We all do the best that we can with the cards we've been dealt, and I'm sure that's exactly what you did. Look around you. Sure, there are some bad eggs here. But, for the most part, a lot of the inmates here are victims of circumstance. Or, haven't you noticed how many poor folks are up in here? It ain't like rich people don't break the rules and commit crimes. They've just got a whole shit-load of money to back them up and get them out of trouble, when need be. I don't know what landed you here, but I'm willing to bet you didn't have some six-hundred-dollars-an-hour attorney defending you. You probably had an overworked, underpaid, public defender like most of us."

"Thanks, Patty. I really needed that."

As much as Marie wanted to be left alone, she was glad Patty had come over. She was right. Before she did anything, including moving forward with her parole process, she had to come to terms with the guilt she was feeling. She finally realized it would serve her no purpose.

"I'll see you at lunch, okay? And, Marie, please eat something. You're the only inmate I know that came to prison and *lost* weight."

Marie chuckled.

"My people in Lobeco wouldn't be surprised. I was always the skinniest girl in our town growing up."

"Where's Lobeco?"

"South Carolina."

Normally, Marie would have ended the conversation by now, but it felt surprisingly good to talk about her hometown. Although many of her memories were of poverty and struggles, she still had some good ones. Despite how things turned out, she still remembered fondly the first time she and Samuel met. She remembered their first kiss and the first time they made love. He *had* been good and loving once. She wondered what had gone wrong. She also realized that as easily and quickly that things had gone from a fairy tale to a nightmare, her life could change from a nightmare to a life worth living. She could remember reading an article once about prison reform long before she could have ever imagined herself in such a place. The article addressed the age-old question of whether or not prisoners had any hope of being rehabilitated. Back then, she had no opinion, one way or another. Now, having lived this life, she thought she knew the answer. As far as she was concerned, *anyone* was capable of rehabilitation. Prison was no different than any other situation. Each person walked away from it with something different. Their experience could be a positive, life-affirming result or it could be one wrought with even more pain and dysfunction. Marie felt she had learned from her experience and she now believed she was possessing a certain strength she never thought herself capable of. She had every intention of using that strength to turn her life around. Not only that, she was going to use that strength to reunite her family. She was no longer afraid.

The end of the day and lights out was the most difficult aspect of prison for Marie. It was when she felt most like a prisoner. However, lately, the end of a day was a symbol of her eventual release. She had even begun to tick off dates on a calendar, leading to her parole hearing.

"Good night, Patty."

In all the years they had shared a cell, this was the first time Patty could ever remember Marie saying good night, or anything close to it.

"Good night. Marie?"

"Yeah?"

"What do you have, a boy or a girl?"

"What?"

"Your kid? What is it, a boy or a girl?"

"Why? Why all the damn questions all the time? Leave me alone! Just...just leave me alone!"

Patty wasn't surprised by Marie's sudden shift. That sort of abrupt change of mood was commonplace when women were locked away. Yet, any discussions of Marie's kid was clearly a special sore spot for her.

Patty was doing consecutive life terms, plus thirty years for murder. She had spent nearly fifteen years in prison so far, having joined the prison system when she was forty-five years old. She and Marie had been here almost the same length of time and were sort of the matriarchs of their cells. However, in all the years that Marie had been in residence, most people knew little about her. She didn't talk much and her case, unlike some of the other inmates, wasn't publicized. The other prisoners had tried to piece together tiny bits of Marie's story, but there was much more missing information than was the case with most of the inmates. Marie did nothing to fill in the gaps.

Although most of the long-term inmates were in prison for violent crimes, there were always those few that left even the most violent shaking their heads, finding it difficult to imagine that certain prisoners could ever actually have it in them to murder someone. Marie was one of those prisoners. Her Bible never left her side and she seldom spoke an ill word of anyone. Many believed that she held on to that Bible so strongly because she didn't want anyone to know what she was writing and concealing between the pages on those little sheets of note paper. Although she constantly mailed letters, she never received *any* in return. Once, when one of the inmates snatched the Bible out of her hand, in an attempt to read what Marie was writing, she beat the woman within an inch of her life. Despite her motherly, quiet demeanor, after that incident, no one ever underestimated Marie as a possible threat again.

She tried to sleep, hoping to dream of the day when she might hold her child once again, maybe even make up for not being a better mother.

"Don't worry, baby. Mama's coming home. Everything is gonna be all right," she whispered to herself. "No one's ever gonna hurt my baby again. I promise."

# CHAPTER NINE

The nightshift was the easiest time to work. It was perfect for nurse Jocelyn Edwards because it meant she didn't have to pay the exorbitant childcare fees for her one-year-old. Although she could tell her husband was getting tired of being Mr. Mom, neither of them had any other choice. His job during the day paid very little. That was why she had taken the job at Montelior. It paid far better than the public hospitals, and based on the schedules of many of the other employees, she was sure she would eventually be able to change her hours, once she had worked there a little longer. If her husband got a better job, she might be able to return to working days, and have enough money to find their daughter a nice pre-school.

Montelior was a long-term convalescent hospital. Most of the patients were either terminally ill, elderly, or both. Often it was a revolving door, since typically, there were only two paths. Either a patient had a remarkable recovery or died. There were not too many that stayed there in *limbo*. Mr. Richardson was one of those patients that happened to be in *limbo*.

Jocelyn wasn't very friendly with most of the other nurses that worked with her. The only person she talked to a bit was Carolyn Switzer. Their lives were similar and she seemed less involved in all the petty gossip that circulated throughout the hospital. The only topic they both seemed to be intrigued with was Mr.

Richardson. He had been a long-term patient for years, when suddenly, he came out of a coma, and recently, he somehow seemed to be rebounding.

"It's sad. I don't think anyone's been here to see that old man since he's been here. It's a miracle that he's not still a vegetable. I thought for sure once he came out of the coma, there would be at least one person that cared enough to be here, but, nothing; no visitors to hear his first words, no happy family members hopeful that he might continue to get better. How often does a patient make this kind of recovery? More often than not, they come here a vegetable and they die here a vegetable," said Jocelyn.

"If it were me, I'd rather they put me out of my misery, awake or not. During the rare moments when he appears *somewhat* lucid, he's still talking out of his head," Carolyn added.

"I was in there one night and I know the man is harmless, but some of that shit he was saying, it scared the living crap out of me. I hightailed it out of that room so fast you would've thought he was chasing me with a knife in his hand."

"Yeah, I've heard him, babbling something about Jekyll and Hyde, and evil and the Lord. I wonder if the accident did that to him, or whether he was already out of his mind?"

Both women turned around when they heard the head nurse enter the room, knowing how much she despised gossip.

"Switzer, I believe your patient in 103 needs his pain meds."

"I'll be right there."

"He's been ringing for the past half-hour."

After Carolyn left to attend to her patients, the head nurse addressed Jocelyn.

"You know, Edwards, the family members of the patients here pay a pretty penny for confidentiality and so that their loved ones are treated with some level of dignity. If you're not on board with that, you could always leave the private sector and return to working at a public hospital."

"I'm sorry, Ms. Williams. I didn't mean anything by it. It's... the other nurses and I consider him a bit of a mystery. No visitors, no specifics as to how and why he was injured."

"We've all been very pleased with your work here, Edwards. If I were you, I would leave mysteries exactly where they belong, between the pages of a book."

"Okay, you're right. I completely understand. It really is none of my business."

"Exactly. Now, I believe you have an hour left on your shift."

"I'll get on it right now."

"I'll take care of Mr. Richardson. You continue your rounds." She turned to the patient. "Now, Mr. Richardson. I believe your catheter needed some adjusting."

Mr. Richardson's eyes bulged with fear.

"This will be a lot worse if you squirm and make a lot of noise and fuss. It's up to you, but I would suggest you lie still and let me do what's necessary."

They both knew none of what she said mattered. The pain that would soon come was inevitable. He braced himself for it, thankful that he was still alive. After she was done, he cleared his throat in an effort to speak.

"You can't do this forever."

"I can do whatever I want, old man. Don't you dare tell me what I can't do!"

"Just kill me. It's what you want."

"Since when do you know what I want? What I want is to make you pay and that's exactly what I'm doing. I waited for so long for you to wake your sorry ass up. Now, all my patience has paid off."

Mr. Richardson's mobility was returning quicker than Ms. Williams anticipated. He managed to press the call button while she was distracted.

Jocelyn returned to assist and noticed the blood on the sheets.

"Oh my God! What happened?"

"He pulled out his foley."

"Shouldn't we call urology?"

"He's fine. I recatheterized. Eventually, the blood will stop and his urine will clear."

After Nurse Williams left the room, Jocelyn approached Mr. Richardson's bed. She planned to clean him up and make him feel more comfortable. She thought she read something in his eyes, as if he were trying to tell her something.

"Mr. Richardson, is there anything else I can do for you?" she asked.

"Help me," he whispered. "Please, help me."

# CHAPTER TEN

No one noticed the dark figure mumbling to no one in particular in anger. The face was etched in a terminal scowl.

"She deserves it. Look at her, flaunting it, daring the world to look upon her evil. It's time for her to join the others."

"When will it all stop?"

"Leave me alone! Let me to do my work. Nothing you say will ever change my mind."

Quickened steps followed a young woman closely, careful not to alert her.

"Look at her. She doesn't know a thing. She's so stupid. So oblivious to her destiny. I'll remedy that soon enough. First, the reminder, then the destruction, then God's work...the purification. I have everything I need right here."

"You can't. Who decided you were judge, jury and executioner? You are not God!"

"I may not be God, but I am one of His servants."

"You sound just like him. I never thought I'd see the day when you would spew his words like so much venom. Don't you know he was sick? It's the reason we're the way we are, you know."

"What way? What are you talking about? We are fine. You keep the world *clean* in your way and I in mine. I would suggest you leave now, if you don't have the stomach for *my* way. Her time has come. God has spoken."

The white handkerchief soaked in a clear liquid silenced a woman returning home from a meeting. Hands ripped her clothing before savagely raping her. As if all of this were not enough, the assailant then dumped her body in the trunk of the stolen car, doused her in the same chemical used to knock her out, struck a match, and tossed it into the trunk to burn, until there was practically nothing left. There was no struggle, no pleas for help. It was very quick, very easy. In the blink of an eye, a life deemed unworthy was extinguished.

"How long do you think you will be able to violate these women and burn their bodies in open view before you're locked away?"

"I place my fate in God's hands. I will stay the course and continue to fulfill His work until He tells me otherwise. When will *you* give *your* life over to the Lord?"

"You and I are on two different paths."

The energy derived from satisfying the purification of the earth was often so intense, it was difficult to be satisfied with just one. As the flames danced in and out of the trunk of the car, there was a certain beauty that could not be duplicated with anything but another. The figure cloaked in darkness longed for an opportunity to satisfy the desire to rid the world of evil. Often, the desire was so overwhelming, caution was nearly forgotten.

"Are you really willing to risk being caught by getting another one tonight, while the fire you started just a moment ago continues to burn? Even you are not invincible."

"I admit it's going to be difficult, but I can wait. I *will* wait. Those who require purification must be carefully chosen and that is what I will continue to do. The Lord depends upon me and I will not disappoint Him. There is a formula to my work, a formula which must be followed with the utmost care. So far, I have gone undetected. My efforts will continue in the same way.

I watched this one ever so carefully. It almost became a game. She was evil in so many ways, not the least of which was her life-long abomination. I had no other choice but to extinguish her as God had intended. The flames are so compelling. Don't you feel it? Don't you just want to dance around it, let it consume you?"

"I'll pass, thank you, and I would strongly suggest you not dance around any flames tonight, unless you're prepared to have the NYPD come and take you away."

"I was simply speaking metaphorically. I can barely contain myself. Only a few more days and I will be able to choose another. Often, it's so difficult to pick just one. I listen to the words they say, I watch their actions, and I try to decide which one is most imperative, but often it is impossible to choose, and I simply choose the one that is the easiest. You'd be surprised at what I must sometimes put myself through in order to carry out His wishes. If you only knew the number of times I defiled myself, in order to best offer these sinners up righteously to the Lord. The sacrifices I have made are immeasurable and will continue without end. You ask me if I'm willing to be caught and I answer a resounding yes! The question you have to ask yourself, is whether you are willing to sit idly by, while our earth is dirtied by the actions of a few."

"All I would suggest, is that if you must continue on this path, that you take it slow. You know Rome wasn't built in a day and neither was the destruction of evil."

# CHAPTER ELEVEN

"You must be Cat."

"Hello, Dr. Phipps."

"So Cat, is that short for something?"

"No, just Cat."

"Have a seat wherever you'd like."

She looked around the room and decided on the couch. The two sat in silence for some time, before Cat finally spoke.

"So how do we do this?"

"However you'd like. This is a safe environment. You can say whatever you'd like, or say nothing at all, if that's what suits you."

"So, you're telling me if I wanna come here and say nothing for an entire hour, that's okay."

"Yes, it is."

"That seems like a big waste of time."

"It's my hope that no time spent here will be a waste."

"I'm not even sure why I'm here. I feel like I keep making the same mistakes over and over again and I'm sick of it. I was hoping that coming here might help me to figure some things out. Nothing seems to bring me much joy anymore."

"What do you think has changed?"

"I'm not sure. There was a time when I could just roll with whatever happened, but lately, I'm not myself. Everything seems to take so much effort. Just getting out of bed to go to work is a chore."

"What kind of work do you do?"

"I'm a dancer, an exotic dancer. A lot of people judge dancers, but I make a lot of money dancing and I've never been ashamed of what I do. The place I work at isn't so bad and all I have to do is dance. I don't have to do anything else, unless I want to. That's the other reason I'm here. When I first started, I had no interest in anything other than dancing. Between tips and lap dances, I made enough money. I thought for sure I'd never do anything but that. Lately, though, I've been doing other stuff. It started with hand jobs and then it was blow jobs. Now, I'm having sex with my customers. It's getting out of control. It's almost like I can't stop it."

"Why do you think you started having sex with the patrons at the club? Are you doing it because you need the money?"

"No, not really. This would all make so much more sense, if I really needed the money. I don't."

"How do you usually feel after you've had sex with someone that's paid you?"

"While I'm...doing it, I don't feel anything. It's after that's scary. I think that's why I'm here. I get so angry after. I don't know why. Nobody's forcing me. It's my decision. But, after I'm done, something happens to me. I get blind with anger. It's gotten so bad, I have to keep changing clubs. After I've been with so many of the customers, I can't stand to see them, and eventually, I have to move on. I've been to three different clubs in the past three months. Pretty soon, I won't have anywhere to work."

"What about your personal life? What kind of sex life do you have outside of the people who are paying you?"

"No men. I do get together with women every now and then, though."

"Do you consider yourself a lesbian?"

"No, not really."

"Straight?"

"Not really. I'm not sure what I would call myself. I'm not sure I want to call myself anything. I just want to be able to feel some semblance of peace."

"You're right. Our goal here is not for you to define yourself. Our goal is to attain exactly what you just said, some level of peace. How have you been sleeping?"

"I sleep okay. I hear all these people talk about insomnia and I can't begin to relate. I sleep like a rock. Sometimes it feels like I'm sleeping too hard. I wake up and it takes me a while to figure out where I am. I listen to people talk about their insomnia and I'm almost jealous. In that split second when I wake up, not knowing where I am or sometimes who I am, that's the loneliest feeling."

"I can imagine it must be. Do you get that lonely feeling any other time?"

"Only after."

"After what?"

"After I've been with them, after the women I meet, or after having sex with my customers, I feel lonely and dirty and angry with all of them for making me feel that way."

"Is there anyone in your life that doesn't make you feel that way, a family member, a friend, a lover?"

"There's no one. I feel like I'm all alone, yet I'm surrounded by so many people."

"You're not alone. I'm glad you came to me."

Candace was happy to find that Cat opened up quite freely and their session continued with great ease.

"Our time is up now, but I'm going to give you my card. I want you to call me whenever you feel like the loneliness you're feeling is unbearable. Can you do that?"

"I guess so, but I may have to call you more than you might expect."

"I wouldn't have given you the card if I didn't want you to call. I trust you to use it as you see fit."

Cat laughed.

"What made you laugh?"

"You don't know how many times I picked up the phone to call for an appointment and then changed my mind. After I finally got the nerve to complete the call, I agonized over what was going to happen here, and whether or not I'd feel comfortable talking to a stranger, but this was okay. It wasn't as bad as I thought it would be."

"I'm glad you're comfortable here. Otherwise, this won't work."

"I'm very comfortable. It's like déjà vu, like I've been here before."

"Good."

Candace pulled out her appointment book. "Do you want to come back the same time next week?"

"Yes, that would be perfect."

Candace watched as Cat left and hoped she would return. More than anything, she wanted to have an opportunity to free Cat from the demons that plagued her, but she knew it would take time. She was hopeful that she would be able to help Cat, but couldn't tell her what was wrong. She would have to show her, in order for Cat to truly free herself from what it was that kept her prisoner. That was the way for all of her patients, including those like Cat that were most likely haunted by secrets.

# CHAPTER TWELVE

"I want those deadbeats out of my apartment now!"

Christina and her lawyer had been back and forth to court for the past six months, yet the Taylors were still there, and hadn't caught up on their rent.

Joshua Sullivan was a good lawyer, but Christina suspected he was one of those bleeding-heart liberals who actually cared about the fate of the poor and downtrodden. As far as Christina was concerned, he could care all he wanted as long as he did it on his own time and it didn't interfere with her business. She wondered if maybe she should go to court and ensure he wouldn't give these losers a chance to lose her more money. What the fuck was she, anyway; the goddamn Red Cross?!

"Christina, I'm doing the best I can, but the wheels of justice often turn very slowly," Josh responded.

"Josh, don't give me that 'wheels of justice' crap. I want them out, now!"

"The holdover proceeding is today at ten o'clock. Unless they have a significant portion of the rent today, they will have to vacate, probably in thirty days or less."

"Thirty days!"

"Yes, I'm sorry, but the Judge is not going to toss a family of four out on the street at a moment's notice, even if they do lose."

"What's this about a significant portion of the rent?" Christina asked.

Josh felt sorry for the family of four who were probably going to end up joining the ranks of the many downsized working stiffs who suddenly became homeless, because they had no money to pay their rent or mortgage, but he had a job to do. The reality was, he was just a paycheck away from being homeless himself. Despite popular misconception, not all lawyers were rich. Josh's grades in law school hadn't been good enough to be recruited by the larger, more successful, law firms right out of law school. Therefore, he had taken the modest inheritance he had gotten from his mother, after she passed away, and opened his own firm. He didn't have a long list of clients, but Christina, along with two or three other frequent clients, kept Josh fed and clothed; and paid off his school loans, allowing him to barely pay the rental on his office space, which he shared with two other attorneys, also in private practice. Therefore, it was imperative he kept the few clients he *did* have happy, or he would be joining the ranks of the poor and downtrodden as well. At this point, he didn't even have enough money to hire his own receptionist and secretary to help out. He and the other two attorneys had put their heads together and decided that they could probably share the cost of hiring one assistant that could help them all. Even with the three of them, they couldn't afford to pay what a secretary would make at one of the larger firms. They would have to find someone with experience enough to do the job well, but who was willing to take much less money.

Like a lightbulb turning on in his head, Josh suddenly had a brainstorm. He looked through his files and found a phone number for Linda Taylor. Unfortunately, it was disconnected. He would have to speak with her before court.

Christina wasn't quite as disappointed as she would have everyone think about the Taylors not paying their rent. As far as she was concerned, it was a win-win situation. She was sure they would not be able to come up with the six months' rent they owed and therefore, they would be evicted and she would get new tenants. She would then be able to raise the rent considerably and make a nice profit over time. This time, however, she would be much more careful about who her property was rented to.

Even her partner, Sebastian, seemed intent on working with the family to ensure they didn't lose their apartment. She couldn't understand it. No one had cared about where she lived when she was homeless. She had been abandoned from the day she was born, simply because of the way she was born. As if that were not enough, the foster homes she was forced to endure were hell on earth. The world wanted to make people like her out to be the freaks, but in truth, it was the people who lived behind those beautiful maintained glass houses that were the sick ones. She could remember one foster home in particular. They tried to break her, but she had always been stronger than any force she was confronted with. While she sat waiting for the Taylors to arrive to court, she remembered the day she decided no one would ever hurt her again.

After having been bounced from one foster home to another, Christina was eager to settle down anywhere. Half of the foster families were simply in it for the support money they received. The other half were the kind of people that always found themselves within close radius to children, wherever they were. One family, in particular, was the Pattersons. On the surface, they seemed normal enough. They were not. From the very first moment Mr. Patterson managed to see Christina unclothed, at the age of twelve, he came up with his own brand of dysfunction. What surprised Christina most was when she realized his straight-laced, perfectly coifed wife, Suzanne, joined in.

Both Suzanne and Tom Patterson were photographers. Initially, Christina was beyond excited when she came to live with them. There were cameras everywhere and they seemed more than willing to share their art with her. They taught her everything there was to know about photography and before things went bad, she thought she would eventually be a photographer herself one day. At first, they encouraged her to take pictures of the landscape, at the zoo, even pictures of ordinary things, like the rain. Then, they encouraged her to take pictures of people. She was fascinated with what her photographs could capture. She even learned how to develop her own pictures. She never saw it coming when they started taking more and more pictures of her. It made sense. In fact, thanks to the museums they visited together, and the photography magazines they constantly bought her, she didn't hesitate when they wanted to take pictures of her with less and less clothing. She justified it, as they did, with calling it art. However, one day, Mr. Patterson wanted her to disrobe completely, and she felt very uncomfortable. The day was etched in her memory.

"Let's take some pictures, Christina."

"Okay."

"These will be true art photos. I want you to take everything off this time. Okay?"

"O...kay," she remembered mumbling.

As she began to disrobe, suddenly, she lost her nerve and stopped.

"What's wrong?" he asked. "Would you feel better if I photographed you and Suzanne together?"

Christina stood rooted to the spot as Tom left the room in search of Suzanne. After he left the room, she thought she was being silly and decided she would take the photos as he had asked, so she went looking for him. That's when she heard Tom and Suzanne speaking.

"Tom, you push too hard. Give her time. She'll give in eventually."

"I don't have the luxury of time. We need the money. Besides which, I didn't see you complaining when you were shoving that white powder up your nose. We wouldn't be in this predicament if it weren't for you and your little habit. Now we're broke and I can't think of any better way to make some money. Do you have any idea how much money we can get for pictures of something like this? This is ten times better than that kiddie porn shit we were pushing. How many photos are there floating around of a kid like this? We'd be stupid *not* to take pictures of it."

"And what if we get caught? You have any idea what would happen if we got caught doing something like this?"

"We won't get caught. We'll take the pictures and sell them the same as we did with the others."

"Yeah, but this is stepping into new territory. This is truly a specialized market. The same people that bought that run-of-the-mill stuff we did might not be into this."

"That's what I've been trying to tell you. It won't be the same people. It's a totally different market, even more underground than the other stuff, and bound to pay even more money. You get what I'm saying? We've hit the fucking jackpot! The best part of it is, she likes taking pictures. She's even easier than some of the others. I agree with you, it's only a matter of time before she's willing to take off all her clothes. But, I'm not willing to wait even a day. If you take the pictures with her, she'll do it even quicker. It'll be a family affair." He chuckled.

Christina stood behind the door, listening. A single tear fell. She had cried many tears before that day. But that single tear would be the last she ever shed. Something clicked in her head while she stood there listening to the Pattersons talk about her like she was the oddity the entire world had always made her out to be.

She decided from that moment, that no one would ever make her feel that way ever again. All the shame she felt for years was suddenly washed away. While the experience hardened her, it also allowed her to make a decision. She could continue to allow others to decide how and what she felt, or she could take control and decide her own fate.

Surprisingly, she took the photos that day. She even helped Tom Patterson to develop them. She then dropped off copies of the photos at her local police precinct. Along with the photos was a note, detailing where they had come from and who had taken them. After leaving the precinct, Christina ran as far away as she could get, and the Pattersons never saw her again.

It wasn't difficult to prosecute the Pattersons, especially given the fact that Mrs. Patterson was in many of the photos.

Life wasn't easy for Christina. She was a twelve-year-old runaway, with no place to live, and she had no intention of going back to foster care. So, she did what most child runaways did. First, she tried living on the street, but that got old pretty fast. Eventually, she met an older girl named Ebony, who introduced her to tricking. It was a hard life, but the older Christina got, the more intent she became on making enough money to leave the life. She decided to return to the world the Pattersons had introduced her to. She discovered there was indeed a huge market for photos of people like herself, and she had no problem with making money from those photos. The difference between what she was doing and what the Pattersons had done was that *she* was in control. From the moment she left the Pattersons' home, she decided no one would ever again control her destiny. She continued to trick for a while, even while selling the photos of herself, until she met a John who introduced her to the investment world. She bought her first property at the age of eighteen, flipped it and used the money to make her portfolio grow by leaps and bounds.

Her earlier experience instilled in her a hatred for photography and she never took pictures of herself or anyone else again. As far as she was concerned, she had paid her dues and would never again have to demean herself in such a way, nor would she allow anyone else to, in any capacity.

Christina never allowed herself the luxury of feeling sympathy or empathy for anyone. She believed that the moment she let her guard down, in even the smallest way, that would be the time when someone would be in a position to destroy everything she had worked so hard to build.

Snapped out of her memories by the sight of her attorney and her tenants engaged in conversation, Christina watched. She couldn't hear what they were saying, but judging by the smiles on the faces of Mr. and Mrs. Taylor, she was sure Josh was not playing hardball.

She decided it was time to make her presence known and got up to walk to the other side of the room to join them. By the time she reached them, the Taylors had already entered the courtroom.

"What the fuck was that all about? Don't tell me the court gave them more time."

"They haven't come before the judge yet, but I may have come up with a solution that could help us all."

"What solution? The only solution I can think of is their eviction and a brand-new set of tenants with enough money to actually pay the rent."

"The only reason the Taylors couldn't pay the rent is because they both lost their jobs. I gave Mrs. Taylor a job at my law office and referred her to an agency that may be able to either pay the rent or loan her the money to pay the rent,until she starts working. Maybe by then, Mr. Taylor might even have a job."

Josh stood there grinning, so pleased with what he thought was a solution everyone would be happy with. He was shocked when he heard Christina's reaction.

"Josh, do you know why I hired you?"

"No, not really."

"I hired you because after doing my research, I realized you were desperate enough to work *real* hard for me. I didn't hire you so you could decide what was best for me. I hired you so that you could enact what I *know* to be best for me. What is it about you men? Do you all think every woman you encounter is a damsel in distress? If you didn't know, let me make things crystal clear for you. I don't need saving by you or anyone."

Josh was practically speechless.

"I don't understand," was all he could say.

"No, you don't, do you? You're fucking useless and now you're fired! Get out of my sight. I would have been better off representing myself in the first place."

As she exited the courthouse onto the street, a strong chemical scent filled her nostrils before she saw nothing but darkness.

# CHAPTER THIRTEEN

C andace sat glued to her television set, watching the news. Another body had been found burned. More than anything, she hoped it was not one of her group members. The reporter's mention of downtown Manhattan and the court buildings in the backdrop kept bringing Christina to mind. She was beginning to become even more convinced that this might not be as random as she at first believed, but instead was focused much closer to home. She remembered Christina discussing her recent visit to housing court to evict one of her tenants. Somehow, she knew it was more than a coincidence. She decided she would call her mentor and ask his opinion.

"Good morning, Harry. I know it's early, but I was wondering if we could get together at some point today. I've got a problem I need to discuss. It's really important."

Harry Little had known Candace for many years. He had been her mentor, her counselor and her friend. In all the years he had known her, he had never heard such tension in her voice as he did now.

"Sure, Candace. You wanna meet for lunch, or did you have something earlier in mind?"

"Lunch is fine. Say twelve o'clock at Amber's."

"See you then."

"Thanks, Harry."

After hanging up the phone, Candace wondered if she should cancel the group meeting. She decided to wait until after she had spoken with Harry.

She turned off the news so she could listen to some music instead. She thought it might calm her. Just as she was turning to her favorite classical station on the radio, the phone rang.

"Hello. Harry, is that you?"

The voice seemed faraway and she could barely hear.

"Hold on one second. Let me turn down the radio."

"Okay, that's better. Can you hear me?"

A high-pitched wail was all she could hear. It sounded like someone crying. She hoped it wasn't one of her patients or someone at the support group.

"I'm here. Just try to calm down so I can hear you. Are you still there?"

Suddenly, the odd sound stopped. Then all she could hear was the raspy sound of someone breathing before a voice spoke.

"God has spoken."

Those three small words instilled in Candace a fear unlike anything she had ever felt. Somehow she knew this was more than a random prank.

Candace quickly showered and dressed. She shut off the radio and turned the news back on, hoping that there might be a special phone number to call if someone had information regarding the recent victims that had been burned. The story was run on the news again and a number was indeed provided. She jotted down the number, tossed it in her purse, and quickly left. Something about being alone in her apartment after the phone call was giving her the creeps.

Although Candace knew it made perfect sense for her to be shaken, under the circumstances, she was sure her concern that she was being followed was more than idle fear. She could feel someone there. Whoever was following her was no amateur stalker. He knew very well how to stay unseen. Yet, she could still feel him there. She made sure she stayed in crowds all the way to Amber's.

As soon as Harry Little saw Candace, he knew something was terribly wrong.

"Candace, what's going on? You're white as a sheet."

"Have you been watching the news recently?" she asked.

"For the most part. Why?"

"Do you know about the burn murders in the news recently? I think they may have something to do with my support group."

"If that's the case, Candace, you know what you have to do."

"It's not easy. My group isn't just any support group. Many of the people in the group trust me to guard their secrets as fiercely as they do their own. How can I betray that trust?"

"Think about the alternative. What if you say nothing and someone else is killed?"

"So, you can see my dilemma."

"No dilemma. Go talk to the police."

Candace considered telling Harry that she thought she was being followed, but she didn't want to alarm him.

"I will. Thanks for making me feel better about this."

"No problem. That's what I'm here for."

"I'm not looking forward to telling everyone in the group. They're not going to like it."

"When you explain to them the alternative, they'll get it. What other choice do they have?"

As they left the restaurant, Candace was suddenly reminded that she thought she was being followed earlier. She scanned the restaurant, wondering if she might notice someone that looked suspicious or maybe even someone she knew.

"Everything okay, Candace?"

"Yeah, I'm fine. Did you drive in by any chance?"

"You want a lift somewhere?"

"Could you drop me off at the recreation center?"

"Of course. When are you going to the police? I could go with you, if you'd like."

"I want to speak to my group first. I was going to cancel to-night's meeting, but if I'm going to the police, they at least deserve to get a heads-up. The fucked-up thing is at our last meet-ing they voted ten-to-five in favor of not going to the police. I shouldn't have led them to believe there was a choice. There are going to be some very pissed-off folks at this meeting tonight."

"Do you keep files on the members of your group?"

"No, you know how groups work; it's like Alcoholics Anon-ymous, very informal. The only files I keep are on my patients. Why do you ask?"

"I was thinking that the police might want to see any files you have on the group members, if you had any."

The recreation center where Candace held her meetings had several meeting rooms and at this time of the day, they were all packed. It was exactly what she needed. She thought it was best to stay in crowds, at least until she spoke to the police.

She made her way to her usual room, where there appeared to be a meeting for anorexics just about to end. She was glad the room was still occupied.

"Hey, Dr. Phipps," the organizer said, after all of the members of the group left.

"Don't worry about cleaning up. My group will be here in a few minutes, and it doesn't look like it needs much sprucing up."

"Thanks! I wanted to take the hubby to dinner tonight, and I would love to go home and take a shower and get dolled up."

"Go. Go. Have fun!"

The room was empty and her group would be starting in twenty minutes. As she threw away random cups, she could feel someone standing behind her. A sickly sweet chemical scent filled the room. She had never smelled it firsthand, but she read enough descriptions of it through the years to know exactly what it was: diethyl ether.

She decided that under the circumstances, it would be best not to turn around, but she did speak.

"Have you come to kill me, too?"

It was that voice again, the same one she had heard over the phone.

"God has spoken."

She hoped if she talked long enough, others would arrive, thereby saving her.

"Surely, God hasn't decided to kill me. I've done nothing wrong. I'm a doctor. I help people."

"You are one of the pestilent spirits. God *has* chosen you."

"I don't think God has chosen me. There must be some mistake."

She knew she was taking a chance that she might anger him even more, but the goal was to buy as much time as possible before someone else arrived, hopefully to save her.

She had done it. She heard multiple footsteps coming up the stairs, only a couple of feet away from where he stood. She would have liked nothing better than to turn around, but she didn't dare, at least not yet.

"Candace! Candace!"

As soon as she heard her name, she knew she was safe and turned around, slowly.

"Wow," Brandy said. "I called your name like twice. You didn't even hear me. What were you thinking about?"

"Nothing. Everything. I don't know."

Candace wasn't sure what to say and decided to wait until everyone else arrived and she could speak to them all at the same time.

"You think anyone besides you is going to show up?" Candace asked.

"There are a couple of people still chatting in the hallway and I saw a couple of people downstairs. Is the person that just left coming back? They didn't look familiar, but then again, who could tell with all those clothes and that hood? I suppose that comment means you heard about the third murder."

"Unfortunately, yes, I did."

"So what do you think, Candace? You think it's someone from here?"

"Who, the victim or the killer?"

"I was actually talking about the most recent victim, but do you think the killer really could be someone from the group?"

"No, of course not. I'm a little distracted today and misunderstood what you were asking."

"It does raise an interesting possibility. I suppose anything is possible. Think about it, all of us are dealing with some pretty heavy shit in this group. I've seen people lose grip for less."

Candace decided she would not tell anyone but the police about what had just happened. More than anything, she wanted to press Brandy for details of what the person that she had passed in the doorway looked like, but she knew that was probably not a good idea.

"By the way, Candace, what the fuck were the anorexics eating in here? Something smells really nasty."

"I don't know, Brandy. I think it might be some sort of cleaning fluid."

"It's awful. Can we open a window or something?"

"Absolutely."

By the time all the windows were open and airing out the room, the only members that were coming had arrived. Their numbers had been reduced from the average fifteen or so to who sat before Candace now, only six members.

"I'm judging from the small number of you who arrived tonight that just about everyone else has watched the news, knows about the third victim, and everyone is understandably scared."

"What news?" one member asked.

"Where have you been, hiding under a rock or something?" Sydney asked.

"I'm the mother of four children, ranging in ages from four to thirteen, and I work a full-time job. That leaves very little time for watching the news or reading newspapers. Just tell me what's going on."

"I'm sorry. I'm a bit edgy myself," Sydney explained. "It seems that they've found another body burned."

"Do they know who it is yet?" the mother of four asked.

"I'm guessing they don't. I'm hoping it wasn't a member of our group that was killed. If it was, then that means these really could be hate crimes. If that's the case, then there's a good possibility that the killer is someone who knows us. After all, it's not like most of us go around publicizing the fact that we come here and why."

"Ladies, I hate to do this, since you took the time to come today, but I'm afraid I am going to have to shut the group down early tonight," Candace advised. "Also, I'm going to end our sessions for a while until we can gain some understanding of what's happening. I hope you all know this means I am going to have to go to the police. Anyone that would like to speak to the police as well should feel free to do so. In the meantime, it's best that you err on the side of caution and try not to go anywhere alone and pay attention to those around you."

Candace quickly scanned the room, taking special note of the members present. There was Brandy, Teri, Cynthia, Kay, Arianna and Nikki. Any one of them could have been the voice she'd heard earlier, but if she were going to make a guess, she had a pretty good idea which of the six it actually was.

First thing the next morning, Candace called the Crimestoppers number that was provided to report any information related to the burn victims that were murdered.

"Hello, my name is Candace Phipps. I'm a psychiatrist and I conduct a support group at a recreation center on Bleecker every week. The second victim of the burn murders was a member of my group. I also believe I'm being stalked and that the killer may be planning to come after me next."

# CHAPTER FOURTEEN

"Watson, wake up. While we were chasing our tails, that mother-fucker hit again!"

Watson could barely raise her head from the pillow. She had a migraine of epic proportions. Over the past several months, her migraines had gotten progressively worse.

"Dammit, Watson! Wake up!"

Simms' relentless pounding on her front door was only increasing the severity of her headache.

"One second! Could you give me a chance to get out of bed?"

Watson stumbled to the door and opened it.

"Hell, Watson, what took you so long? And, were you on a bender last night. You look like hell!"

Simms barged into Watson's one-bedroom apartment.

"Gee, thanks, partner. By all means, come in. Make yourself at home," she said sarcastically. "That is, if I still have a home after the neighbors complain about all the damn noise you're making. Could you knock any louder on my door? There is a doorbell, you know? Especially since it is still morning and I, like most of the rest of the world, was still sleeping. Hell, I've been working around the clock for weeks. What do you expect?"

"Well, not everybody's been sleeping. He hit again. But, this time he underestimated the power of the media. The media coverage has made citizens more aware. This time the fire was reported right away. People are trying to do the right thing. I also think some of them want their fifteen minutes of fame, probably hoping to be interviewed on television or something. Thanks to the calls, this body was discovered early and didn't have an opportunity to burn long enough to destroy all of the tissue and bones. It gets even better. Not only was there a pipe left at the scene; apparently, our fire bug is also a rapist. The pipe had blood and cervical tissue on it. The calls are pouring in on Crimestoppers. One, in particular, seems like it might be promising. A psychiatrist who runs a support group called in. The second victim was a member of her group. We might actually be able to get more information on this one. John and Jane Does make for difficult crime-solving. But with early established identities, we might be able to get a jump on his next victim. I want to stop by and see the psychiatrist first and after that, maybe we should stop by the medical examiner. The full report will take a while, but we can at least get some initial findings, in addition to what the forensics investigator was able to collect at the scene."

Watson could not understand why Simms continued to talk, despite the fact that she was still in the other room.

"I'll be right out. Why don't we go over everything when I'm done dressing?"

"No problem."

While Watson was in her bedroom, Simms figured there was no better time to drain the weasel.

Watson exited her bedroom, dressed and ready to go.

"Aren't you gonna slap on a bit of water?"

"Oh, now you want me to wash. Five minutes ago, you were rushing me like you had no damn sense. Like the corpse was gonna run away somewhere before we got there."

"Should I ask whether you're taking your own car today? After all, if we're riding together, I should know in advance whether I need to keep all the windows open."

"Real funny. You're a laugh a minute, Simms."

"Oh, come on. Where's your sense of humor? I'm just pulling your chain. Besides, judging from all the damn bloody Band-aids in your bathroom, you must have shaved and all that stuff you women do last night before you went to bed."

"What are you talking about? What bloody Band-aids?"

"Okay, now I'm convinced. You *were* on a damn bender last night, weren't you? That's why you couldn't join us at Flanagan's. Is that why you can't remember why the hell you have bloody Band-aids in your *own* bathroom garbage pail?"

"Why are you snooping around my garbage anyway?"

"I wasn't snooping. I was taking a leak and as small as your bathroom is, how many places are there to look?"

"Likely story. If you must know, I had a guest last night. I'm guessing that's where the Band-aids came from. You're so nosy!"

Simms couldn't help but assume her visitor was a man. He also couldn't help but feel a bit jealous.

"You okay, Simms?"

"Yeah, I'm good."

Watson decided she would give Simms a break and rubbed the back of his back.

"My brother was here," she said.

Simms' broad smile was unmistakable.

"That's right. I forgot you said your brother was visiting. Maybe we could all go out and have a beer or something, if we ever get a chance."

"Yeah, maybe."

"So, as I was saying, the forensics guy thinks our guy is also a rapist. Apparently, the pipe had blood and cervical tissue on it."

"That might shorten the list of potential assailants considerably," said Watson.

"Although, technically, I don't know if I'd call it rape. The last victim was killed by the diethyl ether almost immediately. According to the M.E., a large enough dose is fatal. So, instead of a rapist, I guess maybe our guy is a necrophiliac."

"Simms, really? He murdered them, fucked them and then burned them. Rape is still defined as nonconsensual sex, isn't it? Well, I would say that this is pretty damned nonconsensual. As far as the burning is concerned, it's probably nothing more than a means to destroy evidence. The rape is probably the main objective. What I can't wrap my head around is how does he find the time to do all of this and go unnoticed, unless he's murdering and raping them someplace other than where the bodies have been found, then dumping them and quickly burning them after arriving at the scene. It's actually doable, if the guy is fast enough, especially with the ether he's been using as an accelerant. But, why did he leave the pipe this time? There was none with the first two victims."

"Maybe we just think there was none left. Both the first and second victim were burned much more thoroughly than this one. Hell, the first victim was ashes."

"You could be right, or maybe he's just getting sloppy," said Watson.

"I hope you're right, because up until now, this guy has not made many mistakes. He's one of the most elusive killers I've ever seen. If he doesn't make even more mistakes, and soon, I'm afraid this will be one of the few times I won't catch my man, and I can't have that."

"Don't you mean *our* man?"

"You know what I mean, Watson."

"Don't worry. If he got sloppy with this victim, he'll do it again. They all make mistakes eventually."

"Once we meet with this shrink, maybe we'll be able to connect the two victims."

"Let's hope."

"If the shrink's a dead end, there's still the possibility that it's all been random," said Simms.

"I find that hard to believe. Except for the pipe left this time, each of these crimes was executed without fault. It was all too smooth. There has to be some level of planning involved for something to go off virtually without a hitch. There is definitely a connection. We just haven't found it. This guy chose his victims with care and planned his crimes down to the smallest details."

"Hold on just one minute, Watson. Aren't you getting a little ahead of yourself? The medical examiner hasn't even given us his findings on this latest victim. It's a crazy city we live in. This could be a copycat. That would explain the pipe at this scene and none at the first two."

"Are you kidding? You and I both know it's him. Wasn't there a bracelet at this scene as well?"

"Okay, okay, I surrender. I'll admit it's pretty obvious that this is probably the same guy. But, you know what the big word is from the Mayor. We don't want panic in the city. One burned body in New York is just another murder. Two burned bodies and the fear starts to build. But three bodies and there's bedlam. So we need to keep most of these details on the down-low."

"What are you telling me for? You're the media hound."

"Me? Somebody has to stick around while you play the vanishing lady."

"Oh, by the way, Simms, what do you mean you surrender? Surrender to what, may I ask?"

"No comment."

"Is that for me or the media?"

"Both."

There were times when Watson surprised him. One minute, she was the most closed-off, conservative woman he had ever known, and the next, she was flirting with him like it was something they did all the time. He lived for those flirtatious moments. Watson had played many a starring role in the X-rated movies of Simms' dreams, with him as the very willing costar. He had whacked off countless times fantasizing about her. Nevertheless, he never acted on *any* of her infrequent, seductive comments and always chose, instead, to keep it moving. He kept reminding himself that a smart officer *never* shit where he ate. As much as that was probably a good practice in any workplace, he thought it was even more important when your life depended on the level head of both you and your partner. That level head could easily be compromised when sex and emotions were involved.

# CHAPTER FIFTEEN

Kimberly was starting to adjust to Kadeem's presence in her life. He came and went frequently, but she was starting to look forward to when he would return. The more accustomed she became to him being there, the more he was there. However, she knew she would have to address him leaving strange women in the apartment when he wasn't there. She also knew the bracelet she found would need to be discussed, sooner rather than later.

"Kadeem, talk to me."

"What, Sis?"

"You come here out of the blue. You try to get me to write a letter to the parole board for Mom and then you keep disappearing. What's going on?"

"Nothing. Who's disappearing? I'm here. I've always been here and I'm not going anywhere, unless you want me to."

"Really? So what's the deal with the girl you left here?"

"What girl?"

"Come on, Kadeem, stop playing games."

"No one is playing games, Sis. You know that."

Kimberly stomped out of the room and into her bedroom. When she returned, she was holding the silver bracelet she'd found among her brother's things.

"Okay, so if you won't answer that question, what about this?"

"What?"

"Where did this come from?"

Kimberly stood in front of Kadeem, holding the same type of bracelet being left at the crime scenes.

"I think you know the answer to that."

"Would you please stop answering my questions with questions! Okay, so you want to play it like that? Is that what you're saying? Well then, I'll tell you what I know. This exact bracelet has been left at three murder scenes. And those murders started right around the same time you showed up. So please, tell me you got it from one of your skanks or you stole it. Otherwise, I've got to believe the obvious: my brother is a murder suspect. If that's true, then I don't know what I'm going to do, or have you forgotten I'm a police detective? Hell, I'm one of the main detectives on the case. So, please answer my goddamn questions!"

"You, of all people, know I don't have a violent bone in my body. As far as the bracelet is concerned, I really don't know where it came from."

Kimberly couldn't help but acknowledge what he had said and he was right. Since they were children, he was always the one who was sweet and kind and incapable of any violence. That's why it made perfect sense that she would become a cop, and it would have never made any sense for Kadeem. He was the only one who had ever been there for her. If she didn't give him the benefit of the doubt, then who? She decided the only thing she could do was trust him.

"I'm sorry. I guess this case has got me a little frazzled. The pressure is unbelievable and I was fine dealing with the letters from Mom, but now, with the added pressure of knowing she might get out, it's a lot."

"I understand. That's why I'm here. I knew you would need help in handling all of this. You know I'm always there when you need me the most."

"You are, aren't you? I don't know what I would do without you. I would never have survived with *him*, if it weren't for you. You're my lifesaver. Do me one more favor; don't go around flashing that bracelet or giving it to one of your girls. The NYPD is on the lookout for the guy that is committing these murders, and any lead will get noticed."

"Okay."

"Kadeem, have you heard anything about Mom's release?"

"No. I haven't heard anything yet."

"I don't know if I'm ready for her to be back. It'll be like revisiting the past. I want that time to go away. She's a constant reminder of what happened."

"It's funny," Kadeem said. "When I think of her, all I think about is the time of day when Pop was at work, and she would get out the books, and it was just like we were in school. Remember?"

"I don't, not really. So many times, I've tried to remember how I learned the things I learned or if there was any good that happened in that house, but it's all a blank. All I can remember is the things he did to me and our mother doing nothing. I think that's why I decided I didn't want to be a nurse anymore and went into the academy. Every time I cared for a patient, it was like her all over again, taking care of something old and weak, administering to the helpless, yet having no real power."

"Go and get dressed. We're going out," Kadeem said.

"What, no hot date tonight?"

"It's been so long since we've done anything really fun together. It would be good for both of us. Not only that, you need to do something other than work."

"Where are we going?"

"No questions. I know just the place. Don't worry about a thing. I'll take care of everything. I'll even do the driving."

After showering and putting on her makeup, Kimberly dressed

in a pair of leather pants and black turtleneck, only to leave her bedroom and find Kadeem wearing the same thing.

"Oh my God," she said. "We're gonna look like The Bobbsey Twins."

"I'm okay with it. It reminds me of when we were little. I used to love dressing alike."

Kimberly simply smiled.

Kadeem grabbed the car keys.

"Let's go have some fun. I think you've earned it."

Kimberly was giddy for the first time in a long while. Kadeem was right. It was like they were kids again. They jumped in the car.

"Come on, Kadeem, where are we going?"

"You'll see."

Kimberly sat quietly while Kadeem weaved quickly in and out of traffic, wondering if she should say something about his driving.

"You stupid bitch, get the fuck off the road," someone screamed out of their window.

"I would love to get there in one piece," she said.

"Don't worry. Just sit back and relax."

They were in New Jersey at a club called Scenic.

Once inside Kimberly realized she should probably have stayed at home. She felt out of place and spent most of the evening watching Kadeem and the tall, beautiful woman he was dancing with. Her skin reminded her of caramel and her silky, black hair reached past her waist and her legs seemed to go on forever. It was her guess that she was probably a model or something equally exotic. It had always been so easy for him. Neither of them had spent any time with people other than their mother, father and each other. Yet, by the time they both ventured out into the world, she was no different than she was now, mostly shy and uncomfortable with others, while Kadeem always connected well with people. She wondered how two people could grow up in the same household and turn out so different.

Kadeem and his beautiful model friend left the dance floor and joined her. Lani nibbled on Kadeem's neck, all the while never taking her eyes off of Kimberly.

"We look good together," Lani said.

They stayed at the club until the lights started to go up. On the way home, Kimberly was surprised to find that neither Lani nor Kadeem were uncomfortable with the fact that she was giving him head, while he drove home. His intermittent moans and shallow breathing, combined with Lani's sucking and slurping, drew her in. What they felt, she felt. Her breathing synchronized with the rhythm of his. She was helpless to resist it. As they made their way home, their breathing was not the only thing in sync. They both came in unison. Gone was Kimberly's concern about driving safely. All she cared about for the moment was getting off.

She barely remembered going to bed. Surprisingly, she didn't wake in the middle of the night the way she usually did. Thanks to her unusual ride home with Kadeem and Lani, she'd enjoyed the most delicious dream. Incredibly artful lips and hands were all over her body, bringing her to climax over and over again, until she begged for mercy.

# CHAPTER SIXTEEN

K imberly slept uninterrupted until the sun filtered through her bedroom window. When she stretched and turned around, she was surprised to find she was not alone. Sleeping next to her was the woman Kadeem was with the night before.

"Lani! Lani, wake up!"

She shook her awake and her beautiful bed mate yawned and stretched before she kissed her on the lips. Kimberly froze.

"Hmmm," Lani moaned. "Last night was incredible. I've never met anyone like you before."

"What are you doing here? Why are you in my bed?"

"Don't you remember? You didn't have that much to drink last night. Remember, I left my car at the club last night and you invited me to spend the night here?"

Kimberly rubbed at her temples, then shook her head, as if the simple action might make things clearer.

"Are you okay?"

"No. Uh, no. I'm fine. I'm going to go for a run. Is Kadeem still here?"

"Huh?"

"Nothing. Never mind. Make yourself at home. Fix yourself something to eat if you'd like. Whatever you need."

Kimberly changed into her running clothes and shoes and left the apartment. She started out running slowly, pacing herself.

What she really needed was to clear her head and to get away. Ever since Kadeem had returned, she seemed to be losing control of her life. If a perp was doing the things she was doing, she would assume they had a drug or drinking problem. She tried to remember how much she had to drink the previous night. Much like the girl, Lani, mentioned, she couldn't remember having more than a glass or two of wine to drink. That left drugs. She was always so careful with her glass when she was out, so it couldn't have been that someone slipped her something. She thought of something she didn't want to believe. What if Kadeem had been doing this to her all along? She clearly wasn't herself.

Since Kadeem's return, she had been acting strangely out of character. She had been neglecting her work a great deal and her thoughts had been oddly unfocused. Brandon had been working their case mostly on his own. That in itself was uncustomary. Usually, Brandon would have to tell her to slow down. Yet, lately, she hadn't been following up on leads, even though she assured Brandon she would. She knew from the moment she thought of him that was the only person that would be able to help. She had believed everything Kadeem said, without question. Now she wondered if maybe she was being played.

She continued to run, hoping to shake the disorientation she was feeling. Before she knew it, she was at Brandon's place, knocking on the door. Since Brandon's divorce, he had traded a constant string of women. Some lasted longer than others, but in the end they were all temporary. She realized it probably wasn't the best idea to pop up on his doorstep without calling. As she was walking away, the door opened.

"Kimberly, is that you?"

She turned around and came back.

"Yes, Brandon, it's me."

She didn't realize how *out-of-sorts* she looked until Brandon opened the door.

"What's wrong?" he asked sympathetically. "Are you okay? Are you hurt?"

His concerned voice was enough to weaken her defenses, just long enough to let go.

He embraced her tightly and she practically fell into him.

"Whatever it is, it's going to be okay. Come in. Sit down. You want some water or something?"

"Yes, could I have some water?"

"Absolutely."

Brandon went into the kitchen and got her a bottle of water out of the fridge.

"I'm sorry to stop by here unannounced."

"Don't worry about that. You know you're always welcome here. I've certainly popped up at your place enough times without calling."

She smiled.

"There we go. That's better. At least I got a little smile."

"You've always been able to make me smile."

Brandon sat next to Kimberly and put his arm around her.

"Tell me what's going on."

"I'm having some sort of meltdown. My memory has been for shit, I've been distracted, I'm angry all the time and this morning... I...I can't even tell you. I'm so embarrassed."

"You never have to be embarrassed to tell me anything. What happened?"

"My brother and I went to a club last night. I thought it would be fun, but I didn't really enjoy myself. It was an odd evening, but by the end of the night, I figured it was over and I would get a good night's sleep and start fresh in the morning. When I woke up this morning, I was in bed with the girl my brother came home with. I don't even know what happened, but it sure felt like I might have slept with her."

For a moment, Brandon said nothing. There wasn't much he was shocked by, but he had to admit this surprised him a bit. He knew Kimberly was secretive about her personal life, but he didn't believe that she was a lesbian or even that she had an unrevealed freaky side.

"See, I knew it. Now you're shocked."

"I don't shock that easily. I'm considering everything you told me before offering my thoughts, or have you forgotten I'm a detective by trade?"

This time, she laughed.

"Now a laugh. I tell you, I'm taking my act on the road. Maybe I'll stop at Caroline's Comedy Club."

"Stop making me laugh, Brandon. This is serious."

"You ever think maybe that's the problem. Maybe your life has been a little too serious and that's why you're having this melt-down you're talking about."

"I can see where that might be a possibility. But, Brandon, why can't I remember anything? I don't even remember going to bed with this girl."

"How much did you have to drink?"

"Only one or two glasses of white wine."

"Okay. Is there a chance someone, maybe even this young lady, slipped you something in your drink?"

"Even before I became a cop, I've always known to watch my drink when I'm out."

"Let me change this up a bit. What do you think is happening? You must have some ideas."

"Something else I'm embarrassed about. You see, while I was

out running, it occurred to me that all of this started right about the same time my brother showed up."

"Don't stop there. Spell it out to me, plain and simple."

"I'm wondering if maybe Kadeem might be giving me something to make me like this. My brother's always been there for me. He's a good guy. I feel like a complete bitch for even thinking it."

"You and I both know, even weirder things have happened. Strangers don't corner the market on doing fucked-up shit to each other. In fact, most of the fucked-up shit that does happen in this world involves family and close friends."

"I came to the right person, someone as jaded as I am."

"Kitten, we can't help but be jaded. We see the very worst in people every single day. I don't know about you, but it's not the bad things that people do that surprises me. I'm much more surprised by the good things that people do."

"Wow, Brandon, if that ain't fucked up, I don't know what is. I guess that's why we're partners. We make the perfect pair."

He hugged Kimberly to him and kissed her on the forehead. He had never seen her like this. She seemed so small and helpless. He hated to admit to himself that he liked it. She was always so strong and unreachable. It was the closest she had ever allowed him to get to her.

"Whew, how long did you say you were running? You stink," he said, pinching his nose.

She smacked him on his arm.

"Truth be told, I was probably stinking long before I went running. When I woke up and saw that girl in my bed, I ran out of there like the place was on fire."

"So, what you're telling me is you left a complete stranger in your apartment. By the time you get back, she may have backed the moving van up and cleaned you out."

"There's nothing to clean out. Sadly, I have nothing but my principles."

"You have a whole lot more than that, my dear, and I'm not talking about your material possessions."

He wanted to say, *you have my heart*, but bit his tongue, literally and figuratively.

"Maybe my brother is back by now. I should probably call him. Could I use your phone? I left my cell."

"You and that cell phone. You're always leaving it somewhere."

"My battery is dead on my cell, but the landline is up and running."

"Look who's talking. Me always leaving my cell somewhere and *you* never charging yours."

Kimberly called her brother. "Is she still there?

"Kadeem, this has to stop. My job has been suffering. I don't know if the two of us living together is such a good idea."

Brandon could hear his phone ringing while Kimberly was still talking and wondered why she hadn't noticed. He assumed, maybe her brother had hung up on her. Yet, she talked for several seconds while the phone rang. He walked back in the living room when it was clear she was no longer talking.

"Everything okay?" he asked.

"Everything is fine. Thanks for asking."

"I tell you what. I'm starving. I can cook us up one of my Polish feasts or we can go out and get some brunch."

"My vote is for a Polish feast. Can you actually do that?"

"Of course I can do that. I would love the opportunity to try and fatten you up a bit. I didn't think it was possible, but you have actually lost more weight. First, though, you have to do me a favor. *Please* make quick use of my shower, oh sweaty one."

Kimberly stuck her tongue out at Brandon and turned on her heels.

He couldn't care less what she smelled like. He wanted her more than any woman he had ever wanted in his life.

"Yum, something smells good," Kimberly said after leaving the shower.

"I hope you're hungry."

"Starved."

Brandon was busy in the kitchen and hadn't turned around. When he finally did, the sight of her took his breath away. She was fresh from the shower and simply draped in a vibrant blue towel. Yet, her glistening skin and the freshly scrubbed scent of Irish Spring soap made him dizzy with desire.

"I didn't want to put my stinky clothes back on. Would you happen to have a pair of sweats and a T-shirt I could borrow? Brandon?"

His throat was suddenly dry. When he eventually spoke, he had to clear his throat in order to speak.

"Sure, sure. Of course. I'll get you something."

When he returned with clothes for Kimberly, he handed everything to her, only to have it drop to the floor.

They both bent down to pick everything up, bumping heads.

"Ouch," Kimberly said. "If I didn't know any better, I'd think you were trying to get me to drop this towel."

Suddenly, the room was silent and Kimberly wasn't sure why she had made the comment.

"I'm gonna get dressed."

"Okay."

Brandon was sure he would cool off a bit once she returned with more clothes on. He was wrong. Once she came back, wearing his gray sweats and green New York Jets T-shirt, he realized he was truly whipped. If it was at all possible, she was even more gorgeous wearing the sweats and T-shirt. Not only that, he couldn't stop thinking about the sweats he so often wore, being so close to her body.

"You need some help?" she asked.

"No, I'm good. Just have a seat and wait for your taste buds to be tantalized."

"Oh really." She chuckled.

"Really."

"So what are we eating?"

"Well, this is Golabki. It's cabbage leaves with rice and a little bit of meat, and this is kotlet wieprzowy, which is basically pork cutlet."

"It sure smells good. Although, I don't get many home-cooked meals, so I don't have much to compare it to."

"Stick with me, kid. I'll expose you to all sorts of culinary delights. Speaking of which, I forgot the most important thing, the wine."

"I love the bottle. What is it?"

"You're gonna love it. It's a honey wine, made with black currant juice and spices. It's really a dessert wine, but we don't have to stand on tradition. Also, I know what a sweet tooth you have."

Kimberly sipped a bit of the wine and sighed.

"Oh. This is so good."

"See, I knew you'd like it. It's called Kurplowski Royal Mead."

Kimberly and Brandon sat eating and drinking and for a moment their troubles were forgotten.

"You mind if I ask you a question?" Brandon asked.

"Sure. I guess."

"I was a little cautious about bringing out the wine because I didn't want to be responsible for creating a...situation."

"What kind of situation?" she asked.

"Are you in recovery?"

"Recovery from what?"

"I'm going to tell you something," he began. "Don't be angry with me."

"Okay, so now I'm on the edge of my seat."

"Recently, you left your cell phone at work and I tried to stop you, so I followed you. I probably should have stopped when I realized you weren't going home, but I kept going. I saw you at the church. I saw you going to AA."

Kimberly's expression was blank. Brandon couldn't read what she was thinking or whether she was angry or not. He hoped it was a good sign that she hadn't turned the table over or gotten up and stormed out.

"Brandon, I don't know what to say. So this is why you've been acting so strange lately. I can't believe you followed me, like I was some sort of a perp."

"That wasn't my intention. I didn't exactly purposely follow you. I only wanted to return your phone. I thought you would need it."

"Then why didn't you turn around when you saw I wasn't going home?"

"I made a mistake. I got caught up in the moment. You have to realize I care about you. Most of the time you seem like you have the weight of the world on your shoulders. I feel so helpless most of the time. There's nothing I can do for you if I don't know what's wrong."

"What is it about men? You all think every woman needs a man."

"Don't pin that label on me. I wouldn't treat you any different if you were my male partner."

"Really, Brandon? Clearly I'm not the only person not being completely honest. So you're going to tell me that when I got out of the shower earlier, you didn't want to fuck me. Is that something else that would be no different if I were your male partner?"

Brandon wasn't sure what to say and was surprised that Kimberly brought up the taboo topic. He got up from the table and busied himself with clearing the food and dishes away.

"Aren't you going to answer the question?"

Kimberly stood directly behind Brandon, daring him to be honest. His response took her completely by surprise. Without a word spoken, he turned to face her, then grabbed her tightly and kissed her, engulfing her with that same fire she remembered the last time they'd kissed long ago. He then broke the grip his mouth held on hers, grabbed her by the shoulders and held her body away from his, looking directly into her eyes.

"Is that what you wanted? There's *my* honesty. All my cards are on the table. I don't just want to fuck you, Kimberly. I love you, and not like I would love a fellow partner. I love you like a woman. So, yes, I want to protect you. I want everything for you that a man would want for his woman. The only problem is I'm nothing to you but your partner. I want you to be happy, whether you want me or not. Quite frankly, I don't see happiness in you. I don't know what your life is or was, beyond what we do at work every day, but I do know something is wrong. I wish you trusted me enough to open up and tell me."

"You may think you want to know the truth, until you actually hear it."

"There's nothing you could tell me that would change my opinion of you."

"I've got baggage, Brandon; a *lot* of baggage."

"Who doesn't? I've got two ex-wives, an overbearing mother and a father who locks himself in the basement most of the day, building model cars. We've all got baggage."

"Yeah, I guess you're right."

Brandon stepped closer to Kimberly and with his finger, he

tilted her head up to meet his eyes. Once again his close proximity to her didn't allow him to stop his body from responding.

"I thought you didn't want to fuck me?" she asked nonchalantly.

"I don't. I want to make love to you more than anything I've ever wanted in my life."

They kissed. This time the kiss was full of compassion. Brandon kissed her lips, her forehead, her eyes, before sweeping her off of her feet and carrying her into his bedroom. Kimberly's head kept telling her to stop before they went too far, but Brandon's dramatic action not only swept her off of her feet literally, but figuratively as well. Her ability to reason was suddenly lost.

Once in the bedroom, Kimberly was returned to the reality of what was happening. As she tried to speak, Brandon kissed her with such passion, she couldn't help but go with it. Her body responded and all the reasons she had in her head as to why they shouldn't were lost.

"I can't believe we're here. Kimberly Watson is in my bed."

Kimberly's sudden shift was surprising, yet exciting to Brandon. She flipped over so that she was straddling his body and began showering him with kisses much in the way he had been doing to her. First, she kissed his eyelids, then his neck and his lips, while she removed his shirt. Her tongue and lips then traveled the full surface of his chest, biting at his nipples. She enjoyed his response, the masculine moans emitting from him.

"Take off your clothes," he managed to choke out, in spite of his intense pleasure.

Kimberly ignored his plea. Instead she continued to undress him. Her tongue lapped at his manhood, and as if he weren't already hard enough, he grew even more inside of her mouth when she engulfed him.

Brandon wanted to make the moment last and knew that if she

continued at the rate she was going, he would not be able to control himself, at least not this time around. He attempted to move, but his strength was markedly depleted by the things she was doing with her tongue and lips. She stroked him so expertly with her mouth, he was in awe of her. Before he could cum inside of her mouth, he wanted to please her as well. He tried to raise himself up, but she persisted in impeding his movement. Then suddenly, she was removing her own clothing. She stripped down to her panties and Brandon appreciated every bit of what he saw. As he expected, her body was incredible. He sucked her nipples and smoothed her taut belly with his masculine hands as he traveled down to places further south. Once again, Kimberly stopped him. Instead she straddled him backward and rode him relentlessly until Brandon could do nothing more than let go and blast inside of her. Before he could kiss her or lay in bed savoring the after-effects, Kimberly jumped off of him and went straight to the bathroom, locking the door behind her. Brandon lay there confused and wondered what, if anything, he had done wrong.

"Kimberly? Kimberly? Is everything okay?" he called to her outside the locked bathroom door.

"I'll be right out," she responded.

Kimberly returned to the bedroom to find Brandon back in bed. He patted the side of the bed, motioning for her to join him.

"You okay?" he asked.

"Yes, I'm fine."

"You sure?"

"Absolutely. Everything is fine."

Brandon recognized that she did not want to discuss anything that had transpired, and he declined to comment on the obvious fact that she had dressed completely from head to toe.

"I'm going to head out," she said.

"You know you can stay here if you'd like?"

"No. That's okay. I already have enough trouble sleeping. It'll be hard getting used to a new bed and I don't want my tossing and turning to keep you up."

"Can I at least drive you home?"

"No. I'll be fine. Relax."

Brandon walked her to the door and was pleased to find that she at least kissed him goodbye.

"I'll see you at work tomorrow, okay?" he said.

"See you tomorrow, Brandon, and thanks for the brunch."

"Anytime."

# CHAPTER SEVENTEEN

"What you got there, you crazy bitch?"

Before Marie could grab her papers back from Sandy, she was waving them around the recreation room. First, Sandy tried reading them, but Marie was following so closely behind her, she didn't get to read more than a few lines at a time.

Marie was usually the level-headed one in the bunch, but when it came to her Bible and the papers she carried around within, she lost all control. The last time Sandy had done the same thing, Marie beat her so badly, she was in the infirmary for weeks. Patty remembered the incident and did her best to get Marie's attention, so she could caution her. She knew it would take a great deal to get her to focus so she used two words. "Marie! Parole hearing!"

While Sandy was distracted, Patty grabbed the papers out of her hand and punched her hard in the face, knocking her flat. That, of course, the officers saw.

"Mumphrey, you just lost rec privileges for a week."

"Yeah. Yeah. I know the drill."

Marie mouthed the words *thank you* to Patty as she was returned to her cell.

By the time Marie returned to their cell, she had calmed down a bit.

"Marie, let me warn you about something pretty damn important," Patty advised. "It's some trifling folks up in here. I can't think of any place in the world where that saying *misery loves company* means more than here. News travels fast and somebody else's good news travels even faster. So, my advice to you is keep that Bible and those papers well hidden until your parole hearing. That stuff seems to mean a lot to you and everybody here knows it. They're gonna try you by fucking with that thing that means the most to you. Hide it in here and only read or write in it at night, whatever you have to do. But, don't take it out of this cell or you're bound to have issues with it again."

"I hear you and I meant what I said earlier. Thank you so much for helping me out."

"No problem. I'm just being selfish. My people outside forgot about me a long time ago. My family and my man visited for a while, but eventually they stopped coming. It's been years since I've had a visitor. It would be nice to know that somebody on the outside gives a damn about me. Maybe that could be you."

"If I get out, I'll come back to see you. I don't show it very often, but you've been the only friend I've had, both before I got here and now. I was in prison long before I got locked up here."

"It's so true what they say, *everybody's got a story.*"

"When I got married, I thought my life was made. My husband was handsome and smart and all the other girls wanted him, but he chose me. I can remember going to bed at night and praying that a man like Samuel Richardson would want me. I wasn't the prettiest girl and my people were dirt poor, so when he did choose me, I felt like my prayers had been answered. I couldn't have been more wrong. There was something broken inside of Samuel. For the longest time, I thought I broke him, but I realize now it had little to do with me. His problems started long before I came along. Our situation just encouraged him to go over the edge quicker. I've been reading a lot about something called schizo-phrenia and I think that's what was wrong with him."

"Wow. I know all about schizophrenia. My ex-husband's mother was schizophrenic and I think he might have been also."

"I've been wondering for years what we have in common and why I seem to like you so much more than everybody else. Maybe that's our common thread," Marie said.

"You might just be right. Isn't it something, how we find ourselves bound to others by our pain?"

"You said a mouthful there, sister."

In uncustomary fashion, Marie suddenly began to laugh. She laughed and laughed like she had never laughed in her entire life. The word *sister* coming out of her own mouth seemed somehow foreign to her. It was lighthearted and easy. She liked it.

"I'm gonna miss you, Mrs. Marie Richardson."

"I'm not gone yet."

"You will be. That parole board would have to be fools to make you stay here."

"I hope you're right. I'll miss you, too, but I really want to see my kid. Even though I haven't seen her since I got here, she's in trouble. I know it. She's so angry with me. No one can have that much anger and not be in trouble."

"Spoken like a true inmate."

"You know what's funny, though, anger isn't what put me here. I know most people who go to prison for a violent crime say it was self-defense, but in my case it really was. If I hadn't done what I did, my kid would have died. I had to. The only thing that keeps me going is knowing that she's led an exemplary life. My daughter has received all sorts of commendations, and even without the slightest bit of assistance, she was able to not only become an honored police detective, but she also managed to become a nurse before joining the academy. That's what's in that Bible I carry around. Everything I've ever found related to her life, I saved. You wanna see it?"

"The biggest mystery between these bars? Hell yeah, I wanna see! But only if you want to show it to me."

"I do. I really do."

There were pages and pages of newspaper articles, cases she had solved, special commendations, all for Kimberly Watson.

"Why is her name Watson?"

"Maybe she wanted to put as much distance between her father and me as possible, so she changed her name. I don't blame her. I shot her father the same day she was leaving to go away to college. It makes sense that she wouldn't want to be associated with either of us. It probably was the best thing she could have ever done, considering she ended up going to the police academy and all."

"Even though you've mentioned how you should have done more, you must have done something right. Otherwise, how could she have turned out the way that she did. It seems like she has accomplished a great deal."

"Yeah. I'm proud of her. She was able to do all that she has with little to no parental guidance. I just wonder what the cost was."

The next morning, Marie was in better spirits than she had ever been in all her years in prison. In a few more days, she would be meeting with the parole board and *come hell or high water*, she would learn her fate.

It seemed as though things had gotten even better. For the first time in years, she received a letter. It was addressed to her from Kadeem Watson. Her first thought was that maybe she had a grandchild, or that Kimberly had done more than legally change her name; maybe Watson was her husband's name. She ripped open the letter and within minutes, her skin was deathly pale.

*Dear Mom,*

*I'm still trying to convince Kimberly to write a support letter for you to the Parole Board, but she is incredibly stubborn. I know things weren't the best when we were young, but she is so resentful, it clouds all of her thinking. I've joined her again because she needs me now more than ever. There was a time when I could help her through these down periods. I've been able to since we were both little, but it's getting harder and harder now.*

*I truly wish I could come to see you, but Kimberly is so much stronger and she would never allow it.*

*Hang in there, Mom. You'll be home soon and we'll all be a family once again.*

*Love, Kadeem*

Marie's eyes widened with terror. It was starting all over again.

# CHAPTER EIGHTEEN

**J**ocelyn continued on her rounds, but one patient was occupying her thoughts. On the night Mr. Richardson's foley was removed, he had pleaded with her to help him. From that night on, she made sure she paid close attention to him. The more time she spent caring for him, the more things at the hospital didn't add up. She realized it was more than her desire for gossip that fueled her interest. A great deal about the patient, Richardson, was steeped in mystery. Not only that, their head nurse, Ms. Williams, didn't add up, either. She only worked two nights a week. She wondered how she could make any kind of a living working so few days. Even when she was working, Mr. Richardson seemed to be the only patient she focused on. He had no visitors and according to his records, had no family members. Yet, he was staying at one of the most expensive private hospitals in New York. Either he was very rich or someone was paying for his stay, one that had stretched out for years.

"Have you noticed how agitated he's been lately?" Jocelyn asked Carolyn.

"Yeah. Ever since that night Nurse 'Ratchett' caught us talking about him in his room. You think maybe he heard us?"

"No. His agitation has nothing to do with us. I noticed something since I've been here. Every time she comes out of that room, he starts screaming and he always seems to be in a much worse state of mind when she's around. There's something peculiar about her. I asked a couple of the nurses that have been here longer than us where she came from, and she's just as big a mystery as our mystery patient."

"The plot thickens," said Carolyn.

"Well, I've got to clean him up. We better be careful anyway. If she heard us talking, we'd both be in a world of trouble. She would like nothing better than to fire us both."

"Yeah, you're probably right."

Jocelyn left to clean up Mr. Richardson and couldn't help but notice the agony etched across his face as soon as she entered the room. It was something more than what was typical. As always, she spoke to him while she cared for him, hoping to make him as comfortable as possible.

"How are you today, Mr. Richardson? You seem more upset than usual."

"She's here," he responded, his eyes darting around the room. "She's the devil's spawn, you know?"

Jocelyn's first thought was *Nurse Ratchett*, but she reminded herself that this was Ms. Williams' night off. She wondered if paranoia was getting the best of her and that Mr. Richardson was in fact either senile, crazy or both.

"Who's the devil's spawn?"

"The one who pretends."

As Jocelyn removed his clothing to check his bed sores, she was struck by the fact that what she initially saw, and believed to be bed sores, might not be bed sores at all. There was a pattern to the marks on his body. She had seen bed sores and these were no bed sores. In fact, they almost appeared to be scratches. There were odd little marks that bore a strange resemblance to the impressions a mini rake might make if it was pulled across someone's skin. Often when older patients came to be in their care, they bore obvious signs of abuse. But these wounds appeared to be fresh, and this particular patient had no visitors and had been with the hospital for many years. There were never any family members present to do either good or evil. There was only the hospital staff. Now it was Jocelyn's turn to be agitated. If he had no visitors, then the people in whose care he had been placed would inevitably be accused of any wrongdoing. Besides sporadic visits from the head nurse, Jocelyn was the only person that cared for him.

She would have to be careful about bringing up the topic of his injuries, but she would. She had no intention of being blamed for something she didn't do. Before she spoke to anyone, she decided she would speak to the patient first.

She moved in close to him, in case anyone else was near.

"Mr. Richardson, has someone been hurting you?"

He nodded his head.

"Is it Ms. Williams who's been hurting you?"

This time he nodded his head more vigorously.

She expected that would be his response, but hoped it would not. She honestly didn't know how to deal with what she knew.

"Don't worry. I'm here and I'm going to make sure she doesn't hurt you anymore."

For the first time since she had been working there, she saw what looked like a smile on Mr. Richardson's face. She would have to watch him very carefully. In the meantime, she decided to dig a little and find out more about Ms. Williams. She wondered if she had been subjecting other patients to the same abuse as Mr. Richardson.

Jocelyn continued her rounds, secure in the knowledge that Ms. Williams wasn't on duty. After her rounds were complete, she used the time to snoop around. She waited until it was very late to access the personnel files. What she found was enlightening, to say the least. According to her file, Ms. Williams was not new to Montelior. She had started working at the hospital years earlier, left and then returned to work part-time. She began working there as an aide shortly after Mr. Richardson's arrival. She wondered if anyone else had made the connection.

Carolyn went looking for Jocelyn when she realized she had been gone from her post for longer than usual.

"What's going on, Edwards?"

She jumped when she heard her name.

"I didn't want to involve you, but that old man is full of some sort of scratches. Head Nurse Williams is doing something to him. I asked him and he said yes."

"You do know that old man is crazy as a loon, don't you?"

"He may be crazy, but somebody *is* hurting him. I doubt he put those marks on himself and I know I'm not doing it. I'm the only person that cares for him and he's full of what looks like long-term abuse. If anything goes down, I'm going to have a lot more to worry about than just losing a job. I could face abuse charges. I'm going to find proof of what's been going on here, before anyone accuses me of anything."

"I get it, but I would prefer if you do exactly what you said and leave me out of it. I don't want to know anything about what you find out. I was looking for a job for almost a year when I got this one, and I found it just in time for my dirt-bag ex-husband to leave me and the kids and move in with his ex-girlfriend. I've got more debt than even this job can handle, so I can't afford to lose this job."

"I understand. I'll keep you out of it. But, I've got to do this."

"Be careful."

"I will."

"I'm going back."

"No problem. I'll be back in two minutes."

Jocelyn made sure that everything was put back exactly where it was.

She returned to her post and watched the patient monitors. She paid special attention to Mr. Richardson's. Jocelyn was sure Ms. Williams had known Mr. Richardson before he arrived at the hospital, and if she had protected that secret, there was no telling how far she would go, if she felt pushed.

As if on cue, Mr. Richardson's monitor went off.

"I'm going to check on one of my patients," she said to Carolyn.

"No problem."

She entered the room and suddenly was hit with another realization. On the nights when Ms. Williams was not working, Mr. Richardson appeared much more alert. He appeared to be attempting to sit up.

"Wow, Mr. Richardson. You look great. Did you want to sit up?"

"Yes," he answered.

She helped him up and looked him directly in his eyes before asking, "Mr. Richardson, did you know Ms. Williams before you came here?"

"You musn't say that too loud," he whispered. "I'm getting stronger every day and eventually, I will surprise her beyond anything she could ever imagine. Until then, I must remain as I am. She cannot believe me to be a threat or she *will* find a way to kill me."

# CHAPTER NINETEEN

Teri Goldman watched as the kids filed in to school. The school's elite alumni meant many of the parents could be more of a handful than the children themselves. They were often so wrapped up in status that their children's needs and wants were virtually ignored. For years, Teri had considered leaving the school, but it paid much better than the public school system and she reasoned that these kids needed her as much, maybe even more. Some of them placed so much pressure on the kids to succeed, they were in need of Prozac long before they even made it to high school. Teri's own childhood made it easy for her to have empathy for many of them.

"So, you ready for another year of teaching these little bastards?"

Teri turned to find Julie Horton, one of the more jaded teachers. She practically flinched in response to the heartless comment.

"Shhh, Julie. You wouldn't want the principal to hear you, or worse yet, one of the kids. The last thing you want is for one of them to go home and tell their parents what they heard."

"This school wouldn't dare fire me. This is my last year. Thank God. Besides, I know where all the bones are buried."

Teri wasn't sure what that meant but she was definitely glad it was Julie's last year. The last thing any child needed was a teacher like Julie Horton.

"I'm gonna go prepare for my first class. See you later," Teri added.

"Yeah."

It amazed her. Teachers like Julie were honored for their *length of service*, whether they were good teachers or not, but if any members of the faculty or parents had known even a little about Teri's personal life, she would probably have found herself without a job. That reality forced her to make certain decisions about the course of her life that tied her hands. She often reasoned that it was only temporary and eventually, she would be able to lead her own life free of repercussions, but when? It seemed as if she was always waiting for her *real* life to begin.

She entered her classroom, eager to start a new year, only to find the kids had already been up to their shenanigans. Written across the chalkboard multiple times, from top to bottom, were the words *God has spoken*. Teri locked the classroom door and erased the board. She did not want to respond to what was written, as she thought it would serve no other purpose than to lend credence to what had been done. Instead, by the time she completed erasing any sign of what had been written, she opened the door and resolved to never address the issue.

"Good morning, students. My name is Mrs. Goldman."

Teri wrote her name on the board so that her class of ninth-graders could see it in writing: *G-O-L-D-M-A-N*.

"This is going to be a very exciting year for me and, I hope, for you."

Somewhere in the back of the classroom, there was much more raucous behavior going on than Teri allowed.

"Is there something you'd like to share with the rest of the class?" she asked the boy who appeared to be the ring leader.

"Your name is...?" she asked.

"Mark."

"Do you have a last name, Mark?"

He chuckled.

"Doesn't everyone?"

Every year there was *that* kid, one that made even the best teacher reevaluate their choice of vocation. Teri was sure, this year, Mark would be *that* kid.

"I don't know, Mark. Does everyone have a last name? That may be something we can discuss in a later class. For now, I'm sure *you* do, indeed, have a last name and I'd like you to share it with me and the rest of your classmates."

"They all know it."

"Then share it with me then."

"I'm Mark Kissel."

"Okay, Mark Kissel, let's get back to my original question. Is there something you'd like to share with the rest of the class?"

Teri had already seen him and the other boys teasing a quieter, more effeminate boy that sat a couple of seats away. She could guess what they were teasing him about.

"No, there's nothing I'd like to *share*."

"Well then, I guess that means I can get on with teaching *my* class, uninterrupted."

"Maybe," Mark muttered under his breath.

Teri made a mental note to reach out to the kid the other boys had been teasing. She had been on the receiving end of such teasing for more years than she wanted to remember, when she was a kid. If there was anything she could do to ease the stress of dealing with it, she had to.

She took roll call and noted that the name of the kid they were teasing was Daniel Wolff.

The rest of the period carried on without event and as the kids were leaving class, Teri stared pointedly at Mark Kissel. She was sure he had been the one who had written on the board. If he had been the one to write all over her chalkboard, she wanted to make it clear to him that his actions were little more than child's play and that she was not unnerved by it in the least. His return look was one of puzzlement, but she was sure it was an act.

Teri's girlfriend, Sienna, would have called Mark Kissel *a little shit*. However, Teri had a good idea of what these kids were dealing with and tried her best to keep an open mind about every one of them.

When she was sure everyone else was gone, she stopped Daniel on his way out.

"You got a minute, Daniel?"

He was surprised to hear his name mentioned. It seemed as though the only attention he got was negative. Therefore, he was understandably cautious as he approached his new teacher.

"Hi, Daniel. I understand this is your first year at our school. I wanted to mention that sometimes being the new kid can be a bit bumpy, but things will get better."

Daniel tried to be polite and positive, but he really wanted to tell the teacher that his *newness* had nothing to do with the teasing. He had been teased at his old school as well. That was why his parents had decided to send him here; that, and the sudden, overwhelming interest he had developed in a fellow male student. He was *different*. The other kids knew it, his parents knew it, and he knew it. Once upon a time, he had hoped he might change. But, he had finally come to terms with what even these ninth-grade boys recognized. He was much more like the girls than he was the boys. He didn't hate it so much. He wished it wasn't so isolating. It was like being an ugly duckling in a pond full of beautiful swans.

"I know, Ms. Goldman. I'll be okay."

"Will you promise me something?"

"What?" he asked.

"If you need anything, anything at all, if the boys get too out of hand or if you need someone to talk to, will you promise you'll stop by and see me? My free periods are four and six. You can find me here both periods. Okay?"

"Okay."

Teri hoped she had gotten through to him and that he might actually take her up on her offer. She remembered the weighty, all-consuming feeling of isolation.

The first time someone discovered her *secret*, she was five years old. The one advantage she had over many kids like herself was that her parents were very supportive. In fact, Teri sometimes thought they were a little *too* supportive. She wondered why they hadn't expressed more concern about it. No matter what was going on, they never yelled or screamed or even appeared to feel sorry for her. She thought it was all too false. How could parents deal with such a dilemma without more of an emotional response? She had seen her mother and her father get angry and upset about things that seemed far less important than what she was going through. It made her feel like they minimized her pain. She would later learn that they were trying to do their best to help her deal with the cards she had been dealt. They didn't think she would ever be able to if her circumstance was always treated like a life-or-death situation. She'd figured that out when she was a teen. What she couldn't understand was why her parents had made a decision about who and what she should be, long before she was old enough, and had the presence of mind to decide for herself. For that, she didn't think she would ever be able to forgive them.

Each school year, Teri was just as excited as if it were her very first year. She loved kids and was looking forward to the time when she would be a parent. She was sure that's what her girl-friend wanted to talk to her about tonight. They had enlisted the aid of their close friend, Lance, as a donor, and thanks to him, they had been trying to make a baby. Teri felt more loved than she had ever felt in her life. Sienna was a successful model and her career was flourishing, but she was willing to give that up so that they might be able to have a child. It was more than self-sacrificing; it was love. So, when Sienna called and mentioned she had made reservations at their favorite restaurant for tonight, she had a pretty good idea why. She was sure it would be the good news they had been waiting for.

As Teri packed up her things at the end of the day, she glanced out of the window. Daniel, the boy she had spoken to earlier, was speaking with an adult. She assumed it was his father. Yet there was something about Daniel's body language that seemed un-comfortable. Then she remembered what it was like when she was his age. Her body language was probably no different then, sort of awkward and a bit on edge. She watched from the window for a moment, before deciding she was nervous about dinner with Sienna and their new life. That was why she was reading more into a simple conversation between a parent and a child outside school.

She grabbed her things, anxious to find out whether or not it was indeed Daniel's father. She liked meeting parents whenever possible, and especially in cases like Daniel, it would have been nice to meet his father now, rather than wait until parent-teacher conferences in a month or so. Unfortunately, by the time she was out of the building, both Daniel and his father were gone.

She dismissed the entire day from her mind, as she always did when she was on her way home. She *always* made it a point to leave the remnants of the day outside the front door from the moment she walked in. Teri believed that was the only way a healthy, modern-day relationship could survive.

"Sienna, baby, I'm home. What time are our reservations?"

Teri looked around the apartment. Whatever it was Sienna had to tell her must be *big*. She hadn't seen their apartment this clean, since...since never. She wondered if the *nesting* could be starting already. That would be an added bonus, since Sienna was quite the slob.

"Sienna? Where are you? Are you playing hide-and-seek with me or what?"

Teri ran through the apartment, as excited as a schoolgirl. She was sure this was some sort of game Sienna was playing. She went from room to room, only to realize she wasn't there. That's when she saw it: a crisp white sheet of paper folded and placed on the top of the dresser they shared. It occurred to Teri that Sienna probably had to run out and had left a note telling her so, that is, until she opened it. Despite the numerous words written on the page, the one word that screamed out to Teri, was the word *good-bye*. That was all she needed to see to realize something had gone terribly wrong. She knew Sienna better than any other person on the planet. They were devoted to each other. In her heart, she knew there was nothing that would ever separate them. However, that was exactly what the note said. It was brief and to the point and explained to Teri that the *family* they were attempting to achieve was unnatural and wrong, for everyone. Teri felt like she was trapped in a horrible nightmare. The note was real, it was concrete, but there was no way she could have been so wrong about what they shared.

While she searched for clues to what could have brought her world crashing down so abruptly, she walked by their bedroom closet and was suddenly bombarded with an overwhelmingly oppressive, nauseating scent. It smelled pungently sweet and fruity. It was not something anyone would have ever welcomed, nor was it something anyone could ever forget. When she swung open the door, she wasn't sure what sight was more ghastly: that of her lover's belly butchered and laid open, or that of the stranger dressed all in black and dripping blood. There was little time to make any comparison. Within minutes, she was dead.

# CHAPTER TWENTY

I t hadn't been enough to watch the teacher. The students she was impacting had to be watched as well. It was beyond acceptable that she was allowed the freedom to shape the impressionable minds of children. If she was not stopped quickly and dealt the most swift justice God would allow, there would be a multiplication of her dark soul. On one occasion, there was a confused boy begging to be pointed in a righteous direction, being counseled by her, of all people.

"You will not continue to spread your poison amongst the innocents. I will see to that."

That afternoon, an individual shrouded in darkness, anxiously watched Teri Goldman and her students. Teri's fate had already been sealed. The paths of the children were being observed, with an eye to future plans. Of particular interest was a young boy named Daniel. He had already been poisoned by the influences of a contaminated world, and people like Teri Goldman, in particular. He required enlightenment to reverse the damage that had been done.

"Hello, Daniel."

"Hello."

"Do you know Ms. Goldman?"

"Yeah, she's my teacher.

"I also know Ms. Goldman. She has taught me as well."

"What did she teach you?" Daniel asked.

"The difference between what's right and what's wrong."

"What do you mean?"

"Well, what Ms. Goldman is, it's wrong. What she is encouraging you to be, that is also wrong. The only way to be right is to follow God's teachings.

"It is written. *Romans 1:26, For this reason God gave them up to vile passions. For even their women exchanged the natural use for what is against nature. Likewise also the men, leaving the natural use of the woman, burned in their lust for one another, men with men committing what is shameful, and receiving in themselves the penalty of their error which was due.* Do you have a Bible, Daniel?"

"I still have my grandmother's Bible, but I haven't read it in a long time. At first, I stopped reading it because it was too confusing. Then, I stopped reading it because, I guess I stopped believing."

"That's exactly what I mean. When you stop believing in God and His teachings, that is nothing more than the evil trying to take over you."

Daniel suddenly remembered what his mother and father had said about talking to strangers.

"Um...I've got to go, or my parents will be real mad. I'll find my grandmother's Bible when I get home, and read some of it," he lied.

"You do that, young man. Remember, don't allow yourself to be contaminated."

"What did you say your name was?" Daniel asked.

The young boy's craftiness was impressive. He was probably warned against strangers and decided he would do well to have a name, just in case. That was the thing about the most insidious who walked the earth; they were sure to set up distrust for everyone, other than themselves. That's why people like the teacher were allowed to continue polluting the planet with their lies. The darkened figure was buoyed by the boy's request for a name. It was about time one was chosen. He had been waiting patiently for God to send a sign. He was sure this was that sign.

"I am called Mosaic."

That was all Daniel needed to hear to send him running home at breakneck speed. Mosaic was not concerned. Often, to fear God and His messengers was the first step to reverence.

There were high hopes for Daniel, but for now Mosaic needed to purify the evil that was allowed to pollute the minds of so many more innocent children.

The first one had been easy. She opened the door brimming with happiness, for the evil she was prepared to bring into the world.

"They exchanged the truth of God for a lie, and worshipped and served created things rather than the Creator, who is forever praised. Amen. Because of this, God gave them over to shameful lusts. Even their women exchanged natural relations for unnatural ones. In the same way the men also abandoned natural relations with women and were inflamed with lust for one another. Men committed indecent acts with other men, and received in themselves the due penalty for their perversion," Mosaic said, repeating practically the same verse he had mentioned to young Daniel.

In her heart, she hoped this was little more than some religious fanatic in overdrive. Yet, those mere words were enough for Sienna to recognize that this situation could only end badly.

"What are you doing here!" she shouted. "Get out!"

It was so easy for Mosaic to continue the path. She stood there, outraged at her fortress being breached. She believed so greatly that she was the just one and the uninvited visitor was evil. What she didn't know was God's messengers always have an open invitation.

"Why...Why are you here? What do you want?"

"I will gut the evil from your belly, unless you do exactly as I instruct."

Sienna couldn't fathom how anyone could know about her pregnancy. She hadn't even told Teri yet. The realization that this was someone that knew the most personal details of her life scared her even more. She remembered hearing stories of women's bellies being cut open and their babies removed and kidnapped. She reminded herself that couldn't be the case, since she couldn't have been more than a few weeks' pregnant.

"Your presence is little more than a minor annoyance to the task I am faced with, so if you do what I say, maybe I will let you and the abomination that lies inside of you live."

Mosaic handed Sienna a sheet of paper and a pen and instructed her to start writing. At first, she considered refusing, but she had to do whatever she could to save her own life and that of her unborn child. She wrote exactly what he instructed. It pained her to say words that were so untrue and even though she was hopeful that she might be allowed to survive, by the time she wrote the last word, she knew if she didn't do something, she would never leave there alive. She brought the pen down quickly and with enough force to puncture the skin and draw blood, but not enough for the darkened figure to even react. Instead, a pristine white linen cloth, soaked in ether, was calmly brought to Sienna's face.

"Thou shall not lie? That is the least of my concerns. There is no way I could have allowed her and that abomination to survive. Surely she must have known that," Mosaic said.

The sense of triumph felt at being presented with the opportunity to purify not one, but three, made up for the extra work of transporting more than one body. The commandeered vehicle already in place, all that was left was to find a new location to complete the ceremony. Mosaic knew of the perfect place.

It would be hours before the kids returned to school the next morning. No one would be anywhere near the school until then. There would be more than enough time for absolute completion. The symbolism of the location was an added bonus.

As Mosaic prepared, eager to purge the world of evil, he was unaware that someone was watching nearby, fascinated with the ceremony that followed.

"I exorcise thee in the name of God the Father Almighty, and in the name of Jesus Christ His Son, our Lord, and in the power of the Holy Ghost, that you may be able to put to flight all the power of the enemy, and be able to root out and supplant that enemy and his apostate angels, through the power of our Lord Jesus Christ, who will come to judge the living and the dead and the world by fire."

"God, Who for the salvation of the human race, has built Your greatest mysteries upon this substance, in Your kindness, hear our prayers and pour down the power of Your blessing into this element, prepared by many purifications. May this, Your creation, be a vessel of divine grace to dispel demons and sicknesses, so that everything that it is sprinkled on in the homes and buildings of the faithful will be rid of all unclean and harmful things. Let no pestilent spirit, no corrupting atmosphere, remain in those places: may all the schemes of the hidden enemy be dispelled. Let whatever might trouble the safety and peace of those who live here be put to flight by this water, so that health, gotten by calling Your holy name, may be made secure against all attacks. Through the Lord, Amen."

"I am Your humble servant, Lord; one of Your angels, dispatched to earth to rid this world of the pestilent, festering boils of society. I will do Your work, Lord. I will destroy them—those that seek to corrupt and leave us all unclean."

The sickly, sweet liquid, being used to *cleanse*, permeated Daniel's nostrils and for just a moment, made him dizzy and nauseous. He knew he should run, but running was what had brought him to the school. Once again, his father was badgering him. The list of new clubs and teams had come out, and his father couldn't understand why he didn't want to join the football team, or the baseball team, or any other club on the list. He wasn't sure why. Neither of his parents had ever spent any time with him. When he was younger, he was closer to the nanny than either of them. If he had joined a team, they both would have come up with a reason not to show up for any game he might have had. He was sure, when he returned home in the afternoon, they wouldn't even notice he had snuck out in the middle of the night. He did it often. They never noticed. As he watched, he couldn't shake the discussion he'd had with *Mosaic*. His father wanted him to be one thing; his teacher seemed to be encouraging him to be himself. Yet, this *messenger*, who was clearly a killer, seemed to have another opinion about what his path should be.

Long after Mosaic was gone, Daniel settled in on a nearby ledge and watched the fire from a distance. The flickering of the flames was hypnotic, and eventually, he fell asleep. He didn't wake up until he heard the sounds of the sirens approaching. He thought he was hidden away well enough, so that no one would notice him and he could eventually slip away, but apparently he was wrong. He didn't go unnoticed by Detective Simms.

# CHAPTER TWENTY-ONE

"I'm sorry I'm late, especially after calling you so early in the morning," Cat said.

"Oh, no problem at all. It gave me some time to get some personal work done. In fact I was working when you called this morning."

"Still, 1:00 p.m. means 1:00 p.m." Cat seemed jumpy and anxious to speak.

"I did something terrible last night," she blurted out.

"What happened?"

"Well, like I told you the last time I was here, I've been sleeping with most of my patrons at the clubs I work at, and last night I took one of them back to my place. I don't usually do that but I didn't want to go to a hotel and I wasn't about to go anyplace private with the guy. Afterwards, I was done and I wanted him to leave. Usually after the sex is over, most of the guys can't wait to leave, but this guy, he wouldn't leave and all I wanted him to do was leave. And I kept getting angrier and angrier, so I bit him."

"You did what?"

Candace made it a point not to react to what her patients said in therapy, but what Cat said surprised her.

"I bit him. All the signs were there that I should just leave him alone. He's one of those macho jerk types and I knew I shouldn't have sex with him but I did it anyway. He was pretty quick and after he was done, I figured he'd just leave. I couldn't believe it when he rolled over and went to sleep. I kept nudging him to wake up and he wouldn't budge. He grunted at me. I was pushing his body and he wouldn't move. Eventually, I gave up and figured he'd sleep an hour or so and leave. He did wake up in an hour as I predicted, but when he woke up, he wanted to go again. All I wanted was him out of my place, but he didn't get the message. He started climbing all over me and when he started trying to shove his dick in my mouth, I bit him. My intention was just to graze him a bit and get his attention, but all of a sudden there was all this blood. I don't know what happened. It's like I was blind with rage. I still can't believe he didn't beat the hell out of me. I guess he was too hurt to do anything. I just pushed him out of my apartment, and threw his clothes after him. I'm afraid to go home and I definitely don't want to go back to the club I met him at. Essentially, I have no job and no home, at least for now."

"Cat, do you realize how this behavior is now becoming dangerous not only to yourself but to others?"

"Of course I do. That's why I came to you in the first place. I knew it would only get worse. This is the worst it's ever been. I've watched as my anger has grown in intensity and it scares the hell out of me. I keep replaying the scenario over and over again in my mind, and I can't help but wonder what would have happened if I had a gun or a knife nearby. I don't know what's happening to me."

"Can you remember the very first time you had sex with one of your club's patrons?"

"Yes, absolutely."

"Tell me about it."

"His name was Wendell and he used to come to the club about every other night. He seemed like one of those guys that probably had no friends, and I was always fascinated with how he had even found the club in the first place. He had the look of a man who was probably made fun of most of his life. In a way, I kind of felt sorry for him.

"It started with me just being nice to him. He didn't drink alcohol, so I made sure the cola he drank was constantly refilled. Then, I started stopping by to talk to him more than the other patrons. One day I watched him from a distance and I realized he just sat there watching all the girls, motionless. I wondered how that was fun for him. He never got a lap dance and never interacted with anyone. He was solemn. I started wondering if maybe his nights at the club were possibly his only real human contact. One day instead of idle chit-chat, I asked him if he wanted a lap dance. He was so nervous. At first his body was stiff as a board, but I talked to him, told him I liked him and eventually, he began to loosen up. A few simple gyrations and he came right there. It was an odd feeling. I felt sorry for him but I also was repulsed by him. However, I wasn't repulsed enough to ask him to wait until I got off work so I could *really* take care of him. I did. I did things to him that I don't think he'd ever experienced and he was so grateful. He was so socially inept and clumsy. When he left, I'm not sure he knew what he should do. He was stuttering and smiling and after he walked out the door. I saw the two hundred dollars on the nightstand. I wasn't so much offended by the money but I was angry. At first I thought it was the money but I realize now it was more than that. The next time I saw him at the club, he was a different man. He seemed happy. There was a smile on his face. I even saw him talking with one of the other girls. As soon as he saw me, he went from happy to ecstatic. I avoided him the entire night and never returned to that club again. That's the way it's been ever since. I've been prostituting myself and bouncing from club to club."

"Do you have any other feelings about this other than anger?" Candace asked.

"Like what? You mean like shame, fear or pain?"

"Do you?"

"Not really. I think if I had any of those feelings, maybe I wouldn't have had to come here. Isn't that what keeps people from doing things, shame and fear? Otherwise, people would be running around with no boundaries at all."

"I don't know, Cat. Even with fear, shame and pain, people still do all sorts of things. Crimes are committed, lies are told, and fear or shame don't necessarily always keep those things from happening. Would you agree?"

"I guess you're right."

"Cat, you've told me how angry you get. Let's explore the flip side. What makes you happy?"

"I don't know. It's been a long time since I've been truly happy."

"I assume you're not angry all the time. So, there must be brief moments when you're at least content."

"Yeah, there are."

Candace didn't miss the far-off look of contentment on Cat's face and was careful not to interrupt whatever it was she was thinking. Yet, she hoped once the moment was over, she wouldn't simply snap out of it and move on. Candace immediately noticed the shift when it happened. She was back.

"What were you thinking about?" Candace asked.

"Huh?"

"You seemed to be deep in thought for a moment there. What were you thinking about?"

"My brother."

Candace noticed she was smiling again.

"I thought you didn't have any family."

"I do. I have a brother."

"I noticed you smiled when you thought of him, your brother. What is his name?"

"It's Ca...um...It's Caleb."

"What kind of relationship do you and Caleb have?"

Once again Candace noticed that familiar faraway look before Cat spoke.

"We're like two halves of a whole."

"That sounds like a very close relationship."

"We are close. I don't see him as often as I would like, but we have a good relationship. He's a bit of a wild man, but who am I to judge?"

"How often do the two of you get to spend time together?"

"Whenever he breezes into town."

"So, he doesn't live here in New York then."

"No."

"Where does he live?"

"Uh, all over. Caleb doesn't have a *regular* home. He's a bit of a vagabond."

"That must be difficult for you."

"It can be, but somehow Caleb always seems to be there when I need him most. He's in New York now. I just wish he would stand still long enough for the two of us to spend some time together. He's always been such a ladies' man."

"So you and your brother are a lot alike then?"

"No, not at all. I'm nothing like Caleb. He's always been the strong one. He was the one who kept me safe when we were little. He protected me. I would never have survived without him."

"What did you have to survive, Cat?"

"Nothing." She chuckled. "Listen to me overdramatizing. We were like ordinary brothers and sisters. He protected me from *everything*. He was like most brothers and their sister. I think I should go. Caleb mentioned he wanted to get together and I don't want to miss him."

"Why don't you call him? You can use my phone if you'd like," Candace offered.

"No, I have to go."

Cat grabbed her bag and rushed out of the door without so much as a good-bye.

# CHAPTER TWENTY-TWO

"Another rough night?" Simms asked.

"Why do you ask?"

"The clothes. A little boyish, don't you think? And what's with the hoody?"

"What, I can't have a bad hair day?"

"What about the get-up? What are you having, a bad pants and shoes day, too?"

Kimberly was wearing blue jeans and running shoes, attire that her partner was unaccustomed to seeing her in.

"You can question Dr. Phipps. I want to check out the recreation center, inside and out. Maybe someone saw something the night Dr. Phipps said the killer was here."

Simms located Dr. Phipps, and Watson went on her way.

"I wish you hadn't cancelled the session before talking to us, Ms. Phipps."

"I had to. I didn't want my group to be in any further danger. Speaking of which, do you know the identity of the third victim?"

"The name has not yet been released, but yes, we do know the identity."

"Was it Christina?"

"I'm not really at liberty to share that information."

"Detective, please, I need to know. Was it her?"

"Yes, it was. How did you know?"

"She had been talking about taking some tenants to court, right before I saw the news report. I saw the court buildings. I just knew it was her."

"Now that everyone has scattered and you have no addresses or phone numbers, it makes our job that much more difficult. Why did you wait so long to contact us?"

"This is New York. People are murdered all the time. At first, when Caitlin was killed, it didn't occur to me that there would even be any more murders. I assumed it was some random thing and Christina was speculation...until now."

While Simms questioned Candace Phipps, Kimberly combed the street outside the center.

"Looking for something?"

Kimberly turned to find the center's janitor standing behind her.

"Looking for something, little lady?"

Kimberly flashed her badge.

"I'm investigating a homicide."

"Hey, I didn't know you were a cop."

"Excuse me?"

"I said, I didn't know you were a cop."

"Why would you?"

The janitor searched her face for any sign of recognition. There was none.

"Give me a minute here. I'll let you know when I'm done," she said.

Kimberly searched the garbage bin and the surrounding area. There was nothing. She had hoped to find remnants of the ether that was not only being used as an accelerant for the fires, but also to knock out the victims. The distinctive scent was what she was searching for. She found nothing.

While Kimberly considered where she should check next, Simms was upstairs talking to Dr. Phipps.

"Doctor, is there a huge need for a group like this? How many members do you typically get in a given month or so?"

"According to statistics, approximately four percent of all live births are born hermaphrodites. It's a pretty large percentage in the scheme of things. My group typically brought in anywhere from fifteen to twenty-five members a month. I believe there would have been more people in the group if there wasn't such a stigma attached to the condition. Many hermaphrodites are abused both sexually, physically and emotionally because of the way that they are born. The *lucky* ones that aren't abused are ostracized by society as soon as it is revealed that they were not born like everyone else."

"Sounds like an isolating life."

"It is. That is one of the reasons I started the group. I know firsthand about how difficult it can be growing up *different*."

"Really?"

"Yes, detective. You see, I was born intersexed as well. Most people use the term *hermaphrodite*, but we prefer *intersexed*."

Simms wasn't sure how he should respond to what the doctor had said. Suddenly, he realized what she was talking about. It was as if she was suddenly standing in front of him naked. He found it difficult to even look at her.

"See what I mean, Detective Simms? You suddenly have the urge to flee, don't you?"

"No, I...I was trying to figure out if there was any other information I needed from you," he lied.

Dr. Phipps smiled and touched his shoulder.

"Don't worry. It's okay."

"Is there anyone in the group that stands out in your mind

more than anyone else, who you think might have violent tendencies?"

"Detective, they're all different to anyone other than people like me." She chuckled.

"You mentioned that you believed you were being followed. Could you tell whether or not the person that talked to you and frightened you here at the center was a man or a woman?"

"I couldn't tell. The voice was really raspy, almost like the person had a cold, and I wouldn't turn around. I was too scared to."

"If you were going to guess, which would be your *first* guess?"

"Under different circumstances, my guess would probably be that it was a man, but my instincts tell me different. It was probably a woman, disguising her voice as a man. It may not have even been a disguise. Many of the members of my group often live their lives quite androgynous. I do know this, though; the person never left the floor that day and there were only six people in the group, all of which identify as women."

"I'm curious, Dr. Phipps, if these people are considered inter-sexed, why do most of your group members identify as women?"

"I think many of the support groups get members who identify as women because those who identify as men do so in every sense. Like men who are not born intersexed, the stigma attached to males is always greater than that attached to females. Although I don't like encouraging a similarity between intersexed individuals and being gay, it does have one commonality. Women and their sexual persuasions, both emotionally and physiologically, are much more easily accepted than males. You're a police officer. You deal with gay bashing on occasion. Aren't most of your victims male?"

"Point well taken," Simms said. "I'm going to need the names and physical descriptions of the six group members that were here."

"No problem, but all I know is everyone's first name. The

environment here has always been very informal. It has to be that way in order to maintain confidentiality; otherwise, no one would feel comfortable coming."

"I'm going to have a couple of police cruisers keep an eye on you."

"Thank you, Detective. Maybe I'll actually be able to get some sleep tonight. I've been scared to death. I thought I was going to die the last time I was here."

"I can imagine that must have been very scary."

Simms pulled a business card out of his jacket pocket.

"Call me if you think of anything or if you need anything. Feel free to call anytime, day or night."

"Thank you. I might just take you up on that."

Candace considered mentioning that one of her patients displayed obvious symptoms of both multiple personality disorder and schizophrenia. But she realized that would be stepping over the lines of confidentiality since she had never done anything concrete that would demonstrate clearly that she was a threat to either herself or others. Although Candace felt guilty even considering it, since so often the stigma attached to most mental disorders was that the people suffering were highly dangerous. Instead, she conceded that anything her patient had told her indicated no more of a propensity for violence than any other nonviolent patient. She didn't want to be a part of the problem. More than anything, she wanted to be part of the solution.

Simms wondered where Kimberly had gotten to. He didn't imagine that there was that much to look into anyplace other than this room. He hoped she hadn't pulled one of her disappearing acts again.

After searching outside, she decided she would check out some of the other meetings being held inside the center. Her first stop was the front security desk.

"Is everyone required to sign in?" she asked, flashing her badge.

"Yeah," the guard on duty answered.

"Everyone?"

"We try our best to sign everyone in, but every now and then, people get past us, especially if they know where they're going."

"I'm gonna need to see your sign in records for the past month."

"That'll take an hour or so."

"I'm in no rush. I'll be with Dr. Phipps when you have those records ready."

"No problem. I'll get on it right now."

Kimberly found Simms in the hall outside Dr. Phipps' meeting room.

"I asked the security guard downstairs for the sign-in records for the past month. They play real fast and loose with admittance to this place. Anyone could walk in off the street and do whatever they want and go unnoticed."

"It seems like this place is constantly buzzing. I think if someone were able to get in here easily, it would probably be someone who has been here before and knows their way around the place."

"You're probably right. But, you see, we both got in here without signing a thing *or* flashing a badge. How helpful was Dr. Phipps?"

"She was quite helpful. I would say there's a ninety-nine percent possibility of a connection between the victims."

"No shit?"

"No shit."

"So you gonna keep me guessing or what?" Watson asked.

"I don't know. Maybe I should make you beg for it."

"Oh yeah. That's gonna happen."

"Well, since you asked nicely," Simms conceded. "The third victim was also a member of the doctor's group and if she kept any records or we were able to identify the first victim, I'm betting the first vic was probably a member of the group as well. The victims and her group members are all hermaphrodites. Dr. Phipps said they prefer the term *intersexed* but *hermaphrodite* is the word I'm used to. Basically, what it means is they all have both male and female sex organs. That's what the support group is made up of, all of them, including the psychiatrist. The second victim had surgery as a child to make her more girl than boy, and the third victim, Christina Wilson, had both."

"Both, what?"

"She, he, whatever, had a dick and a hole."

"Wow, Simms, do you really have to be so crass?"

"I'm just trying to explain, but if you'd prefer I be more technical, some have conflicting internal and external organs, some have two different external organs, some had the surgery, some didn't, but that's their common link. This guy must have some sort of issue with them. Apparently, this is more common than most people know. There are many variations of intersexed individuals. Some may appear to be women, yet have testicles. Others may appear to be male, but have a normal-looking penis, but also have a hole underneath their penis that is similar to a vagina. But, I don't think that matters to the killer. He obviously hates them all. From what I was able to gather from the second victim's family, she was for all intents and purposes, a female. After the enlarged clitoris or penis, or whatever it was, was removed, she lived her life as a woman. I'm guessing this group has been his main hunting ground, but now that the group is closed, he may need to look elsewhere."

"This should be a lot easier now that we have all this information," said Watson.

"We should visit the families of the victims we've identified. Maybe some names will ring a bell."

"I don't know, Simms. Maybe I should do the talking. You're not exactly known for your tact. You don't want to offend anyone. After all, this is a pretty touchy subject. The victims were pretty secretive about their circumstances, so I'm sure their families didn't make it a habit of sharing this information, either. The truth is, our society is so judgmental of differences, especially sexual ones, that anyone even mildly associated with it probably fiercely guarded the secret. Could you imagine, for example, what might have happened to the lawyer's career if anyone had known she was sexually ambiguous? It probably would have ruined her."

"That would explain her father. Don't worry, I'll show the utmost tact in my questioning."

"I'm going to assume that no one at Caitlin Schwartz' firm was aware of her...situation. Her secretary didn't seem to care for her very much, and I think if she had known, she would have absolutely spilled the beans."

"I think you're probably right. You women can be so catty."

"See, that's exactly what I mean about tact. You just grouped an entire gender together, like we are all exactly the same."

"No, I totally get it. I can't imagine what it must be like to have to tell someone, anyone, that you've got extra parts that make you not one, but two different genders," said Simms.

"It's life-altering," said Watson.

"It can't be easy living life as a freak."

"You see what I mean, Simms? That was so insensitive. I hope you don't plan on using terms like 'freak' when we talk to the victims' families and friends."

"Of course not. If nothing else, I know how to shift up and be a professional when need be."

Before Watson and Simms left the recreation center, the security guard found Watson and gave her the sign-in records she'd requested. While she was talking to the guard, Simms popped his head inside the room Phipps was still standing in.

"Dr. Phipps, you need a lift home?"

"Thanks, Detective Simms. That would be great."

"Simms, I'm gonna look over these sign-in sheets and maybe question a few more people here, see if there's something we missed."

"Okay. I'll see you at the station."

While Phipps gathered her things, she couldn't help but think she had heard the voice of the female detective someplace before.

Simms and the doctor drove most of the way in silence before Dr. Phipps spoke.

"Have you had the same partner for long?"

"Oh yeah, Watson and I have been partners for years."

"I would guess after working with someone that long, you get to be pretty close."

"Yeah, pretty much. Why do you ask?"

"Making small talk, that's all."

Simms assumed the doctor was interested in him and trying to figure out whether or not he and his partner were a couple. He couldn't wait to get her to her destination.

"Do you have family or friends you could stay with for a few days?" Detective Simms asked the doctor as she exited his car.

"No, not really. I might be able to stay with my colleague for a few days. I'll give him a call and ask."

"Is he someone you can trust?"

"Absolutely. I trust him with my life."

"Good. That might be the best thing. If the killer followed you recently, then he probably knows where you live. Either way, I'm going to have a couple of officers keep an eye on you. Thanks for your help. We'll be in touch."

Candace hadn't slept very well for days, so the first thing she did when she got home was eat and then she went to bed. She hoped she would rest a bit easier now that she had spoken to the police and someone would be keeping an eye on her.

Sometime around three o'clock in the morning, the phone rang.

"The judgment of God is swift and without challenge. You may have evaded Him for now, but retribution awaits you," the caller said.

Candace dropped the phone in the cradle and sat shaking in her bed. She considered calling Detective Simms but it was so late. She realized she would never be able to get back to sleep, so she decided to pull her files and go over them. She thought maybe she might find something that rang a bell. She was sure the killer was someone she had come into contact with. Up until now she had been so sure it was someone at the group meetings, but what if it wasn't. Maybe it was one of her private patients. She had very few clients that she would consider violent. However, she thought maybe the killer might be someone obsessed with religion. She couldn't think of anyone right off the bat, but that didn't mean it wasn't someone she had forgotten, or maybe even a patient she hadn't seen in a while.

For hours she pored through stacks and stacks of folders, hoping to hit the jackpot. Somehow she kept coming back to Shelly. Yet, she was still concerned about bringing this to the attention of the police. If she was wrong, the breach of confidentiality might mean losing her license to practice. As she contemplated what she should do next, the phone rang once again.

# CHAPTER TWENTY-THREE

Simms called Watson soon after he learned there was another murder.

"It's showtime, partner. He hit again."

"Where?"

"Prep school at Eighty-second and Broadway."

"I'll be there in fifteen minutes."

"What have we got?" Simms asked the officer on the scene.

"This one's a little different than the others."

"Are you gonna tell me how, or do I have to wait until the movie?"

"This time there's two bodies and the second body wasn't intentionally burned. She's in the back seat. You're not going to believe this. He cut her stomach open."

Simms approached the back seat just in time for Watson to arrive.

"Two victims?"

"Yeah. I think he's unraveling. The body in the trunk isn't fully burned and the one in the back seat is split open."

"Why would he change the format?" Watson wondered.

"Something tells me we're going to figure all this out real soon. This time, we've got a face. We're gonna need some pictures. I've got someone that might be able to make a quick identification."

"Well, we're right near a school. That should be the first place to start."

"The school is starting some kind of a *phone tree* to ensure that the kids don't come in to school today. But, I made sure I told the principal to have all the teachers arrive as usual. This may be a perfect opportunity to figure out how this guy is choosing these locations. This is a completely different neighborhood from the other murders. Why here?"

Watson scanned the crowd.

"You know guys like this usually stick around to witness their handiwork," said Watson.

"You think he's still here?"

"Could be. You never know."

There weren't many people at the school because of the early hour, only a few passersby. However, there was one person Simms noticed right away.

"Hey, kid," he called.

The boy seemed nervous and appeared to be trying to avoid eye contact with Simms, who by now was already headed in the boy's direction.

"A little early for school, isn't it?"

"I leave early so I can have breakfast and use the computers in the lab."

"Where are your parents?"

"At home, work."

Simms recognized that the kid was a bit skittish, so he decided he would tread softly.

"So, you like the school breakfast?"

"Not really, but it gets me out of the house."

"When I was your age, I hated school, but I would have picked a day at home and a home-cooked meal over school any day, least of all, getting to school early. Hell, I used to fake sick, so I didn't have to go to school."

"You didn't live at my house."

Simms watched the kid and wondered if the Bureau of Child Welfare should be ringing his parents' doorbell. This kid was either depressed, abused or both. Either way, he had some issues. He knew the look.

"What time did you get here?" Simms asked.

"About...about...I think, maybe seven o'clock, seven-thirty, something like that."

"Was it closer to seven o'clock or seven-thirty?"

"It was probably seven-thirty."

"By the way, what's your name, kid?"

"I'm Daniel...Daniel Wolff."

"Nice to meet you, Daniel Wolff. I'm Detective Simms. I'd like to speak with your parents. Is there a phone number where they can be reached?"

"Both of their voicemails are always on. They hardly ever return calls," Daniel stuttered.

"I'd like the numbers anyway."

"Okay. Here's my mother's cell number."

"They don't have a landline number I could call?"

"Yes."

"Daniel, I'd like whatever numbers you have for *both* your parents, please."

This was the first time Daniel hoped his parents were actually as disinterested in his life as they appeared to be. If so, they would not have noticed that he was gone all night. If they did notice he was gone all night, he would have to explain to the police why he lied. Surprisingly, it wasn't so much that he was afraid of the killer; it was the complete opposite. He was fascinated and not so keen yet on providing information that would aid in Mosaic's capture. He was sure that he was the only person still alive that had seen the killer up close and personal, and for some reason, he liked that. For the first time in a long time, or maybe ever, he felt special. He wasn't ready for that to be taken away from him.

"Kid, you should probably go home. There won't be any school today."

"Okay."

"That kid knows something," Simms mentioned as he joined Watson.

"What makes you say that?"

"Instinct. He was lying. I could tell. He lied about what time he got here. If I were a gambling man, I would say he's a witness."

"Why would he lie?"

"Why else does anyone lie about being a witness to murder? He's probably scared."

"We'll let him know if he knows anything, we can protect him and his family. Maybe that'll help loosen up his lips."

"You okay, partner?" Simms asked.

"Yeah, I'm fine. I'm just a little tired. I haven't been sleeping well."

"I guess a crazed arsonist, murderer, rapist run amuck in the city could do that to anyone, especially a woman living alone. You do know you have an open invitation to come stay with me if you're afraid of things that go bump in the night."

"I bet I do."

"No really, I mean it. I'll even sleep on the pull-out."

"I'm fine, Simms. Have you forgotten I'm a detective, too? Besides, my brother is there to keep me company now."

"Doesn't sound much like it. According to you, he's out chasing tail every opportunity he gets."

"Very true, but still, I'll be fine. I guess we should get started.

The teachers and staff are arriving and we've got a lot of people to question."

"Don't remind me. My stomach just made a sound like a bear. I haven't had breakfast yet this morning."

"I tell you what, Simms, once we get through this, I'll buy you lunch. I'll even let you pick the place."

"You're on. In the meantime, I'm gonna try to get one of these uniforms to get me some donuts."

"Simms, you're such a cliché." She laughed.

"Yes, I guess I am, but that's what you love about me."

"The word 'love,' though said nonchalantly, hung in the air, like dense fog."

"I'll start with the principal."

"Okay. I'll talk to the school secretary. I believe her name is Mrs. Waterstone."

Mrs. Waterstone was a heavy woman with a thick, Brooklyn accent. Watson was sure she had hit the jackpot before she even spoke to her. She had that look of a woman who knew all there was to know about what was going on with everyone around her.

"Mrs. Waterstone?" Watson asked.

"Yes. This is awful. Why on earth would anyone do something like this at a school, of all places?"

"That's what I'm here to find out. I'm Detective Watson. I'm going to need some information from you this morning. I know this is very difficult for everyone, so my partner and I are going to do our best to get you all out of here as soon as possible. I just have a few questions."

"Any way I can help, I'll be happy to. I don't think there's much I can tell you, though."

"You'd be surprised what information is helpful. To start, did everyone on staff show up today?"

Before Mrs. Waterstone could answer Watson's question, a teacher came running over.

"Paula, have you seen Teri?"

"Your name is?" Watson asked.

"I'm Julie Horton. I'm one of the ninth-grade teachers."

"You mentioned there was a teacher missing."

"I don't know if she's missing, but Teri is always very concerned about the students, about their state of mind and stuff. I'm surprised to see she's not here."

"What's the teacher's full name?"

"Teri Goldman. She teaches the ninth grade also."

"Has anyone tried calling her?"

"I called her on her cell and at home about a half-hour ago, but I got no answer at either number."

"Mrs. Waterstone, I'm going to need Ms. Goldman's phone number, her class list and her address, if you've got it."

"I have it right here. I have all the teachers' class lists. The phone numbers and addresses are in their personnel files. I'll get Teri's file."

Watson tried Teri Goldman's numbers and just as Julie Horton mentioned, she got no answer at either.

"I'll be right back, Mrs. Waterstone; Ms. Horton."

Watson went to find Simms to let him know what she had found out so far.

"Let me see the list," said Simms.

He scanned it quickly.

"I knew it."

"What?" Watson asked.

"From the moment you mentioned a missing teacher and her list of students, somehow I knew Daniel Wolff would be on her list."

"That's the kid you were talking to?"

"I told you. That kid knows something. Let's question a few more people here, then I think we need to talk to Daniel again, and his parents, and send a police car over to Teri Goldman's house."

"You don't think he could be a suspect, do you? How old is the kid, fourteen, fifteen years old?"

"Stranger things have happened," Simms said.

"True, but not so often at Upper West Side prep schools."

"Maybe not so often, but if there's one thing I've learned, it's that anyone is capable of murder."

"Anyone, huh?"

"Yes, *anyone*."

# CHAPTER TWENTY-FOUR

K imberly tossed and turned all night before getting out of bed. Ever since seeing one of the most recent victims with her stomach cut open, she felt as though they were losing ground toward finding the killer, instead of gaining ground. She knew a great deal about serial killers and they seldom changed their MO, yet, this killer had. This time there were two victims instead of one, and instead of being burned, one of the victims was split open and not left in the trunk, but in the interior of the car. She wondered if they might be dealing with a copycat or even worse, two killers working together.

She decided she would call Brandon. He was clearly sleeping when he answered the phone. Kimberly glanced at the clock and realized it was three o'clock in the morning.

"I'm sorry. I haven't been able to get this case off my mind all night. Then, it occurred to me, maybe we're dealing with more than one killer."

On the other end of the line, Brandon agreed that she might be right and added that possibly someone had joined the original killer after becoming a *fan*.

"I'm going in to the station early. I want to check the case files and see if anything rings a bell. I'm sorry for waking you up. Go back to sleep."

After hanging up the phone, Kimberly decided to take a shower before leaving for the precinct. She hoped that she might find something, anything in the files that might help solve the case before there was another murder.

While in the shower, she thought she heard Kadeem come in and called to him.

"Kadeem, are you there? Is that you?"

She got no response, but did hear voices. That's when she realized he wasn't alone. She got out of the shower, wrapped a towel around herself and cracked the bathroom door a bit, hoping to hear the conversation. Kadeem was talking to someone she recognized. The voice was familiar but she couldn't remember where she had heard her before.

"You have to tell her."

"I can't," Kadeem responded.

"If you don't, bad things are sure to happen."

"Even worse things are bound to happen if I tell her anything before she's ready."

"So what are you saying? You intend to continue waiting it out. What kind of plan is that? She needs to know now. If you don't tell her, I will."

"No, you won't. I won't let you."

"Are you threatening me?"

"It's not a threat. It's just the way things are. I will not let you interfere."

"Kadeem, I'm as much a part of this as you are and she will be told, one way or another."

"Yes, she will be, but not until she's ready."

"When exactly do you think that will be?"

"I know Kimberly better than any of us, and I am the best person to decide when it's the right time. If we jump the gun, the result will be devastating for us all. You're so anxious for her to find out. Was it you that left that bracelet lying around for her to see it?"

"I'm so sick to death of you making all of the decisions for all of us. If it weren't for me, she would've never made it as far as she has now. But, to answer your question, no, I didn't leave the bracelet lying around. I'm not stupid."

"I didn't say you were 'stupid.' You and I both know you're far from it. That's what concerns me. You always know exactly what you're doing and quite frankly, I don't think you have Kimberly's best interests in mind. You're only thinking of yourself and as far as you making things happen for Kimberly, you couldn't be more wrong. I'm the one who's kept her going all these years, and it *will* be me that tells her what she needs to know at the proper time," said Kadeem.

When it seemed the conversation between Kadeem and his female companion were over, Kimberly quietly shut the door. She toweled off and exited the bathroom, prepared to pretend as though she had heard nothing.

"Hey, Kadeem. I thought I heard you come in."

"Yeah, I just got here a few minutes ago."

Kimberly looked around the apartment, wondering where the person Kadeem had been speaking with had gone.

"You okay?" Kadeem asked.

"I'm fine. Why?"

"I don't know. You seem a little out of sorts."

"It's this case. It's got me a bit stumped."

"Is that why you're up so early? It's barely five o'clock."

"Yeah, I'm going to the station early. I want to go over some of the case files, see if I can dig up anything."

"What time will you be back?" Kadeem asked.

"Why?"

"I don't know. I was thinking maybe we could spend some time together, like we did when we were little."

"I'm not sure what time I'll be back today, but I'll call you when

I have an idea. Maybe I'll cook you your favorite," said Kimberly.

"What?"

"Have you forgotten already, corned beef hash and cornbread pie?"

"Wait a minute, Sis. That's your favorite, not mine."

"Oh. I'll think of something. So it's a date then. I'll cook dinner, for just the two of us. No girlfriends or uninvited visitors, okay?"

"Of course not."

"I'm going to go get dressed. I want to get to the station before my partner gets there. I would like to go over the files early and uninterrupted, before the day starts."

Kimberly got dressed and was surprised to find that she spent a good deal of time picking out something to wear before she suddenly spoke out loud to herself.

"Snap out of it. You're acting like some college kid. He's your partner. That's it."

By the time Kimberly finished dressing and was leaving the apartment, once again, Kadeem was nowhere to be found.

Kimberly arrived at the station prepared to spend hours poring over case files. She decided to start with the cold case files. After two hours, she was tired and her eyes were starting to feel crossed, but she didn't give up. Instead, she shifted focus and began retrieving many of the solved cases. She had been working so diligently, she hadn't even noticed the sun coming up and the station filling with more and more people. She was reading one file in particular, her face screwed up in an obvious scowl when Brandon arrived. He was standing directly in front of her before she even knew he was there.

"Found something?"

She jumped upon hearing him speak.

"Wow, I didn't mean to startle you. That's why you shouldn't leave your bed in the middle of the night to go over case files; it makes you jumpy."

"I'm not jumpy. You startled me, that's all."

"Okay, whatever you say."

"So, did you?"

"Did I what?"

"Did you find anything in the files? You seemed pretty engrossed in one of the files when I walked in."

"That was nothing. I'm tired. I was trying to focus. My eyes were starting to blur."

Brandon didn't miss Kimberly's haste at tossing the file to the side and wondered what could be there that made her so uptight. He made a mental note to find a way to see that file without her knowing it.

"I need some fresh air. I'm gonna make a coffee run. You want something?" Kimberly asked.

"You know what I want."

"Jelly donut and black coffee, right?" she confirmed.

"Yep. The breakfast of champions."

Before leaving, Kimberly picked up a couple of files from her desk and locked them in her desk drawer. Brandon already knew why. However, he had been in Kimberly's presence long enough to have seen where she kept her backup key. While she was gone, he fished the key from the bottom of her pen holder and took the files and retrieved the one on top. It was the one Kimberly had been looking at when he walked in. It was the only file that had a green sheet of paper sticking out of it. He took the file and quickly made a copy of all of its contents, then returned the file and the key to exactly where Kimberly left it. He folded up the pages and tucked them in his jacket pocket. He was sure whatever was on those pages would make for interesting reading.

# CHAPTER TWENTY-FIVE

Kimberly was surprised to find Kadeem at home when she returned from the precinct. In fact, he appeared to have been settled in. He was intensely writing in a notebook when she walked in.

"What you been up to all day?" she asked.

"This and that."

"That's awfully vague."

"Well, I did some shopping. You needed some beer and while I was out, I replaced your television. How did that happen, by the way?"

"Oh Kadeem, you didn't have to do that."

"Of course I did. How did it get broken?"

"It was just me being clumsy," she lied.

"Is that what happened to the toaster and the bar as well?"

"What are you talking about?"

Kimberly had done her best to clean things up after her temper tantrum. The only thing that she thought anyone would notice was the television. Her plan had been to replace it immediately after breaking it, but time had gotten away from her.

"The toaster is missing pieces and there's a crack in the glass on the bar."

"Oh, that might have happened when I knocked the TV over."

"Really?"

"Yeah, really."

"So, what else did you buy?"

"Nothing. I went to the market and then I saw the Best Buy, so I decided to go in there and look around. They were having a sale, so I figured why not replace my big sister's TV? It's the least I can do."

"Thanks, Kadeem. How much was it? I'll give you the money for it. I was planning to buy a new one anyway. I just didn't have a chance to get around to it."

"No, Sis. This one's on me."

"I'm gonna take a shower, then I'll fix us something to eat. Just make sure you don't go anywhere."

"Where would I go?"

"I don't know, Kadeem; it seems your life is a constant mystery to me. One minute you're there, and the next you're gone."

"Maybe you're not looking in the right places," Kadeem said.

Kimberly turned around as she exited the room and shook her head.

"Yeah, right," she said.

The restorative powers of the shower and Kadeem's presence did a lot for Kimberly's mood, especially when she found Kadeem was still there once she was out of the bathroom.

"What are you smiling about?" Kadeem asked.

"I'm happy, that's all. It's nice having you here. I missed you."

"I missed you, too."

Kimberly put a couple of steaks in the oven, prepared a salad and the corned beef hash and cornbread pie she mentioned to Kadeem earlier.

"You want a beer?" she asked.

"Yeah."

She sat down with Kadeem while she waited for the steaks and pie to be done.

"You never mentioned whether or not you found anything this morning."

"Huh?"

"The case files you wanted to go over? Did you find anything?"

"Not really. I'll try again tomorrow."

"Hopefully not so early in the morning. When do you sleep?"

"I get plenty of sleep. Besides, I can sleep when I'm dead. For now, I've got an important case to solve."

"And your partner, does he get any sleep?"

"What are you talking about?"

"You know exactly what I'm talking about."

"No, Kadeem, I don't. I have no idea what you're talking about. If you're asking me about Simms' sleep habits, I wouldn't know."

"You sure about that. You can tell me."

"There's nothing to tell. We're partners. That's all."

"It's okay you know."

"What's okay?"

"It's okay for you to have a life. You don't have to spend your *entire* life doing penance."

"Is that what you think I'm doing, penance? I'm a detective because I love what I do. I made that choice because I wanted to, because I knew I would be good at it and I am."

"I'm not talking about you being a cop, Sis. What I'm talking about is the way you've given up living. You're alone all the time. It's not healthy."

"I'm not alone."

"I know you're not. You're with your partner, Simms. That's the only person you spend any time with."

"How do you know who I spend my time with?"

"I know everything there is to know about you, Sis. I'm just trying to tell you that it's okay for you to be happy. You *can* let go and have a life. You don't have to stay locked in the past."

"I'm not. It's just that my story, it's not an easy one to tell, and anyone I get close to is going to want to hear the *whole* story."

"Take a chance. You might be surprised at what you find when you do."

"I think the steaks are done."

Kimberly got up to check on the food.

"Kadeem, could you set the table?"

"Okay."

They sat eating silently and when they were done, Kimberly cleared the plate and silverware from the table. She wrapped up the remaining steak and pie and put the food in the fridge. When she turned back around to the table, Kadeem was gone. She called to him, believing he was either in the bathroom or her bedroom, but he was gone, again.

# CHAPTER TWENTY-SIX

*Dear Kadeem,*

*Your first letter concerns me a great deal. I'm concerned that Kimberly may feel we are all against her. Therefore, I think it best you not encourage her to write a support letter on my behalf. I will be fine. If I am meant to leave this place, I will, with or without a letter. In fact, I don't even think it's a good idea that you and I write to one another. I feel very positive that I will be home soon and when I am, you are right, we will all be a family once again.*

*Please take care of your sister and be patient. Soon everything will be as it is supposed to be.*

*Love, Mom*

Marie folded the letter, put it in an envelope, sealed it and put it aside until she could have it mailed the next day.

Ever since receiving the letter from Kadeem, sleeping had become next to impossible, and when she did sleep, it was the same dream night after night, if she could call it a dream. So much of it was more memory than dream. No matter how it started, it always ended the same way: her standing in a corner, while her husband lay on a bed engulfed by flames. Oftentimes she would go to sleep, dream, then wake up and go right back to the same dream again. This was one of those nights. She was grateful when morning arrived and it was time to get up.

She glanced at the letter she wanted mailed and hoped it would arrive quickly. Marie assumed from the letter Kadeem sent that he and Kimberly were together and hoped that he would indeed be allowed to read what she sent. For now, her greatest concern was convincing the Parole Board that she should be freed, and that was all she could concentrate on for now.

Patty was already awake when she got up.

"Two more days, huh?" Patty asked.

"Yeah. Two more days."

"Don't tell me you're getting melancholy about the thought of possibly leaving this place."

"Heck no. I can't wait to go home."

"You've been awfully quiet lately."

"I guess maybe I'm afraid of the unknown."

Marie felt a bit guilty about not being totally forthright with Patty, but she wasn't being completely dishonest. She *was* worried about what she might find if she was allowed to go home. However, she didn't feel comfortable sharing her concerns about the letter from Kadeem and what it meant.

On the *big day*, members of the Parole Board sat squeezed together around a table, sifting through prison, probation and psychiatric reports for countless prisoners. Marie Richardson's file was amongst them. The only thing missing from her reports was any victim statements. Marie had already considered the impact of the lack of any victim or family of the victim to comment. She wasn't sure whether it would work for or against her. She would soon find out.

"This woman survived a sick, violent husband for years, managed to protect her offspring, yet she got all this time. I wonder who the judge was?" queried one board member.

"Not only that, why didn't her counsel appeal the decision?" asked another.

Most would have thought that the decision was an easy one. However, spending that much time in prison changes a person. She may not have been *truly* dangerous when she went in, but chances were pretty good that she could be very dangerous now. Members of the Parole Board were jaded with obvious reason. They saw the reality, that prison rarely helps offenders. Instead, it makes them worse and Parole Board members know that often their decisions can mean the difference between life and death for all concerned.

When the board was satisfied with the information it had compiled on Marie, they invited her to speak with them, asking her questions about her crime, her conscience and her plans for the future. Marie understood the cliche of there being no right or wrong answer, but the truth was, there *was* a right and a wrong answer. The right answer would free her and the wrong answer could clank those bars closed for good. It was a test she couldn't study for, that she hoped she would pass.

The waiting was the worst part. Marie had been informed that it could take anywhere from one to three months for approval, or even weeks, if she got lucky. It was all so vague and she wondered if the ticking clock would now become an even greater enemy. While she waited, Marie decided to make good use of her time. She had been pretty good at homeschooling Kimberly, so she decided to help Patty learn how to read, when she learned she couldn't read very well. Within weeks, many of the other inmates were approaching her, hoping to get help from Marie as well. For the first time in a long time, she felt useful.

One day while she and Patty were in the library choosing a book, Patty asked her a question that surprised Marie more than she expected.

"You gonna teach when you get out of here?"

"I spent so much time trying to stay out of Samuel's way and to just get Kimberly ready for life the best way I knew how, it's never occurred to me that *I* could have a life, a real life. As a teacher. I guess it's not impossible. Maybe not in a traditional school, with a record and all, but I guess there are places I might be able to teach. If you had asked me something like that ten years ago, I would have looked at you like you were crazy. Now, I actually believe it's possible. I hope all this newfound self-confidence doesn't go back into hiding if the Parole Board turns me down."

"Your self-confidence isn't contingent upon your release."

"I guess you're right."

"By the way, do I get a gold star or something for using that big-ass word in the proper sentence, or what? Do I have skills or do I have skills?"

They both laughed.

After checking the New York State Parole Board Release Decisions website for over a month, Marie's decision was available. She was being released. Certain conditions of her parole would need to be discussed. But Marie couldn't imagine that any of it would be that difficult to comply with. She couldn't wait to tell Patty.

"Guess what? I'm free. It may take a month or so, but I'm free."

"I'm happy for you. You deserve it."

"Thanks, Patty."

Marie was so happy, she grabbed Patty and hugged her. Patty was stiff as a board. Marie guessed that she probably would have reacted the same way if the situation had been in reverse. Something about this entire experience had changed her. She wasn't the same woman she was when she'd come here, nor was she the same woman she had become as an inmate. It was a little scary.

"Can you believe that I'm shaking in my boots now that I know I'm getting out?"

"I can believe it. Change is always scary."

"I said all that stuff to the Parole Board. Now I'm wondering if it was real. Am I really prepared to be out on my own? I've never been in charge of my own life. First, Samuel made all the rules, then the prison system made all the rules. I can't even imagine having a meal on anything other than a schedule."

"After a month or so, you'll be well in the swing of things. You'll connect with that kid of yours and make up for lost time."

"I hope so."

"Hope has got nothing to do with it. Think positive. You *will* make it happen."

"What if I just fuck it up again?"

"You didn't fuck it up in the first place, so there's no danger of that happening."

"What am I going to do without you?"

"Write lots of letters, send me a few pictures, maybe even come for a visit every now and again."

"You know I will. We might even get you the hell outta here."

"Don't worry about me, cellmate. I'm a lifer. There's no way they're letting me out."

"That's what I used to think. But, look at me now. I still can't believe it. It's like a dream."

"All I know is you better write me. I'll forgive you if you don't come back and visit. Hell, who would want to come back here after they get out? But, you better fucking write me, or I'll just have to escape and track your ass down."

"I will write, call, send pictures, visit and anything else you want. I might even send you a cake with a file in it."

"You been watchin' them damn black-and-white movies again, I see."

Marie slept like a baby that night. For once in her life, she felt like she had a future. The next day, unfortunately, her silver lining was once again overshadowed by a cloud.

Everyone went to breakfast as usual. Marie took heed when Patty warned her not to bring her Bible and papers out of her cell. However, the lack of Marie's personal effects meant nothing. As Sandy was returning with her tray of food, she dumped the entire tray on Marie's head on purpose. Patty was more correct than she realized. Jealousy, indeed, reigned supreme. By now the news had gotten out that Marie's parole was approved, and women like Sandy were miserable because one person dared to not be miserable.

From the moment the tray hit Marie's head, Patty swung into action. She didn't want Marie to blow her parole at the last minute, and it occurred to her that maybe that was exactly what Sandy was trying to accomplish. Patty knew firsthand that the phrase *misery loves company* was more than a cliché. Sandy had never been much of a fighter and got beat up often. However, this time she came prepared. She had somehow managed to sharpen the edge of her eyeglasses, and when it became evident that she was losing the fight, she took the glasses and shoved them directly into Patty's chest. From the moment Marie saw the blood gushing, she knew there was no hope. Yet, she still tried to save her.

"Help! Help her! She's dying! She's dying!"

"Step back, Richardson."

It seemed to Marie that throughout her entire life, the *officials* only seemed to step in when it was much too late.

Patty died on that floor trying to defend her and protect her parolee status. She looked at her tray of uneaten food. She hadn't even gotten a chance to eat her breakfast. She wasn't sure why that popped into her head, except that eating had always been Patty's favorite thing.

Marie realized that once again there would be a promise that she would not get to keep.

Marie glanced at Sandy as they were taking her away and wondered whether or not the Parole Board had indeed made the right decision.

Marie attested to the fact that her violent action was little more than self-defense. She assured the board that she posed no threat to society and that the shooting of her husband was based on extenuating circumstances.

Yet, as they took Sandy away, all she could think of was how much she would have liked to have killed her, just as *she* had killed Patty.

# CHAPTER TWENTY-SEVEN

It was only a matter of time before Jocelyn figured out that much of Mr. Richardson's physical condition was an act. She often caught him engaging in activity that demonstrated how much better he was. On one occasion, in particular, she was sure she had seen him return to his bed just before she entered the room. She wasn't sure why he was hiding it from her, of all people, but she decided she would stop tiptoeing around the issue and come right out and ask him.

"Mr. Richardson, have you been leaving your bed?"

"Yes. You mustn't tell anyone. If you do, I will never leave here alive," he whispered.

"What are you saying?"

"I think you know exactly what I'm saying. You know who she is, don't you?"

"Who?"

"Mrs. Williams. You've figured it out, haven't you?"

"Mr. Richardson, I don't know what you're talking about. Tell me *exactly* what you mean."

It appeared as though he was going to finally tell Jocelyn the whole story when Nurse Williams entered the room.

"Edwards, is everything okay?" she asked.

"Yes, Nurse Williams, everything is fine."

"You can continue on your rounds. I've got Mr. Richardson."

"I've got plenty of time, Nurse Williams. I can finish up here and also attend to my other patients."

"I didn't say you couldn't. I said there are other patients with a more immediate need. So, please, go attend to them and I will take care of Mr. Richardson."

Jocelyn knew if she tried to go against Ms. Williams, she would lose her job, so she followed orders and left.

"Mr. Richardson, I hear you've been overexerting yourself. We can't have that, can we?"

From her pocket, she retrieved a syringe and injected him with it. He knew it was useless to struggle and remembered the harm caused the last time he had tried to fight her attempts at injecting him with something. The needle had broken off in his arm and the end result was beyond unpleasant. Within minutes, Sam Richardson began to fade away. Drool slid past the corner of his mouth and he struggled to speak. Ms. Williams pulled up a chair next to him. She sat staring at him, her legs crossed and swinging agitatedly back and forth. Despite his slurred speech, he managed to speak.

"You know you can't keep me here forever?"

"You're talking to the wrong person. There are others in the world callous enough to hold another person captive, but not me. I would never be so presumptuous as to control another's life in such a way. If I were you, I would be very careful about who you tell your fairytales to."

He attempted to speak again, but the sedative she had given him was working quickly. Once he was asleep, she withdrew an odd metal object from her pocket and began tracing a path along his skin. Crimson lines appeared on his arms and chest. After she was done with him, she tucked the object back in her pocket, sat, and watched him sleep. The look of self-satisfaction on her face was unmistakable.

Jocelyn stood in the doorway for a moment, not anxious to incur Ms. Williams' wrath at her quick return. She was surprised to find Mr. Richardson sleeping and wondered if Ms. Williams had given him something. She also wondered what she was doing sitting there at Mr. Richardson's side. The head nurse's behavior had become increasingly odd over time and Jocelyn was beginning to realize that she needed to let someone know sooner rather than later. It occurred to her that an anonymous call might be the way to go in order to preserve her job. She quickly left the doorway, glad that Ms. Williams had not realized she was there.

In truth, she was fully aware that Jocelyn was standing there. She simply chose not to respond. Before leaving, she whispered in Mr. Richardson's ear, "Old man, I haven't even begun to make you pay. You can do all the walking and planning you'd like. You *will* be held accountable for the evil you have wrought."

She was well aware that he couldn't hear her, but she didn't care. Her hatred of him wouldn't allow her not to speak.

She exited his room, only to find the other nurses standing around talking.

"No one here has any work to do?"

None of the other nurses liked Ms. Williams. It annoyed them that she was able to work such limited hours. They thought that she was bossy, cold and that her actions were often inappropriate toward the patients and her coworkers alike. Yet, she was allowed to get away with her behavior without so much as a reprimand. However, they were very careful not to rile her, because in everyone's opinion, there had to be someone high up that was protecting her.

"Nurse Williams, it's pretty late and most of the patients are asleep," a nurse named Stephanie said.

"I'm sure there are other duties that can be attended to while the patients are sleeping, or do I need to assign work to everyone?"

Jocelyn made it a point not to respond. She decided that until she arrived at some conclusion about what she was going to do about Mr. Richardson, she was going to keep a very low profile with Ms. Williams.

"Do I?" Nurse Williams asked again.

"No," Stephanie responded.

"Good, I'm glad to hear that. Please get back to work."

Everyone scattered in an effort to look busy and stay out of the head nurse's way. While they were doing that, she did what she often did. Nurse Williams slipped out of the hospital to attend to other matters that none of the nurses needed to know about.

Jocelyn watched from a safe distance as Nurse Williams headed for the exit stairway. She had seen her do that before. Now, with all of her concerns about Mr. Richardson, she wondered where it was she was going and for a moment considered following her. It even occurred to Jocelyn that if she tipped the hospital off that their *part-time* head night nurse was slipping out in the middle of the night, maybe that would be enough to get rid of her. She wasn't quite ready to take that kind of a chance yet. She did resolve that she would clock how long Williams was gone and that the next time she slipped out, she *would* follow her.

# CHAPTER TWENTY-EIGHT

"Yo, Emily! You better get up. Don't you have an early class today?"

Emily whined, stretched and turned over, pulling the comforter over her head.

"It can't be morning already."

"It sure as hell is," Sydney said, chuckling. "It was *morning* when you dragged your ass in here."

"How would you know, sleeping beauty? You know you should have come with me to Plato last night."

"I'm tired of Plato; same people, same faces. It's getting tired."

"You wouldn't have thought so last night. Take one guess who was there."

Before Sydney could guess, Emily excitedly told her.

"None other than Cliff Truesdale."

"So, that was last semester. I won't be revisiting that one *ever* again."

"You see, that's what I tell you about you *bi* folks. Y'all can't make up your minds. It's just plain ole selfish if you ask me. One gender group isn't enough; you gotta fuck 'em all. Meanwhile, women like me can't get no play."

"Emily, you ain't got no damn sense and I would suggest you not offer up your opinion of bisexuality to anyone but me." She laughed.

"You know that shit is true. Why else would you stop fucking someone as *fine* as Mr. Clifford Truesdale?"

"Suffice it to say that the only thing *true* about that boy was his name."

"I don't believe you. No man could have lips like that and not be able to put it down both orally and horizontally. See, I know what the problem is, you're too damn freaky to appreciate some plain-old good loving."

"Baby boy's dick was smaller than mine."

"No, no, no. Don't tell me that. I don't want to know. Seriously, Sydney, tell me the truth. Does he really have a small dick?"

Sydney held up her pinky finger, and with the thumb of her same hand, touched the nail to the middle of her pinky.

"That big," she indicated. "Girl, I didn't feel a thing. I almost had to ask him if it was in yet."

"Now that you've ruined my day, I guess I'll head off to class. You ain't right. There goes another illusion dashed."

Before Emily left, Sydney retrieved a large black vibrator from the side table drawer and turned it on.

"There's always this. Buzzy here is always hard and large and rearing to go."

"Yeah, yeah, yeah, that works sometimes, but when all is said and done, I need a face."

Sydney mimed writing an invisible note in the air.

"Note to self," she said. "Buy Emily one vibrator with a face for her birthday."

Emily tossed a notebook at Sydney and walked out of the door as Sydney dissolved into laughter. She was so glad she had been lucky enough to get Emily as a roommate. She couldn't have been more perfect. She was non-judgmental and over time had become more than a roommate. She was a truly good friend. The two of them actually had quite a bit in common. The only time their opinions differed was when it came to their residence. Emily was constantly complaining about their Columbia University housing, but, despite the sixth-floor walk-up, the roaches and the sporadic leaks in the bathroom, Sydney loved it.

Here in Harlem was the first opportunity Sydney had gotten to live a separate life from her ultra-conservative, ultra white-bread parents. In New York, Sydney could find some semblance of freedom. She felt as though she were living a lie at home in Beverly Hills. If her parents had even a clue of the life she was living here, or what she had been doing when she was at home in California, they would have shipped her off to a convent some-where, or maybe even to some New Age psychiatric hospital, to cure her of her *ills*.

Unlike many of the people she attended group therapy with, her parents had at least allowed her the opportunity to make her own decision as to how she would eventually live her life. What she didn't think they would go along with were the choices she was making along the way, in order to make that decision; if, indeed, she made any decision at all.

As far as Sydney was concerned, in order for her to *truly* make an informed decision, she would need to live a life of duality. She was happy to learn that both in group therapy and in individual sessions with her therapist, her path was a well-chosen one, for her. Despite that she didn't think her parents would approve, there was a small part of Sydney that believed even her parents knew it was the right thing to do. Even the name they had given her was one replete with duality.

So, she took full advantage of her sexually ambiguous name and reveled in her androgyny. She felt she had a handle on things, and unlike many of the people she met with each week for group therapy, she seldom felt as though her circumstances were some sort of curse.

Sydney didn't have a class until twelve, so she decided she would watch a little *Maury* and put some thought into *who* she would be today.

Emily returned from class right about the same time Sydney was leaving.

"You're not going to Plato again tonight, are you?"

"No. No Plato tonight. Why? Did you want to hang?"

"Yeah. I need to get out."

"They opened a new place on Bleecker called 9-4-8-1. We could check that out."

"Sounds good to me. I wanna get my Cuervo on."

Sydney returned from school anxious to get out and with an arm full of bags.

"Did you go shopping again? Can we trade parents, please, or, can we at least trade credit cards? I think mine has a three hundred-dollar credit limit, total."

Emily rummaged through Sydney's bags.

"I guess I'll be hangin' with Sid tonight, judging from your clothes purchases?"

"Sid it is."

"Wow! I thought my days of needing therapy were over when I left home, maybe not."

"You've got the best of both worlds. You've got a girlfriend to do manicures and pedicures with and a guy to keep you safe."

"Right, when was the last time either of us did each other's nails?"

"Is that my fault? You won't let me touch you. You're just afraid I might lay some of that good lovin' on you, like I did when I first moved in."

"Oh yeah, that's it," Emily responded sarcastically.

"What time are we leaving?"

"Let's do happy hour. You know my ass is broke as hell."

"Don't worry, sugar, I got you."

9-4-8-1 was packed with students, mostly from nearby NYU. The music was loud, the drinks were watered down, and the bodies were pressed together like sardines in a can, just the way Sydney liked it.

She was wearing a pair of black jeans, white T-shirt and a black vest. She had taped her breasts sufficiently so that there wasn't any indication that she even had any. Her close-cropped hair was gelled on the sides and spiked at the top and she wore a pair of black horn-rimmed glasses, without corrective lenses. There was a woman at the end of the bar whose eye she had obviously caught. Sydney wasn't sure she was sufficiently excited enough to approach her. Instead, she decided to watch her for a moment. Physical attraction wasn't the most important thing for Sydney. She was looking for a certain *type*. She wanted a woman that liked men. She could usually figure out who fit the bill after simply watching for a moment or two. As she watched the woman that was watching her, she noticed someone else she was much more interested in, standing directly behind her. She reminded her of the actress Halle Berry. Her body was camouflaged by the crowd of people, but if it was anything like her angelic face, Sydney hoped to bury her own face deep in her mound, soon. She crossed the room, anxious to connect with the Halle Berry look-a-like before she got away.

The tall, heavily-botoxed blonde that had been eyeing Sydney from across the room almost seemed angry that she passed her by without so much as a nod.

Sydney stopped in front of her intended target just as she appeared to be walking away.

"Don't tell me you're leaving."

"As a matter of fact, I am. It's a bit too crowded in here for me."

"You can't leave."

"Really, I can't? Why is that?"

"If you do, it will break my heart. You wouldn't want to be responsible for breaking my heart, would you?"

"I've always believed that each of us is responsible for our own individual hearts, no matter what love games we play."

"Okay, if you're going to go, go now. If you speak again, I don't think I'll ever be able to recover from the loss."

"Well, if you put it like that, maybe I'll have one drink with you."

"Thank you. I feel honored that you would brave the crowd to stay and have a drink with me. I'm Sid, by the way...And your name is?"

"Catrina. My friends call me Cat."

"The name suits you."

After about an hour of flirting, even the multiple tequila shots couldn't quell *Sid's* instinct that Cat was a woman with many secrets. It occurred to Sid that some of those secrets might be best left at 9-4-8-1, as she found Emily and they both ventured home. Lust conquered reason and she could barely believe the words as they spilled from her own lips.

"You ready to get out of here?" Sid asked.

"Absolutely. What did you have in mind?"

"Whatever your little heart desires."

"My heart won't be making the decisions tonight. I say we grab a bottle somewhere close by and check into the motel down the block."

"Let me just let my roommate know I'm leaving."

"Something tells me she'll know where you got to."

"Yeah, she will at that," Sid responded, amused.

This was always the uncomfortable part for Sydney. Should she or shouldn't she? Emily always mentioned how surprised she was that *everyone* couldn't figure it out. But, there were often situations where Sydney's lovers didn't *actually* know her gender until they were naked. She was much more careful with men than she was with women, and usually let them know ahead of time. Her caution was simply a way of protecting herself from physical harm. Not every man was prepared for what he saw once she *unveiled* herself.

Once they were checked into The Mercer, things moved much more quickly than Sid expected. The tall, pretty and feline-like *Cat* demonstrated a level of aggression Sid did not expect. The moment Sid unlocked the hotel room door, Cat slammed her against the nearby wall. She held each of Sid's wrists firmly against the wall and covered her mouth with her own. Her snake-like tongue slithered inside of her mouth, flicking here and there, wildly out of control, just before tugging at Sid's lower lip with her teeth, biting her hard enough to draw blood.

"Ouch! Cat! Wait a minute! Can we slow this down a bit? I have to tell you something."

Cat did not respond. She continued on her original path. Then, it was on to Sid's clothing. She ripped open her vest, then her shirt, to reveal the heavy Ace bandage Sid had used to bind her breasts. She ripped the bandage from her body with such force, Sid was surprised at her strength; surprised, frightened and more than a little turned on.

She pushed Sid onto the nearby bed, biting at her nipples, hardening them. Sid squirmed, unsure herself as to whether she was trying to get free or to welcome more of what Cat was delivering in heavy supply.

Cat's mouth and tongue tortured Sid intermittently with equal levels of pain and pleasure, tracing her tongue down to the waistband of Sid's pants. She unzipped the zipper with her teeth and reached her hand inside, before abruptly removing her hand and stopping. Sid was sure her hesitance was because she was repulsed and would now leave.

"I...I was going to...I mean..."

Before Sid could explain, Cat moved back up to meet her face to face and while Sid tried to speak, Cat placed one hand inside of Sid's pants, once again, while the other hand lay flatly atop her mouth. Sid wasn't sure if it was the alcohol she had earlier or some odd scent Cat was wearing, but she suddenly felt incredibly dizzy as a nauseating scent filled her nostrils, just before everything went black.

# CHAPTER TWENTY-NINE

M osaic was fascinated with how much easier it got each time. Those chosen for eradication were also those most ruled by their sickest desires. Therefore, they were easy prey. Often a simple disguise was all that was needed and God's work was done.

It was obvious that this would not be a good night for the numerous layers of dark clothing and hood that had become Mosaic's uniform. The name of the club was 9-4-8-1, and though there was a particular chosen target for the night, the club was filled to capacity with more than enough of the *morally bankrupt*. The sight of bodies bumping and grinding was sickening. The alcohol flowed freely and the vague scent of marijuana wafted through the air. Making way through the oppressive crowd in order to find the bathroom and remove the numerous layers of clothing, Mosaic barely made it to the bathroom before throwing up.

"You okay in there?" a voice asked.

"Yes, I'm fine."

It could be difficult to maintain the veneer of acceptance around such people, but Mosaic was ever-mindful that it was only temporary and that in order to remain undetected, it was necessary to blend in. The person that emerged from the bathroom bore little resemblance to the person layered in black clothing that entered earlier.

It was always so easy. Heads turned and gawked in appreciation, hoping to have the opportunity to engage in some Godless display of debauchery. It wasn't long before the intended target was located. She was despicable. Her attempt at androgyny was pitiful. Anyone with any presence of mind would have been able to tell what kind of abomination was in their presence. What was most disgusting was the lack of shame. She stood there, drawing others in with her evil, taunting and teasing others to join her. Mosaic smiled, fully aware that her days on earth were numbered.

After some time spent drinking and exchanging empty words, it was time.

Things at the club were so chaotic, no one noticed them leaving. This one was especially unnerving, even more so than the others. She had no contrition. Many of them were conflicted and waging an inner battle about what they were. But this one, she seemed to exalt in it, as though she was lucky to have been born what she was. If there were degrees of evil, she would have been the most evil of them all. For that reason, the opportunity to cleanse and purify by removing her from the earth filled Mosaic with an immense feeling of joy.

In order to lure those that needed to be destroyed, sex was sometimes a useful tool. Yet, the sins of the flesh could be much more powerful than expected. Standing in the mirror, begging forgiveness from God, absolution was the best that Mosaic could hope for.

The desire to dispose of the body right there in the hotel room was overwhelming. But that would have been a huge mistake. Instead, a heavy, folded duffle bag was withdrawn from another smaller bag. She was so small, her body fit inside perfectly. However, when it was time to leave the hotel room, Mosaic found it was not as easy to lift the bag containing the body as first thought. Instead, it would have to be dragged across the floor. Getting it from the room itself to the elevator was easy enough. But, the sight of someone dragging a large duffle bag across the hotel lobby floor was sure to draw attention, even donned in the multiple layers of clothing and hood. Exiting from the roof was considered, but if there was no easy exit there, it would cause even greater problems.

It was resolved that the bag would have to be removed through the lobby, after all. Surprisingly, no one seemed to notice, including the hotel staff, who appeared to be bored and disinterested.

# CHAPTER THIRTY

"What are you doing in here?" Candace asked.

"I was early and I figured I would wait. I hope you don't mind."

"How did you get in?"

"The door was open."

Candace knew she hadn't left the door open and she wondered why Shelly had lied. However, she chose not to engage in a dispute with her for several reasons, not the least of which was fear. For quite some time, Candace had been concerned that Shelly was exhibiting symptoms of dissociative identity disorder and possibly schizophrenia. However, recent sessions had confirmed for her that Shelly was clearly grappling with multiple personalities. One thing Candace was sure of was that the condition most often developed as a reaction to childhood trauma. There were also those that believed that having a close family member with dissociative identity disorder made a person particularly vulnerable. Candace realized that it would be very helpful to Shelly's treatment if she knew whether or not one or both of her parents also suffered from either of the disorders. Shelly's frequent lapses in memory, her blackouts and most recently her desire to be called by other names, all were clear indications that she most likely did have multiple personalities. On several occasions, she had even set up appointments and visited her as someone other than Shelly.

"In the future, Shelly, I would rather you not wait in my office, whether the door is open or not."

"I'm sorry, Doc. It won't happen again."

"Have a seat."

"So, are you mad at me?" Shelly asked.

"No, I'm not *mad*."

"You sure seem like you are."

"Well, I'm not."

"Whatever you say," Shelly said sarcastically.

"What about you, Shelly? Are you mad?"

"That's an odd question to ask, or does it mean you haven't really been listening. That's why I came to you in the first place, isn't it? I'm *always* mad."

"Are you really, always mad, or should I say angry?"

"I'm not usually angry or mad when I'm here."

"That's good to hear. What do you think is different here than any place else?"

"I know who I am here. Things are quieter. I can think clearer, even with you talking at me. It seems like even when I'm sleeping, I can't get rid of all of the voices inside my head, picking and prodding at me with all their expectations. All I want to do is make them stop. I just want to be left alone for a minute, so I can think."

"Shelly, there's a medication that I think might help with some of these feelings you've been having."

"I won't take any medication."

"Let me tell you what it is and then you can think about it. You don't have to decide anything now. It's called Seroquel and it will help with some of the impulses you've been having; the anger; the lost time."

"So what are you saying, Doc? Are you trying to say I'm crazy or something?"

"Of course not. You're not crazy. Often a combination of therapy and medication can help strike the proper balance to allow therapy to progress at a better pace. It will allow you some of that peace I believe you are searching for."

"I'll think about it. I don't think it will help, though. I've been on medication before and all it did was make me zombie-like. If I'm going to walk around like that, I'd rather stay the way that I am."

"I hope you'll consider it. It'll be just the thing you need. It doesn't necessarily have to be forever. You could try it and see how you do on it. We can even try some other medications if the Seroquel doesn't work."

"I'll consider it."

Candace realized she should drop the subject and move on to something else.

"How have you been sleeping?"

"Okay, I guess."

"Have you lost any more time?"

"A little. It's probably just stress. I wasn't even drinking the last time."

Candace didn't want to tell Shelly that the fact that she wasn't drinking wasn't exactly a good thing.

"Have you ever kept a diary?"

"Maybe when I was little. I don't really remember, but I might have had a diary when I was a little girl. Why?"

"It might be a good idea for you to start keeping a journal. It doesn't have to be anything too complicated. Write down your thoughts when it occurs to you. I think it will be especially helpful if you do it when you wake up. Often people find journals are very helpful when they're having sleep difficulties."

"Would you read it?"

"I don't have to but it might be helpful in our session. I'll leave it up to you. If you're okay with me reading your journal, then I will. However, you'll have total control of whether I read it or not."

"Okay. I'll do it. I'll start a journal. Hey, who knows, maybe it'll be a best seller," Shelly joked.

With Candace's initial assertion forgotten—that Shelly not spend time in her office when she wasn't there, the rest of the session progressed without event.

"Well, our time is up for today. Have you given any thought to adding another session during the week?"

"I thought about it, but I don't have the time. We'll have to stick to one day a week for now."

"No problem. Keep in mind that the offer still stands."

"Yeah, okay."

Although Candace was careful not to let on that she noticed, it was obvious that Shelly had been searching her office for something. She obviously didn't expect her to return when she did and had left the file cabinet slightly ajar. Candace noticed it the moment she walked in the office but declined to confront Shelly.

As Shelly was leaving, she turned and asked Candace a question.

"You don't tell people what we talk about here, do you, Doc?"

"Of course not; our sessions are purely confidential."

"I hope so, Doc. I don't know what I would do if I found out you were telling people about me."

Shelly's comment didn't miss its mark. Candace's initial low level of fear was replaced with an overwhelming sense of terror. As soon as Shelly was gone and the door was closed, Candace looked through the cabinet, searching for Shelly's file. As she fully expected, it was gone.

osaic stood outside the location where Dr. Phipps regularly held her group sessions. What started as a mission to purify the world was now replaced with anger. It was Mosaic's wish that even one of the members might show up, but there was no one. Dr. Phipps had seen to that. Then suddenly, there she was, Dr. Candace Phipps. Why was she here? There was no reason to be. Any members had been frightened away. It was quite clearly, her time. Following closely behind her, Candace never noticed the figure dressed all in black.

"Hey, Phipps," the security guard said.

The lobby was full of people.

"Hey."

"I thought you cancelled your groups for a while," he said.

"I did. I wanted to stop by in case some of my members were not aware of the cancellation."

"I haven't seen anyone. I think they all know."

"I'm gonna go to my room anyway. I'll be right back."

"No problem."

Before heading to her meeting room, Candace decided to grab a cup of coffee from the lobby. Suddenly, it occurred to her that she was being watched. Then, just as suddenly, the feeling was gone. She shook her head and whispered to herself, "Candace Phipps, get a grip."

"You okay?" the security guard asked, when he saw her talking to herself.

"Yeah, I'm fine. Just working some stuff out in my head."

"Okay. These fire murders are freaking everybody out. I can imagine it must hit really close to home for you."

"I didn't realize you were aware of the connection."

"Are you kidding? News travels fast. Everybody's been talking about it. My wife didn't even want me to come to work. Members of other groups have been talking about it as well. Some of the other groups have even lost members. Haven't you noticed how empty it's been here, compared to in the past? People are scared."

Candace looked around. Even though the lobby was pretty crowded, she realized the guard was right; there were less people than usual.

"Could you do me a favor?" Candace asked the guard.

"Sure, anything. What do you need?"

"I'm going to my room. Could you ring my phone in fifteen minutes?"

"Absolutely. You sure you don't want me to go with you? I could if you'd like."

"No, I'm sure everything is fine. It's just a precaution. I'm starting to realize it won't hurt me to be as cautious as everyone else is being. Until now, I don't think I've been taking this as seriously as I probably should."

"I know that's right. It's not enough that this nut job is killing people, but the way he's doing it. I can't imagine what those people must have gone through. I hope they were dead before he burned them. That's a horrible way to die, being burned to death."

"Yeah, it is awful."

Candace headed over to her meeting room, careful to proceed with the utmost caution. As soon as she entered, she knew the killer had been there. She should have run immediately, but it was difficult not to gaze in awe at what was scrawled across the walls. In bright red letters was the word *abomination*, written several times. Also written on the walls were multiple passages from the Bible. She read the first she noticed. *Corinthians 6:9 Or do you not know that wrongdoers will not inherit the kingdom of God? Do not be deceived: Neither the sexually immoral nor idolaters nor adulterers nor men who have sex with men nor thieves nor the greedy nor drunkards nor slanderers nor swindlers will inherit the kingdom of God. And that is what some of you were. But you were washed, you were sanctified, you were justified in the name of the Lord Jesus Christ and by the Spirit of our God.* Candace continued on, reading the next verse which read: *Corinthians 12:21 I fear that when I come again my God may humble me before you, and I may have to mourn over many of those who sinned earlier and have not repented of the impurity, sexual immorality, and sensuality that they have practiced.* She continued reading, mesmerized by it all. Then, suddenly, there was a passage she recognized. Those red letters in particular jumped out at her even more than the others, halting her breath and curdling her stomach. They were words she had heard before, not in a Bible or even written somewhere. She had heard these exact words spoken. She had long had her suspicions but now she was sure. She knew the killer and the killer knew her. She was also convinced that all those many times she felt as though she were being followed, it was more than paranoia. She was on the killer's list.

She wondered why she hadn't been killed first, then realized that her death might be meant to signify an ending. She, more than anyone else, represented what the killer believed was wrong with the world. She was sure of it. The killer was planning for her to be the last. Her first thought was to call the detective whose card was in her pocket. Then, the thought dawned on her that the killer had come to her, possibly for help. What kind of doctor would she be if she didn't find a way to do just that. She was torn. Her logic and her survivor's instinct told her that the first thing she should do was call Detective Simms. However, her sense of obligation told her she should find a way to break through to her patient's psyche. She believed so much in the power of her profession that she was convinced she could turn everything around, if she only had enough time. She stood there waiting, bracing herself and cautiously aware that she would need to be prepared, but also hopeful that her skill would afford her the time to both save her own life and that of others, including her patients. She realized if she were prepared for the killer's arrival, she would at least have a fighting chance. Before she could turn to watch the door, she felt a strong hand gripping her right shoulder. Before turning to meet her executioner, she read the words once again. *Colossians 3:5 Put to death, therefore, whatever belongs to your earthly nature: sexual immorality, impurity, lust, evil desires and greed, which is idolatry.*

"I've been waiting for you," she said.

As much as she wanted to deal with the issue at hand, she was relieved to find that it was the security guard standing behind her.

"What the heck happened here?" he asked.

"I don't know."

He gazed at her for a moment.

"You're pale as a ghost," he said.

"I'm just a little shaken up. I'll be fine."

"Should I call the police?"

"Don't worry, I'll take care of that," Candace said.

"You sure?"

"Absolutely."

"Is there anything I can do?"

"As a matter of fact, you could walk me to my car, if you don't mind."

"Of course. Of course I will."

The guard stood there, suddenly aware of what was written on the walls.

"Whoever wrote this is stark raving mad," he said. "My wife is always on my case about not going to church and I always tell her, I don't need to go to church to pray or be a good man. I also always tell her that anything, even religion, can be a bad thing when it becomes an obsession."

After calling Detective Simms and assuring him that she didn't need either him or a squad car to come and get her, and that she was okay to drive to him, she got in her car and headed in the direction of the address he had given her.

# CHAPTER THIRTY-TWO

K imberly sat in her car outside Brandon's apartment, watching. She could barely remember driving there. She wasn't even sure herself why. It was as if she were on surveillance, ducking every time she thought she saw or heard someone coming. That's when a car pulled up. She recognized the driver immediately. It was Dr. Phipps. She was immediately confused. Her first thought was, what was she doing there? Then, inexplicably, she was jealous. Eventually, her jealousy was replaced with blind rage. She pounded her fists on the steering wheel and considered storming into Brandon's apartment, but thought better of it. Instead, she sat in the car, talking to herself.

"There's nothing to worry about, nothing. He loves me. He's always loved me. No one can take my place. I'm the most important person to him and always will be."

As if in answer to the silence, Kadeem suddenly appeared.

"Sis, what the heck are you doing? I've been looking for you everywhere."

Kimberly jumped, before turning to find Kadeem looking in at her on the driver's side window.

"My goodness, Kadeem, you scared the crap out of me."

"You gonna let me in or what?" he asked, pulling on the driver's side door.

"Do me a favor, get in the back," Kimberly said.

"What are you doing skulking outside your partner's place? This doesn't look like perp surveillance to me. Don't tell me you've turned into a stalker," Kadeem said.

"I should be asking you that question. Did you follow me?"

"Of course not. I was looking for you and I thought maybe you'd be here."

"How did you know where Brandon lived?"

"You told me."

"No, I didn't."

"Yes, you did."

"Whatever. What was so urgent that you couldn't wait until I got home?"

"I was worried about you."

"Yeah, sure you were."

"No, really. You have to admit, Sis, you have been acting a tad bit strange lately, breaking up LCDs for no apparent reason; your edginess; your forgetfulness. I was concerned. This case is starting to get to you."

"I'm fine. It's the people around me that are making me feel like I'm crazy, like you and all your girlfriends."

"What girlfriends? I'm a lonely, lonely man," Kadeem said, with a smile.

"Of course you are and despite what you may think, this is work, so I'm gonna have to ask you to meet me at home."

"Whatever you say. Don't get caught."

Kimberly couldn't help but think that Kadeem should have been a cop. His stealth movements never ceased to amaze her. She looked through her rearview mirror and within minutes, he was gone.

As was usually the case, Kadeem's presence had gone a long way to calm her and she was able to better gather her thoughts, just in time to see Brandon and Dr. Phipps leaving. She wondered where they were going and decided she would follow them. She ducked down in her car and waited for the two of them to get into what she assumed was the doctor's car, since it wasn't Brandon's. They drove away and Kimberly waited just long enough to go undetected, before following them. She knew Brandon would notice her easily if she didn't keep a reasonable distance behind them. It appeared they were headed toward Long Island. After about forty-five minutes of driving, they were pulling up in front of what appeared to be a two-acre property right outside of Lake Ronkonkoma. A middle-aged man opened the door and quickly embraced Candace. He then shook Brandon's hand, before closing the door.

Kimberly wondered what was going on. Brandon seldom kept secrets from her, but he had never mentioned any of this. What was he doing with a witness and who was this man whose home they were at? He seldom handled matters related to a case without letting her know what he was doing. The entire situation was very odd. Kimberly didn't think she should wait. The area was much more secluded than the city and the chances of Brandon noticing her car were highly likely. She decided she would return to Brandon's place and wait.

Inside Harry Little's home, Candace was attempting to come to terms with the reality that there was a killer on the loose and that she was most probably the next victim. She was also coming to terms with the fact that she was not quite ready to turn the killer in to the police. In her mind, she thought that all she needed was more time with *her* patient.

"Harry, I'm so sorry to put you out like this. I didn't have any place else to go."

"Stop it. You're not putting me out at all. What kind of friend would I be if you couldn't at least count on me for a place to stay?"

"I don't want to put you and Pearl in any danger."

"Don't worry. I doubt anyone will find you all the way out here."

"I don't know, Harry. Someone's definitely been following me."

"What do you think, Detective?" Harry Little asked.

"I'm going to get some officers out here to keep an eye on you all, but I won't lie, I don't think I'll be able to keep them here for long. If the killer is the person that's been following Candace, he or she is getting sloppy, and I'm hoping whoever it is will slip up enough and get caught."

Brandon couldn't help but notice Harry whispering to Candace. Candace appeared agitated by whatever he was saying.

"Am I missing something here?" Brandon asked.

"Candace, you need to tell him," Harry said.

"I can't."

"Candace, I can't help you if you don't tell me *everything*. Now, what's going on?" Brandon asked.

"She's got a patient, a patient who is suffering from multiple personalities and schizophrenia."

"We don't know that for sure," she lied.

"Candace, come on. You're a pro and you and I both know, from everything you've told me, that it's true."

"It's because I'm a professional that I don't want to jump to conclusions here. I've spent my entire career trying to fight against all the prejudices and generalizations associated with a psychological diagnosis, and one of those generalizations is that everyone that's suffering from schizophrenia or multiple personalities is either incapable of functioning or dangerous. It's simply not true. I've been doing this long enough to know it's not true."

"Aren't schizophrenia and multiple personalities pretty rare?" Brandon asked.

"You'd be surprised; not as rare as you would think. With medication most can live relatively normal lives," Candace said.

"I understand all that, but I still need some more information on this patient."

"You don't understand, Detective. I owe my patients a certain level of confidentiality. It's my responsibility to help them to get better. What kind of doctor would I be if I gave up simply because the person's illness was more serious than most? I would be no different than an oncologist who gives up on a Stage 4 cancer patient. As doctors, we are charged with healing, not giving up. That responsibility is no different for me as a psychologist than for any other doctor."

"I completely understand that, but it's a different issue altogether when murder is involved."

"We don't know for sure that she's the murderer."

"You're right. We also don't know that she's not, and you have not indicated to me a strong level of belief that she's not."

"I'll think about it. There is more involved here than a question of integrity. I could also lose my license."

"I hate to do this to you, but if I have to, I'll get an injunction to pull your records."

Candace simply shrugged.

"I'll sleep on it and call you tomorrow," she said.

"Don't worry, I'll talk her into doing the *sensible* thing," Harry offered.

"Sure, like it would be so easy for you if it were one of your patients."

"Actually, I think it would. Candace, you and I have been colleagues for years. I have nothing but the utmost respect for you, but this is not about integrity. This is about life and death; not only yours, but others."

There was nothing else left for Candace to say. Harry Little walked Brandon Simms to the door and said good night while Candace contemplated what she was going to do next and what her decision might cost her.

# CHAPTER THIRTY-THREE

K imberly had a key to Brandon's apartment that he had given her long ago. She only used it once when he was sick at home with the flu. She decided tonight would be the second time to use the key. Her plan was to be waiting for him when he arrived.

Kimberly sat in the dark, waiting. She wasn't sure why, but she was in a dark place and had no desire to absorb even the smallest bit of light. Brandon, being every bit the cop, sensed someone was there immediately and entered cautiously, his gun in hand. The lights of a passing car warned Kimberly that he was prepared to strike and she spoke quickly.

"Brandon, it's just me. It's Kimberly."

"Kitten, what are you doing here?"

It had been so long since he'd called her that. The last and only time he had was years ago when they shared a very surprising and passionate kiss. The pet name still had the same effect now that it had on her then.

"You're not angry?" she asked.

"Do I look angry?"

He stepped closer, not quite touching her, but close enough that she could feel the warmth of him all around her. The heat of his eyes bore through her like lasers, his gaze focused intently upon her face. Sporadic flashes of light cut through the darkness each time a car passed by outside, illuminating the beauty of her glistening face. Then suddenly, with little more provocation than her presence, his body responded to the closeness of her. The hardening of him closed the distance between them and she could now *really* feel him. For the first time in a long time, her mind was free. She could see or think of nothing but him.

"Brandon, I don't know if I can," she said.

"I don't understand. What's holding you back? We've been together before. I know what you feel like. I *love* what you feel like."

"You don't know, not really. If you did, you would never say the things that you do."

"Baby, there is nothing that you could tell me that could ever change the way I feel about you. You have to know that."

"You say that now, but all that would change if I ever, if I...If you...I'm so empty."

"There's nothing empty about you, Kitten."

One minute her voice was steeped in melancholy, then suddenly her words were husky with desire.

"Fill me up," she demanded. "Fill me up!"

Kimberly backed Brandon against the wall, her hands groping wildly at the hardness between his legs. She nibbled at his neck, inhaling his musky, manly scent. He was positively intoxicating. She unzipped his pants and reached inside, eager to feel him in her hands. The sticky feel of pre-cum between her fingertips excited her even more. Their bodies sweaty from passion and too many items of clothing, Brandon stripped off her shirt, then his. He looked at her with that familiar look that she enjoyed so much, a look that said she was the most beautiful thing he had ever laid his eyes on.

"You are so fucking beautiful," he said, as if reading her thoughts.

Then suddenly, he knew. He understood why, out of the all the women he had married, dated, fucked and worked with, she was the one that he couldn't let go of. For the longest time, he thought it was little more than a simple case of wanting what he couldn't have. But now, he knew he could *have* her, or at least somewhat. That wasn't what fueled him. It was all that she represented. Wrapped in that one stunning package was a living, breathing contradiction. One minute, she was saucy; the next, she was sweet. She could be cocky as hell, then suddenly melt into a pool of insecurity. Sometimes, he thought his sole purpose in life was to save her, until she turned around and saved him. They had only been intimate twice, but both times, she had proven herself to be anything but insecure. Lost in thought, the slap across his face stung and shocked him, yet made him even harder than before.

"Have I lost you? Where did you go?" she asked.

"Just thinking about how incredibly lucky I am."

"Then show me."

Kimberly plunged her tongue deep inside of his mouth, enjoying the echoes of his moans trapped between the seal of their lips. She encouraged the rotation of their bodies so that she was against the wall and began removing the remainder of her clothing. Brandon stopped long enough to take in the sight of her black lace bra and panties.

"Oh my God," was all he could say, as he took all of her in with his eyes.

He traced his fingertip across her chest, then down to her breasts, first one, then the other. As he focused on her right nipple, he could feel it harden beneath the trail he was leading. The flimsy covering of the lace bra did nothing to conceal her hardness. Then, suddenly, she turned again so that the front of her body was flat and plastered against the wall. Brandon rubbed his body against hers, his cock finding a comfortable place between the folds of her pleasantly rounded ass cheeks. She poked her ass toward him, teasing him.

"Do you want it or not?" she asked.

"Hell yeah."

"Then take it."

Brandon reached down, anxious to feel her hot wetness on his hands and Kimberly stopped him. She raised her arms above her head.

"Grab my wrists!" she demanded.

Brandon did as he was told. Kimberly guided his cock toward her with her movements, writhing and squirming erotically against the wall. As he entered her, she was so tight Brandon wasn't sure what hole he was filling. Quite frankly, he didn't care. All he cared about was making the feeling last as long as possible. With each thrust, his grunts and groans got louder and louder. Brandon could hear nothing from Kimberly and wished he could see her face better. He angled his face so that he could kiss her lips, reaching and hoping to see a bit of the joy he was experiencing written across her face as well. A single glance told him all he needed to know. The sight of her biting her lower lip, the squint of her eyes and the rapid rising and falling of her chest, gasping for air was more than he could stand. He couldn't have controlled his explosion if he wanted to. As he emitted a sound akin to a growl, Kimberly screamed out in unison. Brandon couldn't have imagined anything more perfect, that is until Kimberly once again quickly left his side to head directly to the bathroom. As she had done before, as soon as she exited the bathroom, she quickly left, leaving Brandon wondering why.

After tossing and turning all night, Brandon realized he had been so caught up with the case, and the sudden shift his relationship with Kimberly had taken, he had forgotten about the files he'd snuck out of her desk and copied. Under the circumstances, he decided there was no better time than now, to find out what she could have been so intent on hiding. He got out of bed and retrieved the papers from his desk.

The name on it was *Marie Richardson*.

"Hmmm, who are you, Marie Richardson, and why doesn't our Kimberly want anyone to know anything about you?" he said aloud as he began to read.

That's when he saw Kimberly's name listed as a potential witness. Marie Richardson was her mother. Now he understood why she was unwilling for him to see the file. She was ashamed. He almost felt guilty for having pried. He decided he would never do something like that again. Kimberly was his partner and so much more, and he would have to do his very best to trust her, no matter how mysterious she appeared to be.

# CHAPTER THIRTY-FOUR

When Kimberly returned home, Kadeem was sitting in the living room, waiting for her.

"Somebody's been fucking," he sang.

"Kadeem, do you have to be so crass?"

"Oh, so now I'm crass. I can't help it. I can smell it all over you. It's making me horny."

"I really don't want to talk about this with you."

"Why not? I thought you could tell me anything."

"Nobody tells anyone *everything*."

"You do, Sis. Have you forgotten? I know all there is to know about you."

"I'm not going to discuss my sex life with you."

"And here I thought we shared everything. No fair. I share everything with you. Don't I?"

"I don't ask you to. Sometimes you share a bit too much."

"You say that like you don't enjoy it. You know you do. Almost as much as you enjoy fucking that partner of yours."

"What makes you think Brandon and I are anything more than colleagues?"

"Well, to start with, when I got here he was Simms; now he's *Brandon*. Always remember, I miss *nothing*."

"This is one of those things I want only for me. I don't want to share it with *anyone*."

"I hate to break it to you, but you have no control over that. I'm in here," he said, pointing at his head.

"I'm tired. I'm taking a shower and then I'm going to bed."

"I can't sleep. Can I borrow your car? I wanna go for a ride."

"Kadeem, I need my car for work tomorrow. Make sure you're back first thing tomorrow morning."

"I'll only be gone for an hour or two."

"Kadeem, I'm serious. I've been fucking up enough lately at work. The last thing I need is to not have transportation."

"I thought you detective types doubled up," he joked.

"I'm serious. Bring my car back."

"Aye, aye, Sir," he said, saluting.

Kadeem picked up the keys to the car.

"Wait, Kadeem. Before you leave, go with me down to the basement. The super said I could store some things down there. I could use some help carrying everything."

"So now I have to do menial labor to get the car for an hour or two."

"Aw, poor baby," Kimberly responded.

Kadeem grabbed one box and Kimberly grabbed the other. Once in the basement, Kimberly saw Troy, from 4G, also putting some things away. It seemed all he did now was stare at her, and when there was anyone else around, he was whispering to the neighbors, while he stared at her. He was starting to get on her nerves. She decided she would ignore him and do what she had come down to the basement to do.

"You done?" Kadeem asked.

"I'm done. There's more in the apartment, but we can bring those down another time."

"So does that mean I'm dismissed?"

"Just help me move these to the back and tape them up, then you can go."

The entire time Kimberly and Kadeem moved and taped the boxes shut, Troy watched, shaking his head and whispering to himself.

"What's his problem?" Kadeem asked.

"I don't know what the fuck is wrong with him. All he does is stare all the time. I'm starting to get sick of it. I'm starting to get sick of him."

"Ignore him," Kadeem offered.

"I've tried that."

"You want me to talk to him? I'll do it right now," Kadeem insisted.

"Kadeem, don't. That's the last thing I need. He's probably already got everyone in the building thinking there's something wrong with me. Who knows what stories he's telling them?"

"Now you're sounding paranoid. Don't let that asshole fuck with your head."

"Let's get out of here. That's good enough," Kimberly said as she affixed the last piece of tape to a box.

As they were leaving the basement, Kadeem walked close to where Troy was standing and rammed his shoulder into his as he passed.

"What the fuck is your problem?!" Troy screamed.

"I don't have a problem. Do you?" Kadeem yelled back.

"You crazy bitch! I'll be happy when they lock your ass up. You don't belong around normal people!" Troy screamed.

"Why did you have to do that?" Kimberly asked. "All that'll do is make things worse."

"It might, but damn, it felt good doing it."

While Kimberly and Kadeem left, Troy continued to stare, dumbfounded.

Kimberly's dreams were fitful throughout the night. About three o'clock a.m., she was awakened by the sound of a car horn.

It took a few seconds before she was fully awake and by the time she was, she realized she was in a car heading straight for on-coming traffic. At first she thought she might still be sleeping, then she realized nothing could be further from the truth. She swerved just in time to avoid running into another car. She managed to get the car on the right side of the road and sat there, badly shaken. As if avoiding what could have been a catastrophic accident wasn't enough, she sat there in her car for several minutes before realizing she had no idea where she was. Once she thought her head was clear enough, she started the car up and drove enough to figure out she was all the way in Long Island. She remembered sleepwalking when she was a little girl but nothing like this had ever happened to her. Was it possible that she could have driven herself all the way here while she was asleep, or was someone messing with her mind?

# CHAPTER THIRTY-FIVE

Marie's final weeks in prison were hopelessly solemn. All the happiness she initially felt was easily minimized with Patty's death. She found herself returning to the same old withdrawn Marie. After Patty died, she declined to tutor any more of the inmates. Even the library no longer held its former charm. She spent the rest of her days marking off time. From the moment Patty was gone, Marie removed herself from the world she had lived in for so many years. As she saw it, Patty was the only thread that held her to this place. She knew Patty didn't believe that she would have visited. But she had every intention of coming back to visit. She was even looking forward to looking into whether or not the hopes of Patty being paroled were as hopeless as she led on. None of that would happen. However, there was something she could still do.

Marie realized that long before she met Samuel Richardson, she believed in God and she still believed. Her faith over the years had been understandably shaken, but, she did still believe. She decided there was one promise to Marie she could keep. She started the first letter the night before her release.

*Dear Patty,*

*What do you say to someone to whom you owe your life? Just when I thought no one cared whether I lived or died, you came along. You were loud-talking and ate faster than any human being I had ever seen before. But, when all was said and done, you were the best friend I ever had. From the moment I realized that's what we were, friends, I wondered what life would have been like if we had met on the outside. Would I have been the religious girl, with 2.5 children and sensible shoes and you, the sexy, bad girl that made my life interesting? I guess we may never know.*

*I will say this, though, save me a place up there and we'll continue a friendship that didn't have near enough time here on earth.*

*Love,*

*Skinny Marie*

Marie stuck the letter to Patty in front of her thick volume of news articles and pictures of her daughter, Kimberly. For the first time in years, Marie got down on her knees and prayed.

"Heavenly Father, as I embark on this journey of discovery and endeavor to lend a helping hand to my daughter, guide me, oh Lord, down the most righteous path and please welcome my sister-friend Patty into your comfort. Amen."

Marie did something else that night she hadn't done in a long time. She cried. She wasn't sure if the tears were of happiness or of sadness, but guessed that they were probably a combination of the two. When she was all cried out, she dreamed of Patty Mumphrey as an angel. That's when she remembered something she'd asked her mother when she was a child. One Sunday evening, after spending the early part of the day at church, they were sitting down for dinner, when Marie asked her mother if people died but were not gone forever, why hadn't anyone ever returned and let the world know there was a hereafter. Her mother's response to her was, "They return all the time. That's what dreams and miracles are."

Marie smiled. She had gotten her dream; maybe she'd have her miracle as well.

"Good morning, Patty."

That was now the way she started every day. Marie remembered how forgotten Patty felt when she was alive. She didn't want her to feel forgotten now. She made sure every morning she acknowledged her presence. She thought it was only right. After all, Patty had made the supreme sacrifice for her.

# CHAPTER THIRTY-SIX

"Do you want to lose your job or what?" Carolyn whispered to Jocelyn.

"What are you talking about?"

Jocelyn stood there staring at Nurse Williams' back.

"Everyone is noticing. People are talking. When you're not in Mr. Richardson's room watching him, you're staring at Williams and watching her. You know she doesn't like you. Hell, she doesn't like anyone. She probably can't wait to give any one of us the ax."

"She's the one that needs to be fired. It's criminal. She's been hurting that old man. The scratches on his body, the foley mishap, it's all been her. Worse than that, I think she had a prior relationship with him before she came here to work. *Coincidentally*, the two of them came here right about the same time. It was all in her personnel file."

"I told you I didn't want to get involved in any of this. I don't want to know anything about what you did or didn't find in someone's personnel file. There's one thing I do know for sure: you're *not* supposed to be fishing around in employee personnel files."

"Yeah, and patients are not supposed to be getting abused by the staff, either, but it sure as hell happens."

Carolyn was suddenly angry. Jocelyn's comment sounded more like an accusation and she knew why.

Many of the patients at Montelior were senile and could sometimes get unruly. There was one old lady that used to call Carolyn a bitch all the time and she would sometimes kick or hit her when she was trying to care for her. One day in particular, when Carolyn was trying to dress her, the woman bit her, hard, on the hand. At first, she barely reacted, then a few minutes later, she returned with a heavy towel, soaked in water, and wrung it out. She proceeded to beat the old woman with the towel until she was so exhausted she couldn't hit her anymore. Jocelyn was the only one that saw it, and for a moment she considered turning her in. Instead, she approached Carolyn and was upfront about what she had seen. Carolyn told her she had been having an especially bad week, both at home and at work, and when the old lady bit her, she lost it. She told her she had never done anything like it and would never do it again. Jocelyn agreed not to report her, then out of curiosity asked her, "Why the towel?" She explained that she knew it wouldn't leave marks. Jocelyn didn't turn her in, but for the longest time, she wondered if Carolyn had told her the truth about never having done anything like it before. After all, if it had truly never happened, how did she immediately know to use the wet towel to beat the woman so that she wouldn't leave any marks?

Jocelyn decided Carolyn was probably right and she should leave her *completely* out of all of it. As far as Jocelyn was concerned, her beating that defenseless old woman was an indication of the difference between the two of them. She also realized that she should probably be more careful about showing both Mr. Richardson and Nurse Williams so much attention. She not only needed her job for the money, but if she was no longer at Montelior, there would be no one to watch over Mr. Richardson and keep him safe. Just as the thought occurred to her, Mr. Richardson rang his call button.

"You wanna get that, or shall I?" said Nurse Williams.

"No, I'm on it," Jocelyn responded quickly.

Once inside Mr. Richardson's room, it was clear he had already been *tended to* in some way. That's when she realized there was more to the energy she witnessed him secretly demonstrating. Yes, he probably didn't want Nurse Williams to know how much better he was getting, but looking at him now, drool hanging out the side of his mouth, she knew he was being doped up with something that wasn't necessarily prescribed by his doctors. Obviously, Nurse Williams was well aware of Mr. Richardson's progression, or she would have had no need to drug him.

She dabbed at his mouth with a cloth before checking his body. Suddenly, he grabbed her hand. She was surprised to find how much strength there was in his grip. What was even more surprising was when he spoke.

"You know who she is, don't you?"

"No, Mr. Richardson, I don't. Can you tell me who she is?"

Although he was still capable of speaking, the drugs were greatly limiting his ability to think clearly.

"She's trying to kill me. She wants to punish me for what I did."

"What did you do?"

"All I wanted to do was right a wrong. She should never have been born. What kind of a life could a person like that have? I was really trying to save her from a lifetime of pain. Then one night I was sleeping and when I woke up, the flames, they were all around me. I could barely breathe and my arm was on fire. I knew it was her. From the moment it happened, I knew."

"Who is she? She's not your wife."

"No child, of course she's not my wife."

"Then who is she?"

As Jocelyn anxiously waited for him to respond, he quickly

stopped talking and even shut his eyes. She wanted to believe that it was the drugs working but she knew that wasn't it. She turned to find Nurse Williams standing behind her. This time she did nothing to conceal her anger. It was obvious she was seething.

"Get out!"

"Now wait a minute, I..."

"I said, get out!" Williams yelled.

Initially, Jocelyn was going to stand her ground and challenge Williams' anger. After all, how could Williams justify her reaction to anyone? To defend it would have to mean revealing what was really going on. However, something about the look on Williams' face frightened Jocelyn, and she knew challenging her was the last thing she should do. Instead, she stormed out of the room, past all her nosy coworkers, watching and waiting to hear the latest gossip.

Carolyn's face was the first Jocelyn saw. Her expression was full of reproach and Jocelyn was in no mood for *I-told-you-sos*, so she avoided her and instead chose to leave the floor entirely.

"I'm taking my break," she said, as she walked away.

Nurse Williams followed close behind.

# CHAPTER THIRTY-SEVEN

The last thing on Jocelyn's mind was food, so she decided to use her break to clear her head. She found an empty room and stretched out on the bed. She couldn't figure out which emotion was overwhelming her more: the anger she felt toward Nurse Williams, or the disappointment she felt toward herself. When she discussed what was going on at the hospital with her husband, much like Carolyn, he had cautioned her to mind her own business and reminded her how many bills they had to pay. Now, she would probably have to go home and tell him she was unemployed. The last thing she expected was to go to sleep, but she did. She slept for almost an hour, a full thirty minutes past her break. She jumped up and looked at her watch, realizing how late she was.

"Oh shit!"

She straightened her uniform and headed toward the door. When she swung it open, a dark figure was standing in the doorway, blocking her path. Her confusion only lasted a moment. It was well past visiting hours and the person standing in front of her didn't appear to be anyone she knew, not that she could tell. Whoever it was was wearing so many layers of clothing and their head was covered with a large hood. At first she could barely distinguish whether it was a man or a woman, then she knew exactly who it was.

"What are you doing here, and why are you dressed like that?" she asked.

"God has spoken," was the response.

"What? What did you say?"

"Come with me. There's something you need to see."

"What?"

"I have something to show you. You need to see this."

Jocelyn didn't like this one bit, but she wasn't sure what to do next.

"Just give me a second. I need to call my husband. I promised him I would call while I was on my break, but I fell asleep."

"You can call him after."

"After what?"

"Come with me now and I'll show you."

Jocelyn reluctantly followed. Her phone was in her uniform pocket, set on silent. So many times people on her phone contact list had mentioned her dialing them at all hours by accident. One time in particular her husband mentioned hearing her entire conversation with one of the nurses on the floor. She remembered being quite relieved that it wasn't one of those nights when she was complaining to Carolyn about him. She stuck her hands in her pocket, hoping to re-create the same cell phone *accidents* she often apologized for. Now more than ever, she needed that phone to call someone, anyone. She wasn't sure what was going to happen next, but somehow it wasn't going to be good.

Two floors above, Carolyn was complaining to another nurse about Jocelyn not returning from her break.

"You think Williams fired her?" the nurse asked.

"I wouldn't be surprised," Carolyn responded. "I told her to mind her own business but she refused to listen."

"Mind her own business about what?"

"Nothing."

Carolyn knew the nurse was trying to get the latest hot gossip and she had no desire to feed the frenzy.

After about three hours, Carolyn was convinced Jocelyn had indeed been fired. Although she had no intention of asking Nurse Williams, she was sure she would be able to tell whether or not she had fired Jocelyn by the look on her face. As the hours ticked by and neither of the women returned, Carolyn started to get worried. She wondered if somehow they had gotten past her and were in Mr. Richardson's room. She made her way to his room, convinced that was where she would find both Jocelyn and Nurse Williams. Not only were they not there, neither was Mr. Richardson. The situation had progressed well beyond an employee that may or may not have returned from her break. Now there was a patient missing, a patient that was presumed incapable of walking. She would have to alert someone. Before she did that, she decided she would enlist the other nurses and search the floors. They searched for an hour before conceding that Edwards, Williams and the patient, Richardson, were nowhere to be found.

"We need to alert security now. Otherwise it's gonna be our asses if anything fucked up happened here tonight," said Carolyn.

"This is some bullshit," said another nurse. "I work nights for a reason. I've gotta get my kid ready for school. I can't work any overtime. As soon as we call security, everybody still here is stuck."

"I know damn well you're not talking about overtime and your kid going to school when we've got an infirm patient missing, on *our* watch."

# CHAPTER THIRTY-EIGHT

"Hello, Dr. Phipps."

"Hello, *Kimberly?*"

"Yes, we spoke to one another on the phone. I mentioned wanting to meet with you. Is there something wrong?" Candace asked.

Candace realized she was staring and obviously Kimberly was aware of it as well. Kimberly's presence in her office told her everything she needed to know and it granted her the opportunity she was hoping for. Suddenly, so many things were brutally clear.

"Yes, you did mention wanting to discuss something,; you just didn't mention what. I guess I'm just wondering if you're here about the murders."

"I am *sort of* here about that, but indirectly. I've been having some *difficulties* and I thought you might be able to help."

"By all means. I'd be happy to help in any way I can, Kimberly."

"It's the case. It's a lot of things. I just haven't been myself lately."

Candace sat silently, careful to listen without interrupting.

"I've always been so together. I worked full-time at a hospital while I went to school. I eventually went to the Police Academy and I made detective younger than most. But there's something about this case that's unraveling me."

"I assume by *this case* you mean the burn murders."

"Yes. Of course."

"Has this case been any more difficult to solve than any others?"

"No, not really. Don't get me wrong, it's been plenty difficult, but I've had cases that were much more difficult than this one. Hell, every year there are cases that go unsolved."

"So, is there something about this case that is impacting you in some personal way?"

"No, of course not."

Candace didn't miss the agitation when she mentioned the possibility of a personal connection. She hoped that Kimberly would make the connection on her own.

"I've been sleeping with my partner, which is so out of character for me. I don't know what came first. I find myself asking whether the sex came as a knee-jerk reaction to the stress, or whether I'm stressed because of the sex. I've never crossed that line before. Until now I've always believed that work and personal life should be kept separate, especially when it comes to cops. I've been screwing up at work. It's not like me. I'm usually so on point, so pulled together."

"It's perfectly reasonable to expect that a case such as this might increase anyone's level of stress, and with stress comes our natural responses to stress. Everything you've mentioned is perfectly normal. Unusual sexual alliances, mishaps at work, insecurities. All of those responses make perfect sense."

"I wouldn't exactly call what happened between Brandon and me *unusual*."

"I'm sorry, I misspoke. I meant *unusual* in the sense that it was different than what you might usually do."

"Oh."

For a moment it seemed to Candace as though Kimberly was relaxing a bit, then her face suddenly dissolved from a smile to a frown.

"Was there something else you wanted to say?" Candace asked.

"No. Is there a bathroom I could use?"

"Yes, it's right outside the door on the right."

Candace waited for Kimberly for several minutes until she heard a loud noise coming from the hall. She left her office and when she didn't see Kimberly or anyone else, she stood outside the bathroom door, preparing to knock. She thought she heard loud voices arguing and pressed her ear to the door to hear better.

"Are you stupid or something? What do you want to do, ruin it for all of us? Why on earth would you come to see her?" said one voice.

"I'm sick of protecting you. I'm tired of all the secrets and lies. If it wasn't for you, I wouldn't have had to come here. Why don't you just leave me alone. Go away!"

"Maybe you should be the one to go away. If it wasn't for me, you wouldn't have that nice shiny badge. Have you forgotten the sacrifices I made for you? I took all of it, all of the pain, all of the hurt, while you curled up in a ball somewhere acting like none of it ever happened. Now you want to play the all-powerful super-hero cop. It's too fucking late for that! You're so fucking weak. If it's not me, it's Kadeem. If it's not Kadeem, it's that partner of yours. Do you ever take care of yourself? Now you're here at Dr. Phipps' office. Why? Why on earth would you choose to come here of all places?"

Candace was sure she recognized both voices. One was, of course, Detective Kimberly Watson. The other voice was most definitely Shelly. As much as Candace would have liked to continue listening to the exchange between the two, she didn't want to be discovered, so instead she rushed back to her office and sat down as if she had never left. Shortly thereafter, Kimberly returned. She seemed no worse and sat down as if nothing had happened.

"I'm sorry for keeping you," Kimberly said.

"No problem at all."

"How does this work? I guess if I'm a client, I must have used up most of my hour."

"Don't worry about the time. I don't have another client after you."

"You sure?"

"Absolutely."

"I hate to mention this, but I hope it goes without saying that this is confidential. I wouldn't want the department or my partner to know that I've visited you."

"Of course. I am bound to complete confidentiality, unless someone's life is in danger."

"Of course."

"Would you like to continue the session?"

"Yes."

"Do you have any leads on the burn case?"

"Huh?"

"The case, do you have any leads?"

"What does that have to do with anything?"

"Your stress and a lot of the changes you've been going through seem to be a direct link with the case you're working on."

"I don't think so. Okay, I admit some of it might be the case, but it's so much more than that. I don't think it's as simple as that."

"So what do you think it is?"

"I don't know. I guess that's why I came to you."

"I'm glad you did. I am curious, though. Out of all the psychiatrists you could have gone to, why did you choose me?"

"Somehow, I felt like I should be here. It almost felt like I had already been here before."

Candace could sense Kimberly's earlier agitation when she'd asked her about the case, but when she mentioned being glad that she had come to see her, she softened a bit.

"I'm glad, too. It feels like this is the first normal thing I've done in a really long time."

"Do you sometimes feel like you're not normal?"

"All the time. I've never felt like I was like everybody else. I've always been different."

"That must be difficult."

"You have no idea."

"I think I do, but what I think or anyone else thinks doesn't matter. It's what *you* think about *you* that's important."

"Sometimes I feel like I just want to rest. It all gets so overwhelming I just want to lay down and sleep and let it all pass me by."

"It sounds like you may also be a bit depressed."

"No, not really. I don't think I am anyway. I'm tired."

"Fatigue is one of many signs of depression. You know you can lie down if you'd like."

Candace was surprised to find that Kimberly took her up on her offer and stretched out on the couch. She was even more surprised when she drifted off to sleep. However, what followed wasn't surprising at all. In fact, it made perfect sense to Candace. Kimberly began to speak, yet, not surprisingly, the voice Candace heard bore no resemblance to Kimberly's.

Candace withdrew the handheld voice recorder she often kept in her desk drawer and pressed the "record" button. She was careful to do all of this very quietly. She didn't want to break the hypnotic state Kimberly appeared to be in. She was also well aware that she might need the recording at a later time.

Amidst her tortured wails and alternating states of anger and confusion, there was something else. Once again, words were repeated to Candace which she had heard before. Kimberly's voice reverted to something other than her own. It was a raspy, almost manly voice, spoken through exaggerated breaths. It was the voice

260 Michelle Janine Robinson

she barely recognized as the one she had heard on the phone, but the words were unmistakable.

"*God has spoken.*"

Just as quickly as Kimberly entered her trance-like state, she left it. She sat up and began speaking incessantly. This time, the voice was different, yet still not Kimberly.

"So Doc, what do you think? What are we going to do about our girl here? She is clearly unraveling like a roll of yarn."

During the time that Candace had treated Kimberly, Shelly, Kay, Cat, Kadeem...and Daniel, the only two that had ever acknowledged each other, were Kimberly and Kadeem. Candace believed that made perfect sense since they were brother and sister. However, this was the first time one of the personalities other than Kadeem or Kimberly had acknowledged each other. For the first time, Candace was confident that she was having a breakthrough. Shelly's acknowledgment of Kimberly in therapy, was the first step toward the discovery that they were all one and the same. Once Kimberly, Shelly, Kay, Cat, Kadeem, Daniel and any other personalities that were wrapped in the one package, were revealed, the *real* person could step forward. Candace was convinced that person would be Kimberly. She was also convinced that Kimberly was not the killer and that it was one of her other personalities. She was sure it was Shelly, but she couldn't be one hundred percent sure.

"Hellllllooo," Shelly said, dragging her words exaggeratedly. "Did you hear me, Doc? What are we going to do, because quite frankly, I think she's off her rocker. Not only that, her state of mind is fucking with the others as well. If we don't fix her and quick, we're *all* going to end up behind bars, and I'm not having it."

Candace knew her words had to be carefully chosen. They were moving forward, but she was well aware that even one word or tone of voice could set them back.

"Why would you end up behind bars? For what?"

"Doc, stop fucking with me, okay? I'm not Kimberly or even Cat or Kay, for that matter. You and I both know the deal; the others, not so much."

Candace was sure she had ruined things by underestimating Shelly, but she was surprised to find that Shelly continued to speak.

"Mosaic needs to be trapped and despite the fact that I am probably the only one here who's stronger than Mosaic, it can't be me. Kimberly has to do it. She has to kill him, once and for all. I thought she had, a long time ago. It was after her father, the pig, was burned. I knew it couldn't have been Kimberly. It's not her style. The old man had been taunting her one night. She was only twelve or thirteen years old. She was a fragile little thing and then out of nowhere, Mosaic showed up. He used the same stuff, that ether, to accelerate the fire. It was the same stuff that old bastard would use to knock Kimberly out. Her father would use just enough of the ether to knock her out and then do some really sick shit to her. I don't think he even gave her the ether to keep her from feeling the pain of it. I think he was afraid of either his wife or the neighbors hearing what he was doing to her down in that basement.

"She was born with both you know, a dick and a pussy, and he actually thought he was doing *God's work* by cutting it off. By the time that poor excuse for a mother found her, she was bleeding to death. It was surprising to find that her mother was actually good for something. She nursed Kimberly back to health, but without a real doctor and a hospital, she could do nothing to restore Kimberly, cosmetically. She was so worried about her husband being locked up, she never took Kimberly to the hospital. Her father mutilated her so badly she was disfigured for life. What could have been a viable penis was destroyed, neither completely present nor completely gone. Somehow, though, she never could shake the feeling that it was still there, intact. It's the craziest thing. It's like those stories you read about war veterans who lose an arm or a leg and can still feel it itching. It was right about that time that Kadeem was born. The mind is a bitch, ain't it?"

"It most certainly is," Candace agreed. "How did you feel about Kimberly's father?"

"I don't think I felt any way about him. I was the one he fucked, but I could handle it, so I took over for Kimberly when it was time. What pissed me off about it though, wasn't the sex. It annoyed the hell out of me that he thought he was the one in control. He wasn't. He would say these things to me that he thought was demeaning and he thought he was hurting me when we were having sex, but I'm the one that controlled everything. I decided when it was over. I decided how much enjoyment he did or did not get out of it. Unfortunately, those times when I decided I didn't want him to enjoy it, Kimberly was the one that paid the price. He would punish her something awful, but at least she never had to have sex with him. That would have been much worse for her. He would yell and scream at her about how he should have been given a boy, like it was her fault. There were times when I would laugh out loud, because it was kind of ironic. He went on and on about how entitled he felt to have a son, yet, he had cut off the one thing that might have made that possibility a reality. He was a crazy, evil old bastard.

"Then, one day, suddenly Mosaic arrives," Shelly continued. "Once the fire started and I saw his arm burning, I thought for sure we could all wave good-bye to the dirty old bastard. Then, all of a sudden, here comes Kimberly. She puts out the fire and destroys Mosaic. It was the craziest shit I ever saw. For the life of me, I couldn't understand why she would save that old man's life and destroy the one person who could truly have saved her. Even

after that, he continued to torture her. She would go days sometimes without eating. He had made these *tools*, or at least that's
what he called them, and he would hurt her with them. The thing
that amazed me more than anything though was her mother.
The mother acted like she was deaf, dumb and blind. Then, all
of a sudden one day, she's like Superwoman to the rescue. When
she fired that gun, I wanted to pop me some popcorn and wait
for that bastard to bleed out. Then, once again, here comes fucking
Pollyanna, Kimberly. She called the police. She actually saved
the motherfucker's life. The mother went to prison for shooting
him, Kimberly went away to school, and I, I got to watch over
the sick fuck. At first I was a volunteer at the hospital, then years
later, I returned. Now, I get to decide when. I get to decide how,
all the time. It's so much fun."

"He's still alive?" Candace asked.

"Of course. What did you think, I killed him? Death would be
way too good for him. He needs to suffer and he has in various
ways throughout the years. If it were up to me and I had the
access, I would do the same to that sorry-ass mother of hers. She
was just as bad. Maybe I will have my chance. She's getting out
of prison soon."

Everything was suddenly starting to take shape for Candace.
Despite her earlier beliefs that Shelly was probably the killer, she
was now sure she was not. But who? Who was this Mosaic
personality? Was it one of the others or a separate personality
unto itself? Shelly seemed convinced that the killer had also been
the personality that had set the fire all those many years ago.
However, given what she recently learned, Candace was just as
convinced it was not. There had never been a murder until now.
Not only that, everything both she and the police knew about
Mosaic seemed to indicate that the intent was to destroy anyone

that was anything at all like herself, or Kimberly. Mosaic's beliefs were identical to Kimberly's father. Therefore, it would have been unlikely for Mosaic to have tried to kill Kimberly's father all those many years ago. If anything, he would have championed her father. Candace was convinced that either one of the other personalities she had met was the killer or Mosaic was newly contrived. What she couldn't understand was why? All of the other personalities made sense. Shelly was Kimberly's champion. She was the strong one. Cat was the beautiful, alluring one. Kay was sexually free and Kadeem was the brother her father always wanted. Not only that, he was the male side of her she had lost, when she was butchered by her father. Daniel was the person-ification of innocence. He could have been easily molded into any one of the personalities. But why was Mosaic created? It suddenly dawned on her. Mosaic personified Kimberly's father. He represented all of her father's ravings about good and evil. The only way to truly destroy Mosaic would be to destroy her father. The only aspect of that idea that didn't make sense was why her father had yet to be destroyed. According to Shelly, they all had access. If Candace could reveal the answer to that question, she could end the murders and Mosaic would most likely disappear forever.

# CHAPTER THIRTY-NINE

C andace was still riding the fence as to whether or not she would eventually have to involve the police. In the meantime, she decided she would pay a visit to Samuel Richardson at Montelior. As the truth began to slowly unfold, she had done her best to avoid Detective Simms, even going as far as leaving her colleague's home, so that the police couldn't find her. She was intent on drawing Kimberly's mental break to a conclusion and she wouldn't be able to do that under the watchful eye of the police. Unfortunately, the first face she saw upon arriving at Montelior was Detective Simms.

"What brings you here?" he asked.

"Patient follow-up, that's all."

"Oh really, and who is your patient?"

"Detective Simms, are we back to that again? Is this even the same case?"

"Dr. Phipps, you may think you have me fooled, but I don't fool that easily. This case is connected somehow and something tells me you know exactly how it's connected. All I can say to you is be very careful about how you proceed. This whole thing might blow up in your face."

"Detective, much like you, I, too, am not easily fooled. I take great pride in what it is I do and I never want anything more than to assist my patients in living their healthiest life. I take that mission very seriously, just as seriously as I'm sure you take police work."

Candace glanced over at Detective Kimberly Watson, silently wondering if it was indeed Kimberly at all. She also wondered if she would be able to tell the difference between Kimberly and her other personalities without being in a session with them.

As Detective Simms walked away to join his partner, Candace followed.

"Dr. Phipps, this is a police investigation, so I would appreciate it if you would move to wherever it is you say you were going, unless of course, you have something to add to the investigation?"

"No, nothing at all, Detective."

"Okay then, good-bye."

Candace didn't need to be any closer to Kimberly than she was now. She could tell that she was unraveling as quickly and obviously as Shelly had warned. The disheveled clothing, the confused expression, the labored gait, were all indications that Kimberly was heading straight for a psychotic break that no one would soon forget.

Candace realized that it was probably best for her purposes to do exactly as Detective Simms had said. She wasn't sure what they were investigating, but if he didn't yet know about Kimberly's father, she wasn't going to be the one to tip him off.

"I'm here to see Samuel Richardson," Candace said.

"Really?" one of the nurses on duty queried sarcastically. "Well, you ain't the only one who wants to see Samuel Richardson, or did you not notice all the cops in this place? Mr. Richardson is missing. An elderly patient, who can barely walk, has suddenly gone missing."

At first, Candace was as confused as everyone else. She had come here anxious to speak with Mr. Richardson. She'd hoped to figure out a way for Kimberly to symbolically *destroy* him, so that she and the other personalities, including the killer, could move on. Obviously, someone else had figured it all out and gotten there a lot quicker than she had.

That meant only one thing. Mosaic had most probably gone to protect Mr. Richardson and the next move would now be to kill her and eventually Kimberly as well.

Candace was sure Mr. Richardson was still somewhere in the hospital. She made her way to his room and poked around in his things, wondering if any of it might lend a clue of his location. She was well aware that the police were all over the hospital and hoped they had completed their run-through of Mr. Richardson's actual room. That's when she felt it. A small trickle of liquid landed on her face. She was sure it was urine. She looked up and right above her was a vent. Mosaic had obviously shoved him into the vent in order to protect him. It was then that Candace realized she could not do this alone. She would have to enlist Detective Simms' aid.

She wasn't sure how Mosaic had accomplished getting Mr. Richardson inside of the vent, but Candace was sure that she lacked the strength and capability to get him out. She turned to leave, only to find Kimberly blocking her path.

"*Kimberly?*"

"What are you, blind? Of course I'm not Kimberly."

"*Shelly?*"

"No, it's me, Daniel. Mosaic sent me to help. We are God's chosen. We must respect the weak and righteous. Mr. Richardson must be protected at all costs."

That's when Daniel approached Candace aggressively. She considered screaming, but wasn't sure what the outcome might be. She reminded herself that while Daniel was still just another of

Kimberly's many personalities, he was also a personality that was a child and therefore might be subject to the same reactions a real child would have.

"Daniel, you don't want to hurt me, do you?"

"You won't be hurt. You will join the others in the Kingdom of Heaven."

"But before I join the others, I will hurt. Mosaic is going to smother, poison and burn me, just like he did the others. I am a doctor and I assure you, Daniel, that *will* hurt.

# CHAPTER FORTY

**W**hile Shelly tried to avoid making contact with the nurses, for fear of being recognized as the night nurse, Ms. Williams, Brandon Simms questioned anyone and everyone.

"It's funny," one of the nurses said. "I'm not accusing anyone or anything, but..."

"The smallest bit of information could be more helpful than you realize."

"Okay," she conceded. "The night that Mr. Richardson and Nurse Edwards disappeared, the head nurse kind of also disappeared. She's not missing like Edwards, because she called in, but the night those two disappeared, was the last night anyone saw Nurse Williams."

"Can you describe her?"

"Of course. I actually thought I saw her when you guys arrived, but someone told me it was a police officer, not Nurse Williams."

"So, she looked like Detective Watson?"

"I guess. Is that the officer that's here?"

"If I set you up with a sketch artist, do you think you could describe Nurse Williams well enough to produce a drawing of her?"

"Heck yeah. I know her face almost as well as I know my own. Much like everyone else here, I don't like Nurse Williams very much. She's a bit of a ball-buster and we would try to warn each other when she was on her way. I know her face *quite* well."

"I need a sketch artist down here, pronto," he yelled to no one in particular.

Brandon knew the officers were all so intent on making an impression, they would jump at the chance to aid a detective in whatever capacity.

"No problem, boss," was the response from one of the uniformed officers.

"Please don't call me 'boss,'" Brandon said.

"No problem, won't happen again."

Brandon almost chuckled out loud. He was sure the officer was about to add the word *boss* at the end of the sentence. He wondered if he was such a goof when he was wearing a uniform. It had been so long he could barely remember.

He turned and looked for Kimberly. However, for the first time, he wasn't surprised about her disappearance. He was sure that once the sketch artist arrived and the drawing was complete, the answers to all the questions he'd had for so long would be answered. Unfortunately, he wasn't sure whether or not he would be prepared to hear the truth. He remembered something a doctor had once said to a victim's family, as they waited to learn their loved one's fate. The doctor had told the family to *hope for the best, but prepare for the worst*. At the time, Brandon couldn't believe that someone, especially a doctor, would say something so fucking stupid. Somehow, though, he now understood the meaning of what that doctor had said. And he was going to do just that: hope for the best, but prepare for the worst.

The sketch artist arrived quickly and despite that Brandon seldom stood around while a witness was helping to create a sketch, he did this time. Before the face was even finished, his question had been answered.

"Hey, you know, Simms, this looks an awful..."

Before the artist could finish the sentence, he stopped him.

"I know. I know. But let's keep that to ourselves for now, okay?"

"No problem here. I just draw the sketches. I leave the police work to you guys. My lips are sealed."

"Thanks, I appreciate that."

"I will say this, though, I hope we're both wrong. I've always liked Watson. She's a sweet girl. I remember when she rescued that Mexican girl from those sickos. She was relentless and it didn't stop after she caught her man. She did everything she could to save that girl. She has a good heart."

"You're right. She does," Brandon agreed.

From the moment the sketch started to take form as Kimberly's face, Brandon was torn between putting out an all-points bulletin or not telling a soul and attempting to locate her himself. It was the sketch artist's comment that helped him make up his mind. He was right. Kimberly was a good person. He realized badge or no badge, he had to be the one that found Kimberly. He had to figure out what had gone wrong. He wasn't sure what it was he had figured out, but one thing was for sure, Kimberly knew who the killer was. That's when he remembered the file on her mother that she had hidden from him. He also remembered her elusive brother, Kadeem. He was sure that one of them was indeed the killer. Since her mother had been locked away and was not yet set for release, that meant it had to be Kadeem. Since Kimberly's mother was the easiest to locate, he decided he would speak to her first and find out all he could about Kadeem and the relationship between him and his sister.

By the time Brandon arrived at the prison, he was surprised to find that Marie Richardson had indeed been released.

"Did she say anything when she left?" Brandon asked one of the correctional officers.

"No, but then that wasn't rare for Marie. I don't think I heard her speak more than a couple of times in all the years that she was here."

One of the other officers joined them.

"She did do something that was a bit odd, though. Marie was one of the quieter, less violent prisoners. The only time she would blow her top was when someone touched that Bible of hers. She carried it everywhere. No one ever really got a chance to look at it up close, but there were always pieces of paper hanging out of it. And one day, when one of the prisoners snatched it out of her hand, a picture fell out of it. A lot of the prisoners have valued possessions in here. She wasn't any different than most. The only difference was, most of the prisoners take those possessions with them when they leave. It's the damnedest thing; with all the fuss Marie made about that Bible and the contents, she walked out of here without it. None of us could understand it."

"Is it still here?"

"Yeah, as a matter of fact it is. I held on to it. Marie was an odd one, but she was one of the few that seemed like she regretted her decisions. She actually seemed to be a good person, for the most part. I was hoping she'd be able to find it easily if she ever came back for it."

"I'd like to take a look at it," Brandon said.

"Certainly. Detective, can I ask you a question?" the officer said before she walked away,

"Of course, what is it?"

"Marie's not in any trouble, is she? She just got out. I hope she didn't get into trouble already."

"I don't think she has, but if there's any possibility that she might, I want to stop her before she does."

"Enough said; I'll get the Bible."

After looking through the Bible, it didn't take Brandon long to put all the pieces together. Suddenly, everything made perfect sense. The odd behavior when they had sex, the secrecy, the obsession with her mother's file. He couldn't believe he had been so blind.

The officer glanced over Brandon's shoulder as he looked at the pictures.

"I was so surprised when I saw those," the officer said. "Who knew Marie had twins? Let alone any children."

"She didn't have twins," he responded.

"Really?"

"These aren't twins. It's the same child."

Brandon looked once again at the photos of *a* child he was sure was his partner, Kimberly Watson, when she was a small child. In some of the pictures, she was dressed up to look like a boy; in others, like a girl, and in still others, she wore nothing at all. However, he could see how the correctional officer might think the pictures were of twins. In some of the pictures, the child was clearly a boy, while in others, it was obviously a girl. Brandon wondered what kind of hell Kimberly had been subjected to and by who.

He finally realized there was a connection between the missing old man and nurse at Montelior, and the burn murders. Samuel Richardson was Kimberly's father, who had been shot by her mother several years earlier. He also realized that her brother, Kadeem, was probably little more than a figment of her imagination; or to use the clinical term already provided to him by none other than Candace Phipps, Kadeem was one of Kimberly's multiple "personalities."

"Fuck!" he said out loud and to no one in particular.

"Everything okay, Detective?" the officer asked.

"Not really. A psychiatrist who doesn't know how to mind her own fucking business is about to be killed."

"Anything we can do here?"

"Not really, unless you can tell me where Marie Richardson went?"

"I think maybe that can be done," the officer said, smiling.

Brandon kissed her on the cheek.

The officer was gushing.

"She arranged a cab when she was released. We can probably find out where the driver dropped her off."

"You may have just saved a life."

"All in a day's work, I always say."

"I know that's right."

# CHAPTER FORTY-ONE

Within minutes, Brandon was knocking at the door of a room being rented by Marie Richardson.

"She ain't home."

"And you are?" Brandon asked, flashing his badge.

"Aw shit, she just got out of prison; is she in trouble already? All I get is convicts, and they all seem to end up right back in trouble again. I'm getting out of the business. The revolving-door aspect of renting to repeat offenders is very stressful."

Brandon looked him over and immediately decided he didn't like him and that with all his talk, he, too, was probably an ex-con.

"My heart bleeds for you and I never said she was in trouble. I just need to know where she is."

"I can't help you there. All I do is rent rooms. I'm no den mother."

"Clearly," Brandon said.

He looked around the dilapidated structure, and once again, was reminded of why he took an immediate disliking to the man in front of him. Brandon did nothing to conceal his feelings and the man noticed it immediately.

"Well, if there's nothing else, I have plenty of work to do."

"There is something else. I need to get into her room."

"My tenants have an expectation of privacy. You got a warrant?"

Brandon suddenly grabbed the man, wrapping his shirt around his fist and slamming him against the nearest wall.

"Don't you fuck with me, you scum bag! You *really* don't want to make an enemy of me. Otherwise, I might be forced to make this place my pet project. When I'm done with you, you'll no longer be an ex-con. You'll be back in prison reaching for your ankles and this place will be condemned. So, are you gonna open up the fucking door or what?"

"Calm down, calm down! I didn't say I wasn't going to open it. Just give me a chance to get the key. I'll be right back."

"I'll go with you, in case you get any bright ideas about running away."

"I'm not going anywhere."

"Good, because I'm right behind you."

After the landlord retrieved the key, Brandon went inside.

"Feel free to disappear," he said to the landlord.

He watched as he scurried away, like the rat he was.

Brandon looked around the room and the first thought that sprang to mind was no wonder ex-cons became repeat offenders. Living conditions like these would make anyone want to go out and commit a crime. Within minutes, however, he had hit pay-dirt. Sitting on the fifty-nine-dollar dresser compiled of what was probably mostly cardboard, was a pamphlet from Liberty Travel. Brandon immediately dialed the number for the location closest to where Marie was staying.

"So, she plans to hightail it to Los Angeles," Brandon said out loud. "That would most certainly violate her parole requirements. There must be a serious reason why she would decide to do that just a few days after being released. Mrs. Richardson, how much do you know?"

Brandon was pissed to find that the smarmy landlord had returned and caught him talking to himself.

"Didn't I tell you, you weren't needed here."

"I was just trying to warn you, you know, before she ran. The woman I rented the room to, she's on her way up."

"Make yourself scarce," Brandon said, before adding, "Thanks."

"No problem, man."

"Now go, really. I don't want her to know I'm here."

The landlord pulled the door shut, locking it and quickly left.

When Marie Richardson turned her key in the lock and entered, Brandon was waiting for her.

Brandon was surprised to find that she didn't try to run, and she didn't seem at all afraid.

"You must be Mr. Brandon Simms. Oh, I'm sorry, I'm sure you prefer Detective Brandon Simms."

"How do you know my name, Mrs. Richardson?"

"I've been following your career for years. You work with my daughter, don't you?"

"Yes, as a matter of fact I do. Do you happen to know where Kimberly is right now? I need to find her."

"I don't know where she is, and even if I did, I doubt she would want to see me."

"Why is that, Mrs. Richardson? Does it have anything to do with her father?"

"Well, Brandon. Can I call you Brandon?"

"Feel free."

"Well, Brandon, I think maybe Kimberly blames me for her childhood."

"What kind of childhood did she have exactly?"

"Excuse me if I sound a bit skeptical about your intentions, but it seems to me you may know the answers to these questions already."

"Not really, Mrs. Richardson. I learned more about Kimberly today than I've known about her in all the years we've been partners. Do you know what it feels like to think you know *all* there is to know about a person, and then to suddenly find out it's all been a lie?"

"I'm an expert on that topic. I ran away from home to be with a kind, handsome, giving man only to learn that I'd married a monster. Now, let me ask you a question. Have you *been with* my daughter?"

"By *been with*, am I to assume you mean have we had sex?"

"That's exactly what I mean."

"Yes, we have."

"Did you notice anything different about her?"

"No, I didn't notice a thing, but in all fairness, I didn't get a chance to see much. Kimberly made sure of that."

"Kimberly wasn't born like most girls. In fact, I don't know if you could call her a girl at all. She was born one of a small number of what is called Mosaic hermaphrodites. Kimberly has both male and female internal reproductive organs, and once upon a time, she possessed both male and female external sex organs as well. Can you imagine the effect of such a child on a man raised and groomed for years to be a preacher, then suddenly ostracized by his father? Sam, quite literally, lost his mind. He took all of that pain, anger and emotion out on Kimberly. He did terrible, awful things to her and I'm ashamed to admit, I didn't do very much to stop him. I really was very weak. I understand why she hates me so."

"What makes you think she hates you?"

"In all the years that I was locked away in prison for shooting her father, she never visited me, never answered even one of my letters. I was sure that shooting Samuel, to protect her, might make up, at least a little, for not standing up and defending her sooner. It meant nothing to her. I think she hates me as much as she does him."

"Why did you keep those pictures of her, the ones you kept in your Bible?"

"When Kimberly was young and growing up, she had an imaginary friend she called Kadeem. He wasn't really an imaginary friend; he was more like an imaginary brother to her. She liked the pictures. She would say one was her and the other was Kadeem. It was all she had, after Samuel did what he did to her."

Brandon was afraid to ask.

"What did he do?"

"I always tried to stay at home, or return home as quickly as possible when I had to go out, because I knew things could only get worse without me there. One day, I got into a car accident and by the time I returned, there was blood everywhere. I asked Sam what happened and he told me that Kimberly had hurt herself, and I believed him. As sick as Sam obviously was, he never lied about the things he did to her. He believed in what he was doing. He believed it would bring us all closer to the Lord."

Brandon sat listening to Kimberly's mother, wondering who was crazier, the mother or the father, and how Kimberly had fared as well and for as long as she had. The poor thing had been cursed with two complete psychos.

"Well, anyway, as I told you earlier, she had *both*...But when I checked Kimberly to make sure she was okay, it was gone. Her penis was gone and she was so pale. I couldn't take her to the hospital, so I did the best I could to treat her myself at home. Surprisingly, she survived. Sam convinced me she had done it herself and for the longest time, I believed him. She was a little girl and I thought maybe she was confused when she did it. She was so young. It wasn't until Kimberly was going away to college that I realized it had been Samuel all along. I found him in her room with this strange tool he had created. It was some sort of metal contraption. It looked like a rake, with an odd sort of a hook at the end. That's when I knew it had been him all along. Can't you see, that's when I knew I had to save Kimberly. I had only bought the gun to threaten Sam, if need be, but when I saw him standing over her with that, that thing, I knew I had to defend her at all costs, so I shot him."

"One more question," Brandon said. "What are the tickets to Los Angeles for, or better yet, who are they for?"

"My family, of course."

"Your family, meaning?"

"Kimberly, Samuel and me."

"What makes you think Kimberly, or even Samuel, will be willing or even able to go with you to Los Angeles?"

Brandon watched as she simply stared off into the distance, with a blank expression on her face.

"Do you know where Kimberly is?" he asked.

"No, I don't, not for sure. But if I were going to guess, I would say she's not far away from her father."

She had been with her father earlier that day and the hospital was where she had been spending some of her *lost* time, when Brandon didn't know where she was, but he didn't know where she was now.

There was one thing he was sure of; the last people Kimberly Watson wanted to see were her parents, the very same people whose name she had abandoned as her own and changed in order to distance herself from them as much as possible.

# CHAPTER FORTY-TWO

Brandon was sure, if anyone could figure out where Kimberly was, he could. After all, they had worked closely together for years and had shared a level of intimacy few partners ever shared. Yet, he couldn't deny the truth. Despite his belief for many years that he knew all there was to know about her, she had been hiding secrets so great, it would take him quite some time to understand he really didn't know Kimberly Watson at all. He did know one thing, though, he *had* gotten through. Their connection, while brief, had existed. That is why he knew he was the only one that could save her. Then suddenly, as if a light had been turned on in a dark room, Brandon knew where she was.

The very first time he and Kimberly had shared a kiss had been after a bust at a garage downtown. Girls were being trafficked in from Mexico to serve as sex slaves. He and Kimberly had worked on the case for months and eventually were ready to bring the group down that was trafficking the girls. That was one of the few cases in which he had witnessed Kimberly off her game. She was distracted and emotional, and Brandon had assumed that because some of the stories were so horrible, it hit closer to home for her because she was a woman. One girl, in particular, seemed to get to Kimberly. She had been sold to some sicko who had raped and tortured her for days. By the time the police found her, she was so badly mutilated, she would never be able to have children. It was the one and only time Brandon had ever seen Kimberly become so attached to anyone, least of all a victim. She had done everything in her power to find the person who had hurt the girl and when she did, she beat him so badly Brandon was worried she might kill him. When it came time for Kimberly to answer to charges of brutality, he had backed his partner and told the bigwigs she'd acted appropriately under the circumstances and had followed all protocol. Police work was one of the few things Brandon not only took seriously, but also did with great integrity. The incident with Kimberly had been the first time he had ever lied in the face of allegations of police brutality. After the issue with the pervert had been put to rest, and Kimberly had done everything she could for the young girl, she made it her mission to stop the ring that was trafficking the girls. And that's exactly what they did—together.

The night of the sting, after everyone had been arrested, they were sitting in the garage where everyone had been busted and it simply happened. Kimberly was raw with emotion and still feeling grateful that Brandon had backed her the way that he had. The two of them sat in the car and she mentioned how important it was to her to save girls like Lupe. It was only now that Brandon realized why it was so important to Kimberly and he wished instead of kissing her that night, he had encouraged her to talk more. He wondered if he had, would she have been able to open up to him and maybe things would have been different. The kiss they shared was brief, yet passionate, but he always remembered her words afterward: "I've never felt safe before, but today, here with you, I feel safer than I've ever felt and I don't want to lose that." The man in him wanted nothing more than to not only continue the kiss, but also to take their union away from the garage and back to his place. But the partner in him understood what she was trying to say and left it alone.

Brandon knew Kimberly would go back to where she felt safe and he was guessing that dank, smelly garage was probably where she felt the most safe. He just hoped he would get there before it was too late.

# CHAPTER FORTY-THREE

By the time Brandon arrived, Kimberly was not alone. She had a firm grip on Candace Phipps, and Kimberly's thoughts were so splintered, she could barely gather her thoughts enough to figure out what she should do next. She searched for Kadeem amongst the sea of voices and faces.

Candace recognized the look on Brandon's face. He had obviously figured everything out. However, his confused look seemed to be surrounding Kimberly's rapid descent into madness. Candace, too, believed, that there would be more time. However, the addition of Kimberly's parents to the mix had changed the dynamics of the situation.

"Her parents are here!" Candace yelled to Brandon, by way of answer to his questioning gaze.

"Shit! I told her to stay away!"

"Well, she didn't listen," Candace said. "They're outside. Their presence accelerated a breakdown that would have otherwise proceeded much more slowly. If it were not for that, I might have been able to help her."

"Shut up! Shut up! Everybody, stop talking," Kimberly demanded.

"Okay, baby, we'll be quiet," Brandon said.

"Kadeem!" she shouted. "Where are you? I can't see you anymore."

"I'm here, Sis. I'm right here."

The prattle of incessant voices was driving her closer to the edge.

"You're so fucking weak!" Shelly said. "I tried to help you, tried to teach you how to survive and what did you do? You succumbed to the likes of a man. What kind of a dumb whore are you? How the fuck did you end up with a badge? You're spineless. You're nothing. You're less than nothing, with your constant whining and complaining. *Kadeem, help me. Kadeem, where are you? Kadeem, what should I do?* Pathetic!"

"Shut up!"

"Make me! Prove that you've got a backbone," Shelly taunted.

Kimberly held on to her ears, trying to block out Shelly's voice, trying to block out all the voices.

"Don't listen to her, Sis. She just wants you to be like him. Why don't you shut up, Shelly! You're the one that's nothing!"

"Kadeem, there you are. Where were you? I'm scared. I'm so scared. Tell me what to do. I don't know what to do."

"We're going to get out of here, okay?" Kadeem said.

"Okay."

"You don't need all of them," he said. "You only need me."

"I know, Kadeem. I know, but they won't leave me alone."

"Stop talking! Would you all please just stop talking! I can't think."

Brandon suddenly noticed the handkerchief Kimberly was holding, and sniffing the air, he realized it was probably doused in enough ether to bring the entire place down and them with it.

"Brandon, baby, I can make you feel so good. Come with me," Kay said.

"Kimberly, please, let her go. There's enough ether on that handkerchief to kill her instantly. Once you've done it, you won't be able to take it back. That's not what you want. I know it's not.

Candace is your friend. She's been trying to help you," Brandon pleaded.

"Why do you keep calling me that? My name is not Kimberly! I'm Mosaic."

"Don't listen to her. I'm Cat, my name is Cat."

"Shut up. I said shut up, all of you!" Kimberly screamed.

With one hand, she held on to Candace while she intermittently massaged her temples with her left hand, the same one that was holding the handkerchief soaked in ether. Judging by the overwhelming scent filling the room, Brandon was sure there were two lives in danger. She kept touching the handkerchief to her own head, forgetting the damage that a small bit of the diethyl ether could cause.

"I don't think you want to hurt Candace," Brandon said. "She wants to help you. The two of us are going to get you the help you need, but you have to let her go."

"No!" she screamed. "You're just trying to trick me. You want to divert me from the path God has chosen for me. You're jealous of my relationship with God."

Brandon wasn't sure what he could say that wouldn't set her off. He decided to try something different.

"What do you want?" he asked.

"I want to go home. I don't like it here anymore. All I want is to go home."

"Where is home?"

Confused again, she began massaging her temples, the cloth dangerously close to her face.

"You and I are not so different, you know. We both want the same thing. We want to rid the world of evil. I kept hoping you would understand, maybe even join me. He's the only one who understands," she said.

"Who? Who understands?"

"He's my only friend. As soon as he found out the truth, he was there to help me every step of the way. I don't know what I would have done without him."

"Who? Kadeem?"

"I don't like it here anymore. I want to leave. Why don't you just let me leave?"

"I'll let you leave, but you have to let Candace go."

"I don't believe you!"

Brandon would have said practically anything to save not only Candace's life, but also Kimberly's and his own.

"I tell you what. You can send Candace over to me and lock us both in. I won't even try to come after you. Just let her go."

"I don't think I can let her go. She hasn't been cleansed. It's my destiny to carry out His wishes. You don't know what she is, but I do. She's an abomination. She hides beneath her imaginary beauty, but underneath all the beautiful clothing and makeup, she is nothing more than a twisted abomination."

"You mean like Kimberly?"

"Stop it! Stop mentioning Kimberly. I don't know this person! Stop trying to confuse me!"

"I'm not trying to confuse you. You and Kimberly were friends once and I don't want you to forget her."

"A friend," she muttered, confused.

"Yes, she's a friend."

"Stop it! Stop trying to trick me!"

"I'm not trying to trick you."

Brandon watched as Kimberly jerked her head around, looking behind her, speaking to someone standing near the door. Brandon saw no one.

"Daniel," she said, smiling. "I knew you would come. I knew you were one of his disciples."

That's when Brandon realized, somehow she had been so impacted by the young man named Daniel, he was now one of her many personalities. It was Brandon's guess that Daniel represented the young brother she had lost when the personality she knew as Kadeem had grown up.

Brandon hoped she would be distracted long enough so that he could make a move and quickly end the standoff.

"Daniel, you are truly one of His chosen."

Kimberly acted before Brandon had a chance to. She pushed Candace toward Brandon and ran toward the door, her hand contorted as if she were holding something or someone, judging from the conversation she was having. Once on the other side, Kimberly locked the door and barred it.

"Did you take care of everything?" she asked. "Good, good," she responded.

"What about Kadeem? Where is he? I can't leave without Kadeem."

She got into the driver's side of her car. Then she saw him. Kadeem was right there, as he had always been, sitting in the back seat.

"There you are," she said. "I thought you had left me."

"Didn't you believe me when I told you I would be here as long as you needed me?"

She suddenly felt more confused than ever. She realized she was still holding the white cloth soaked in ether and dropped it on the dashboard. Yet, her vision still seemed to be unfocused. She stared straight ahead, looking at Kadeem's reflection in her driver's mirror, with Daniel sitting right next to him. As hard as she tried to focus her eyes, the images of both Kadeem and Daniel contorted, disappeared and returned, making it difficult for her to see either of them. It was like watching a program on television, with a signal that was not connecting. The images swiveled back and forth, crackling and all full of static, as they were intermittently joined by Shelly, Kay, Cat, and countless others.

"Kadeem, I don't know what's happening. My eyes. I can barely see you."

"I'm right here. As long as you need me, I'll be right here."

Suddenly he was back and her vision was completely clear. His image in the mirror was perfect.

"I was so scared. I thought Daddy had hurt you and made you go away from me, like the last time. I need you to take care of me. I'm so scared."

"Don't worry. I'm right here, Sis."

She started to cry.

"I can't see you! What's happening? I can't see you anymore, Kadeem. You're fading again. Come back!"

She only saw Daniel, sitting in the back seat, and wondered why he wasn't speaking and finally, he did.

"Mosaic, it's only a matter of time before Brandon is out and the entire area is swarming with police."

Kimberly continued to alter the octave of her voice to fit, for not only Kadeem, but Daniel as well.

"You know why I'm fading, don't you, Sis?" the practically male voice said. "You have to let me go."

Except for her throaty voice, the silence within the confines of the simple black sedan was deafening.

Then, as if she were suddenly a ventriloquist's dummy, a familiar voice returned.

"I don't think I can, Kadeem. I need you."

"Not really. You don't *really* need me anymore. You're going to be fine. The only way you can get better is if I go away."

"Please don't go," she cried.

The sound of his voice faded slowly away and for the first time in a long time, he was silent. Along with the distance of his voice, his intermittent reflection eventually faded away, until it was completely gone. Kimberly and Kadeem were no longer one person. He had been a brother she'd created to ease the pain of loneliness and abuse. He'd stepped in to represent that part of her that was male, when her father was doing everything he could to destroy her. Now it was all clear and she no longer needed him. Yet, Mosaic still existed. Turning, she noticed for the first time, the body of Nurse Jocelyn Edwards in the back seat.

"Daniel, you thought of everything. Thank you. I was right. You are truly the best of His servants."

Jocelyn's body was moved from the back seat to the trunk and placed on top of a tire, just before closing the trunk completely.

"If we don't leave now, they'll come for us. It's only a matter of time."

Her voices shifted from one to another to fit who was speaking.

Still a bit flustered by Kadeem's departure, she did exactly as the voice of Daniel told her and exited the car. As Daniel, she tossed a lighted match directly onto the dashboard and the white cloth soaked in diethyl ether. The quantity and the explosive properties of ether were far greater than she'd anticipated, and the force of the explosion ejected her from the area of the vehicle.

# CHAPTER FORTY-FOUR

"Don't get too used to flying solo, Simms. We've got a new detective coming from the Twenty-fourth Precinct. He'll be here next week, so enjoy your solitude for a few more days. And Simms, I've been *real* patient, but you've got to get your act together, and soon, because my patience is wearing thin."

Simms had spent months drinking and fucking to forget and when that didn't work, he simply stopped coming to work. When it was apparent that he would lose everything, he at least managed to drag himself into work each day. However, his alcohol consumption and random women were replaced with a mean side that made it impossible to keep a partner. Although his Captain didn't believe it was intentional, he did believe that subconsciously, Simms was hoping that eventually he would piss everyone off and be forced to go it alone.

After years of working with Kimberly, he now felt closer to her than he ever had. He now understood so much more about secrets. They could eat you alive if you let them.

Simms knew that the day Kimberly *died* would be permanently etched in his memory. After she left the garage that day, locking him and Candace inside, they heard the explosion. Brandon had hoped to get to Kimberly quickly enough to avoid exactly what he knew would eventually happen. The scent of the ether filling the garage told him everything he needed to know. There was enough ether soaked into that small cloth Kimberly was holding on to, to kill everyone, including herself. He did eventually free both himself and Candace, but not quickly enough.

He kept replaying that day over and over in his mind, like some terrible film he couldn't stop watching. While his Captain ragged him for being a fuck-up, he stopped listening and replayed the events of that day once again.

"Candace, stay here," Brandon remembered saying. "Close the door and don't open it until I come back and get you."

By the time he got outside, there was little left of the vehicle. Kimberly lay several feet away. He was sure she was dead. Then he saw her head move slightly and her beautiful eyes open. He ran to her and held her closely in his arms, feeling her warmth and remembering what it felt like to hold her.

"Kimberly, why didn't you come to me? I would've helped you. Why didn't you trust me?" he asked.

She stirred. He was sure she was dying, yet surprisingly, she seemed to be springing to life.

"Kimberly! Oh my God! Don't worry. I'm going to get you some help. Just hang on."

"You still trying to save the world, partner?"

A smile spread across her lips and all Brandon wanted to do was to save her, not just from death, but from prison and mental facilities and the prying eyes of the public.

"I'm going to go get some help. You're going to be fine, just fine."

"Yes, Brandon, I am," she agreed.

He went back to the garage, opened the door for Candace and looked for a phone. After calling 9-1-1 and telling them to send the police and an ambulance, he tried to think of what he was going to tell everyone when they got there. He quickly returned to Kimberly to make sure she was comfortable while they waited for the ambulance to arrive, but by the time he got back, she was gone. He realized, in her condition, she couldn't have gotten far on her own. That's when he remembered her parents. For a moment, he considered going after them. Instead, he decided, this would be one time he wouldn't get *his man*, or in this case, his woman.

"Good-bye," he whispered.

Brandon returned to the garage to free Candace.

"What happened?" she asked.

"She's gone."

"Is she alive?"

"No," he lied.

"Maybe it's for the best."

"I don't understand."

"She suffered enough. What kind of a life would she have had anyway, locked away in a prison or some mental institution somewhere? Why do you think she did it, really? I think I understand, but I'm still not completely sure."

"Kimberly created all of her personalities to survive the pain of overwhelming abuse. The cop, the fiercely strong Shelly, the innocent temptress, the protective brother, the child who was so easily molded, even the killer, were all aspects of her personality. Her father had made her believe she truly was evil, and she had waged an inner battle during her entire life trying to destroy the evil inside. It was only when her old life converged with her new that the evil inside could no longer remain hidden. Mosaic became all that her father represented. As long as her father lived, Mosaic could never be destroyed. The murders would have inevitably continued."

# CHAPTER FORTY-FIVE

"Simms! Are you listening to me? That's exactly what I'm talking about. There you go, zoning out again. You've still got some time. You wanna take a week off before your partner gets here next week? It'll give you a chance to clear your head and start fresh."

Simms was fully aware that the countless weeks he'd spent drinking, fucking random women and not showing up for work couldn't go on forever. His Captain had been much more patient than he'd expected, but at this point, his patience was wearing quite thin.

"Cap, I heard you. I'll think about it," Simms responded.

While Simms stood there, pretending to pay attention, Detective Wickham knocked on the door.

"Come in!" the Captain yelled.

"Did you see this?"

"What, Wickham?"

Detective Wickham stood in the doorway with a sheet of paper in his hand.

"This just came off the wire. It seems as though the folks in Los Angeles may have a copycat on their hands."

Simms could feel the blood draining from his face. He already knew where this was going. He also knew this was no copycat. He was the *only* one that truly knew.

There had been no one around to dispute Simms' version of what happened that day, so he made sure that everyone believed that Kimberly Watson's body was the one that had been burned to ash in the trunk of the car after the explosion.

"What copycat?" the Captain asked.

"There was a burned body found in California. In Manhattan Beach, of all places."

"Yeah, so."

"So, guess what they found near the body?"

"What the fuck! Are we playing Twenty Questions here or what? What the fuck was found?" the Captain yelled.

"One of those damn bracelets, of course!"

If Simms were honest with himself, he would have admitted that he wasn't all that surprised. More than anything, he wanted to believe that she was cured and had truly found some way to lock every one of her personalities away, but it was wishful thinking on his part. He was aware what the rest of the day held for him. He would go to his desk, maybe agonize for an hour or two, then do a bit of soul searching. He might even try to convince himself that he had nothing to do with any of it, not anymore. But, eventually he would make the only decision he could make and go right back into his Captain's office and ask for the week off he'd offered earlier. He knew exactly where he had to be. However, he didn't want to let on that he was affected by what he had just heard. He silently got himself together before coming back with his characteristic sarcastic retort.

"Wickham, you got nothing better to do than watch cases outside our jurisdiction? Aren't there enough crimes right here in New York City for you to deal with?"

"Hell, man, I thought you'd want to know. You gotta admit, it's some crazy shit."

"Yeah, That's exactly what it is, *crazy. It's some crazy shit executed by some crazy* motherfucka that wants a little airtime, riding on media attention from a case we already solved, right here in New York City. I'm sure he'll get exactly what he wants."

"Can we all get back to work now, men, or did you want some tea and crumpets for your coffee klatch?" the Captain asked.

Simms walked away, eager to access his computer. He Googled *body found burned in Los Angeles* and immediately saw what he was looking for under a link for cbs2.com.

He plugged in his earphones and listened. Anxious to get past the numerous advertisements, he found it difficult to sit still as he waited for something, anything, that would tell him this had nothing to do with *her.*

*"A burned body was found at Manhattan Beach today. It was stuffed into a trunk and mostly destroyed. Officials have not yet determined whether it was the body of a man or a woman. Despite the condition of the vehicle and the body, a silver bracelet was found in close proximity, barely affected by the blaze. Apparently, the situation closely mimics several murders committed in New York City several months ago, in which a veteran police detective was killed. Both Detective Kimberly Watson and her assailant, whose identity remains unknown, perished in a fire. Both bodies were so badly burned, positive identification of Detective Watson could only be determined based on DNA retrieved from a phalanx bone found at the scene. Teeth available at the scene were determined to not be those of Detective Watson and were believed to be those of the assailant. Positive identification of the killer has yet to be determined, as records available for dental comparison have not produced a match. Tune in tonight at eleven for more on this story and others."*

After listening to the news report, Simms waited a while, then went back to his Captain's office.

"Cap, I'm going to take your advice and take a few days off before my new partner starts."

"Great. Finally, someone's taking my advice. Just make sure you come back here in tip-top shape. You've used up all your second chances."

"No problem. I'll be back bright-eyed and bushy-tailed, ready to break in my new partner."

"You'd better be!"

In truth, Simms wasn't sure whether he'd be back or not. Only time would tell.

# ABOUT THE AUTHOR

Michelle Janine Robinson is the author of the Zane Presents novel *More Than Meets The Eye*, published June 21, 2011. She is also the author of *Color Me Grey*, published June 1, 2010. Both books were published by Simon & Schuster/Strebor Books. Michelle's short story contribution *"The Quiet Room"* was a featured story in the *New York Times* bestseller *Succulent: Chocolate Flava II*. She has contributed to several other anthologies, including *Caramel Flava*, *Honey Flava*, *Purple Panties* and *Tasting Him*. In 2009 *Tasting Him* won the IPPY (Independent Publisher) Award for Erotica. Urban Reviews listed Michelle's first book, *Color Me Grey*, as one of the best reviewed books on UrbanReviewsOnline.com for 2010. In February 2011 Michelle was voted *Writers POV Magazine's* Annual Winter Writing Contest Winner of the Year and in March 2011 Michelle was voted a National Black Book Festival finalist for Best New Author of the Year. Look for two new novels by Michelle in 2013, *Strange Fruit* and *On The Other Side*. Michelle is a native New Yorker and the mother of identical twins. Visit the author at www.michellejaninerobinson.com, www.facebook.com/michelle.j.robinson and Twitter @MJanine Robinson.